Tacos, Tarot, and Murder

A Cozy Magic Midlife Mystery

Silver Circle Cat Rescue Mysteries
Book 6

Leanne Leeds

Tacos, Tarot, and Murder
Silver Circle Cat Rescue Mysteries #6
ISBN: 979-8-9900434-2-8

Published by Badchen Publishing
2709 N Hayden Island Dr.
STE 103131
Portland, Oregon, 97217

The cat could very well be man's best friend but would never stoop to admitting it.
— Doug Larson

Contents

Chapter One

THE BRASS BELL ABOVE THE DOOR LET OUT A cheerful chime as I bustled behind the café's oak counter, refilling the sugar jars and adjusting the tidy displays of baked goods from local merchants. Golden morning sunlight streamed in through the tall, arched windows lining the front wall, bathing the cozy room in a warm glow. I breathed in the mingling scents of roasted coffee beans and cinnamon as I worked, enjoying the moment of calm before the usual morning rush.

Pete Granger, the friendly bookshop owner, strolled up to the counter, the floorboards creaking under his footsteps. "Morning, Ellie!" he called out. "The usual, please."

I grabbed a clean, white mug with a cartoon cat face and the funny saying "You had me at meow" from the shelf. "Dark roast with a dash of cream and three lumps of sugar?"

"You got it," Pete chuckled, his mouth twitching up in a smile. He leaned on the counter, the early morning sunlight from the windows setting his silver hair aglow.

"Coming right up, Pete," I said. "How's business?"

We chatted while I prepared his coffee, and as as Pete took his drink, a streak of orange fur leaped onto the counter.

"Well, good morning, Marmalade," he chuckled, stroking the tabby between her ears. She purred, nudging Pete's hand for more attention. "You might disagree, young lady, but I don't think you need any coffee."

Marmalade let out a soft meow.

"Oh, is that so?" he chuckled.

The Silver Circle was an excellent place for our cats to socialize before they were adopted into loving families. They moved between tables and chairs, tails swishing as they relaxed in the territory they felt they owned. Some curled up in pools of sunlight that streamed through the windows, while others batted at stray napkins or chair tassels.

Pete settled into a plush green armchair near the front window, steaming mug in hand. A smile played on my lips as I busied myself tidying the counter top, the sweet scent of baked goods curling through the café.

The bell over the mantrap door jingled again as someone new entered the café area. I looked up from arranging the baked goods.

"Hey Mom!" called my daughter Evie from the

lobby as she breezed down the staircase from the second floor. Her cheeks were flushed, and wisps of hair had escaped her messy bun. "Sorry I slept late. I wasn't feeling that great."

"Hi, sweetie, and no problem," I smiled. A feathered cat toy dangled from her belt loop and swayed back and forth as she approached to give me a brief kiss on the cheek. "You're just in time. I could use some help. It's getting a little busy."

Evie grabbed a green apron from behind the counter and tied it around her waist, falling into our café routine. The mid-morning rush was beginning as regular customers filtered in.

The silver-haired ladies from the Thursday morning knitting circle arrived, already chattering away as they settled around their usual table. A clutch of high school students on their way to school sauntered in next, ear pods in their ears. They grabbed a window seat, laughing at something one of them said—though I didn't know how those kids heard anything with those things stuck in their ears.

The bell jingled again and Augusta Walton bustled in, her arms laden with boxes of fresh pastries from her bakery. The sweet, yeasty aroma filled the café as Augusta and Evie exchanged morning pleasantries.

A plump calico cat named Duchess hopped onto the counter beside them, her fluffy tail swishing back and forth. She padded over and then stood up on her hind legs to peer inside the pastry box. Her nose twitched as she sniffed the array of baked goods.

"Shoo, Duchess," laughed Evie, nudging the cat away. "These are not snacks for you!"

Cecelia Goddard, the local real estate agent, picked up Duchess. "How about we strike a deal, Duchess? Your delightful company at my table in exchange for my making sure something delicious finds its way to you," Cecelia told the cat.

Duchess purred, always eager for snacks.

The door opened again, and Evie's face lit up, her hazel eyes sparkling as her boyfriend Matt entered the café, looking as handsome as ever in his faded jeans. His brown hair curled around his collar, and he gave Evie a crooked smile I could tell made her heart flutter even with the pacemaker steadying her heartbeat.

"Hola," he said as he walked over to give her a quick kiss. "Looks like business is booming today, no? You having a good morning so far, mi amor?"

"It's going great now that you're here," Evie grinned, her cheeks flushing pink. She loved it when Matt stopped by the Silver Circle on his way to work on whatever case Lodestar assigned him. Even on the busiest days, his warm, easygoing presence lifted her spirits.

"I love to hear you say that," he said, planting a quick kiss on her cheek. He looked over at me. "Hey Ellie, how's the day going?"

"Can't complain," I said. "Can I get you anything, Matt?"

"Just an Americano for me. Need that caffeine boost before I go catch a cheating husband in the act."

As I frothed milk for Matt's coffee, Evie sidled up next to him, slipping her arm through his and gazing up with an adoring smile. He grinned down at her, eyes crinkling at the corners. They stood hip to hip, swaying to the jazz music playing overhead.

Watching them banter and laugh made my heart glad. They complimented each other so well—Evie's creative spirit lighting up whenever Matt was around, while his steady kindness gave her confidence. It was beautiful to see my daughter so happy and carefree with him, especially after the medical challenges of her childhood.

"Excited for... um, for..." asked Evie, her expression clouding with frustration. "The thing in the square this weekend with the dancing?"

"Cinco de Mayo this weekend? I'm looking forward to it," grinned Matt as he deftly handled Evie's inability to recall the words she was looking for. "My grandmother's been talking nonstop about the festival. Seems like everyone in Tablerock is planning to attend."

"Will you dance with me at the town square?" asked Evie. "I'm not the greatest at dancing, but I've been trying to learn salsa from TubeTrek."

"Well, then you know more than me, I think," laughed Matt. "I'd probably end up stepping on your toes with my two left feet. I have not been practicing my salsa moves—because I don't have any salsa moves."

Matt and Evie's playful banter continued as I finished preparing his drink. I added a splash of cream to the dark roast blend, the beans ground by our local roaster that morning. I slid the mug across the counter, the rich, earthy aroma of the coffee bringing a smile to Matt's face.

Matt brought the mug to his lips, savoring the aroma before indulging in a deep drink. "Mmmm, that's just what I needed."

Evie poked him in the side with her elbow, eyes alight with mischief. "Getting a little coffee fix for your addiction there?"

Matt chuckled and drew her into a one-armed embrace. "Don't worry, you're the only addiction I've got."

"All right, all right," she said, rolling her eyes.

"I have to get going. I'll see you later on this afternoon," he called to Evie. With a wave, Matt headed out the door, the cats watching as he left.

Evie gave a dreamy sigh as the door swung closed behind him.

The morning rush wound down as the clock neared noon. I made my way to the front door, flipping the sign to "Closed" and turning the lock. This was only the second week of our new lunch closure policy, implemented to give the cats—and the staff—some downtime midday without people interacting with them. It still felt unusual.

Evie finished wiping down the tables while I straightened up beneath the counter. "It's so nice not to race around serving lunch," she said. "And I think it's a good thing for the town, too. We don't need to compete with the other lunch places."

The back door to the kitchen swung open and Keisha Washington, our café manager, emerged, untying her apron. "Kitchen's all cleaned up and restocked for the afternoon," she reported. "I'm going to run a few errands, but I'll be back before the afternoon rush."

Evie gave her a thumbs up. "Sounds good, Keisha. Enjoy your break!"

"Yes, enjoy! Why don't you take your lunch break, too, sweetie?" I suggested. "I've got things handled here. Since we're not serving lunch anymore, there's not that much to clean up."

"You sure, Mom?" asked Evie. "I don't mind staying to help."

"Positive," I assured her.

"Okay, then I'll head upstairs and make us both some lunch." Evie smiled, untying her apron. She gave me a quick peck on the cheek before grabbing her messenger bag and heading upstairs.

One by one, the morning volunteers and employees slipped out the front door for lunch, calling out cheerful goodbyes.

"Enjoy your lunch! See you in an hour!" I said, waving to Kelly, one of our regular volunteers.

"Have a good one, Darla, Frances!" I said as Evie's best friend headed out with Laurie's veterinary assistant.

As the last volunteer disappeared out the door, the shelter seemed to settle into the new midday lull. The incessant ringing of the front desk phone stopped. The chatter and laughter of volunteers and visitors faded. Even the cats grew more languid, draping themselves across sun warmed windowsills to doze.

I took a deep breath, embracing the calm quiet. The only sounds were the gentle humming of the ceiling fans and the occasional jingle of a cat collar as they shifted in their sleep.

"Oddly quiet, isn't it, Digby?" I asked the one-eyed cat.

Digby glanced up from grooming himself, pausing mid-lick. He blinked his one good eye at me and gave a raspy meow, as if only half listening. After holding my gaze for a moment, he returned to licking his fur, more focused on removing a knot than conversing. His attention soon drifted again to the rectangle of sunlight inching across the floor, where he stretched out to soak up the warmth.

I chuckled to myself.

Clearly, I would not get any riveting conversation out of Digby right now. The old tabby had priorities, and a sunbeam nap took precedence over anything I might have to say.

I climbed the majestic stairs up to the second floor of Wardwell Manor, where Evie and I lived, along with the cat's private areas on the second and third floors. With each step I ascended, more perked up ears and twitching whiskers appeared over the banister rails above.

By the time I reached the midway landing, a cacophony of impatient meows and yowls rang out. The pitter-patter of paws on hardwood grew louder as the horde of furry residents raced up and down.

It was their lunchtime, too, and they were ready.

They swarmed my feet, nearly tripping me in their eagerness. Their plaintive cries echoed through the stairwell as they jockeyed for position. I gripped the railing to avoid falling over from the writhing sea of whipping tails and butting heads.

"Patience, my goodness!" I called over the din, but their pleas only grew more insistent as they herded me up the remaining steps. "If I fall down the stairs and break my neck, none of you are getting soft food."

Well, that wasn't quite true.

And they knew it.

As I reached the top step, the swarm of felines enveloped my feet in a writhing sea of fur and tails and guided me toward their food bowls, their plaintive meows rising in a hungry chorus.

I sighed, a smile tugging at my lips. "Do we have to go through this every single day? I know you're not starving. You certainly know you're not starving."

Their yowls grew more insistent—showing that they did not, in fact, know that.

I scooped kibble and gushy cat food into the rows of ceramic bowls lining the second floor shelter kitchen—vermilion, sapphire, emerald. No sooner had the first pieces hit the floor than the ravenous furry mob descended, a flurry of swishing tails and twitching ears.

The room filled with the sounds of enthusiastic crunching and slurping as they devoured their meals. A calico named Callie licked her bowl clean, then tried nudging her neighbor out of the way for more. I eased her back.

"Save some for everyone, Callie," I chuckled.

Just then, Evie entered holding two tuna melts. The smell wafted through the kitchen, and a dozen noses lifted into the air, nostrils flaring. Two dozen eyes locked onto the sandwiches. Tails froze mid-swish.

Evie paused. "I shouldn't have carried these in here."

The cats abandoned their bowls one by one, drawn by the tantalizing scent of tuna. They padded toward Evie and the sandwiches like mighty lions stalking gazelles on the African plains, slowly and deliberately with predatory eyes fixed on the plate in her hands.

"You know we can see you, right?" Evie backed toward the door, clutching the tuna melts away from the approaching felines. "All right guys, not for you," she said. "Go back to your gushy food."

The cats continued their advance, slinking low and slow across the floor like tigers stalking prey through tall grass. Muscles tensed beneath slick fur, ready to pounce. Bright eyes remained locked on the tuna prize, never blinking.

"Oh, crap." Evie spun and darted away down the hall. "I'll meet you in the small kitchen!"

After Evie darted out the door with the sandwiches, the cats paused, ears twitching. For a moment they remained poised, as if contemplating giving chase. But then, one by one, their postures softened, and they all settled back at their bowls to resume their interrupted meals.

That afternoon when we reopened, it was bustling as usual.

This time, Evie worked behind the counter, busy preparing orders and chatting with customers, while I moved around the seating area, refreshing empty mugs and delivering baked goods, the ever-present smile on my face belying the effort it took at my age to keep up with all these youngsters.

At the far end of the counter, Police Chief Ed Yarbin and Dr. Anthony Canter sat in their usual spots for their Thursday afternoon coffee and conversation.

Chief Yarbin gripped his heavy navy mug, steam rising from the black coffee inside. His brow was furrowed as he listened to Dr. Canter talk, offering an occasional grunt in reply. He took intermittent sips, glancing around the café over the mug's rim.

"So, Ed," Dr. Canter began, setting his coffee mug down with a clink, "That big Cinco de Mayo festival is coming up this weekend. The whole town gets pretty lively. Are you looking forward to all the celebrations?"

Chief Yarbin let out a long sigh, shoulders slumping. "Looking forward to it? More like bracing myself," he muttered with a dismissive wave of his hand. "Every year it's the same thing—that festival brings ten times our usual crowds. And with bigger crowds comes more headaches for me and my officers. More public drunkenness to deal with, petty thefts and fights breaking out... It means a mountain of extra paperwork and overtime. So no, I can't say I'm looking forward to it."

Dr. Canter waved his hand. "Oh, lighten up, Ed! So there's some rowdiness—it's all in good fun! The festival is great for our local businesses. Brings in lots of tourist dollars. And it's just one weekend a year, after all. You can handle it." He leaned back smugly in his chair.

The police chief gripped his coffee mug tighter, jaw tense. "Easy for you to say, Anthony. You get to enjoy the celebrations while I'm left dealing with the aftermath. You don't have to worry about crowd control or keeping the peace. So forgive me if I'm not brimming with excitement."

The café door swung open, setting the entry bell jingling. Councilman Cornelius Hammond strode in, waving cheerfully at the other patrons. Spotting Chief Yarbin and Dr. Canter at the counter, his face lit up.

"Afternoon, gentlemen!" he called out in his booming voice as he made his way over to them.

Before either man could respond, Councilman Hammond pulled out the empty seat next to Dr. Canter with a scrape, removed his jacket, and plopped himself down. The chair wobbled slightly under his gigantic frame.

"Don't mind if I join you two for a bit, do you?" he asked as if they had a choice.

Dr. Canter shook his head in amusement while Chief Yarbin grunted, returning to his coffee.

"We were just discussing the Cinco de Mayo festival coming up," the doctor explained, turning in his seat to face the councilman. "Our friend Ed here has some... reservations about the whole thing."

Councilman Hammond chuckled. "Let me guess—you're less than thrilled about all the extra crowds and policing it'll bring, eh, Ed?"

Chief Yarbin crossed his arms, grunting in confirmation.

"Now Ed, try to look at the big picture," the councilman continued, gesturing with his hands. "Events like this are vital for local business—all the tourist dollars pouring in gives them a boost. And it puts little Tablerock on the map, brings tons of positive attention to our community!" He clapped a hand on the police chief's shoulder. "The festival is good PR, if you think about it that way."

"I heard this argument already." Chief Yarbin just shook his head, unconvinced.

Estella Garcia, wearing her trademark colorful shawl, walked in to the café. "Buenos dias, mi amigos!" she said as she approached the counter. Estella, who was practically Tablerock's matriarch at the tender age of sixty-eight, was a bundle of spicy but loving energy. She was also my daughter's boyfriend's grandmother.

"Estella! Your usual?" I asked, smiling.

"Yes, por favor, Eleanor," Estella replied in her lyrical Spanish accent. As I prepared her coffee, she glanced over at Chief Yarbin, Dr. Canter and Councilman Hammond chatting at the end of the counter. Her eyes glinted mischievously. "Ay, you three together over there—that looks like trouble waiting to happen, no?"

The men looked over as Estella made her way, shuffling a bit to make room.

"You know what they say—when you men get together, always expect trouble!" She wagged her finger at them, but her eyes were dancing. "But me, I like a little trouble." Estella gestured at the empty seat between the Chief and the Councilman. "You gentlemen wouldn't mind if I joined you, would you?"

She didn't wait for an answer before sitting.

"We were just discussing your Cinco de Mayo festival," Dr. Canter explained after Estella had settled at the corner counter. "It seems our police chief here has some reservations."

"Aye! Me, too! Me, too!" Estella chuckled. "Ah, yes, it is always dramatic around festival time! We Mexicans take our love of telenovelas too far sometimes, yes?"

Evie, who was refreshing water bowls nearby, turned. "What kind of drama is happening this year, Abuela?"

I froze in surprise, the coffee pot hovering mid-pour. Abuela?

Since when did Evie call Estella that?

As I regained my composure and set the pot back down, my mind raced. Clearly Evie and Matt's relationship had progressed more seriously than I realized if she was embracing his grandmother as family.

A swell of emotion rose in my chest.

My little girl was growing up, forging her own life and connections. It seemed like just yesterday Evie was this tiny thing in a hospital bed, tubes everywhere, fighting just to make it to adulthood. Now here she was, a strong young woman comfortable calling her boyfriend's grandmother by the warm, familiar term.

Where had the years gone?

I stopped myself, pulled my head back into the conversation, determined not to get too sentimental. I could reflect more on Evie's milestone later—my nostalgic trip down memory lane was causing me to miss the latest town gossip.

Can't have that.

Estella sighed, taking a sip of her cinnamon latte before continuing. "Aye, and then there is Rosa Vargas—she is on the festival planning committee, yes? Already she is making a big fuss, insisting that only restaurants should compete in the margarita contest. The day before the contest!"

"But Luna's tarot shop has won that contest like, what—five years in a row?" I said. "That would mean Luna couldn't even compete."

"Yes, Luna's margaritas are legendary around here," Councilman Hammond recalled. "Rosa's are good, too. But Luna's are something special."

"She's probably a witch," Yarbin mumbled.

"You really don't enjoy this time of year, do you, Ed?" The doctor waved his hand. "You know what? Don't answer that. You've already made your feelings clear." He turned back to Estella. "What else is giving you heartburn?" Dr. Canter said with a grin, clearly enjoying the gossip. "Unburden yourself."

"Well..." Estella lowered her voice. "I heard that Diego Gomez and Luna had a nasty breakup recently. And now, at the planning meetings, Luna is accusing Diego's new girlfriend Blanca of... how you say—sweeping her feet?"

We exchanged confused glances, eyebrows raised. Apparently, this odd phrase was as foreign to all of us as a dog groomer at a cat convention.

"It is an old Mexican superstition—they say that if

someone sweeps your feet with a broom, it will bring you terrible luck and ruin your life."

"Really?" I asked.

"Well, that you'll be single forever, which is the same thing, no?" Estella leaned in, whispering, "Luna claims Blanca came to her shop and swept her feet. She says this is why Diego left her, and why she is having such bad fortune."

"That's the most ridiculous thing I've ever heard," Chief Yarbin huffed.

"Really?" Estella said, frowning. "You do not believe? Let me sweep your feet right now and we will see!" She looked around the cat café, presumably for a broom to assault the police chief's work boots. "Maybe Mrs. Yarbin would like a change, you think?"

Yarbin snorted—but he also moved his feet a little further under the counter.

"I don't know, Ed," Dr. Canter said. "Who knows what's real and what's not? I dated a Brazilian woman once who was very superstitious. She used to sprinkle salt around the bed to ward off evil spirits."

"I guess it worked, since you're not with her anymore," Yarbin deadpanned.

Estella smiled at Yarbin before continuing. "Anyway, the breakup is making the planning meetings very dramatic. Shouting, crying, accusations flying everywhere! Diego says he still cares for Luna, but she needs to move on and stop blaming Blanca for their issues."

"Yikes," said Evie. "No wonder you compared it to a telenovela, Abuela!"

Estella chuckled. "Oh yes, there is never a dull moment during Cinco de Mayo time! But I am sure it will all work out in the end. We Mexicans are passionate people—we fight hard, but we also love hard." She smiled at the group.

"Brazilians, too," Canter added.

Yarbin turned to stare at him in bewilderment. "And you wonder why you're still single?"

"I don't wonder," Estella said flatly.

I busied myself wiping down the counter while Evie pretended to be engrossed in refilling the creamers.

"Well, all this talk reminds me I need to review the security protocols for the festival," Chief Yarbin grunted, gulping down the last of his coffee. "Best to be prepared for any trouble that might arise. Nice chatting with you all."

As the chief took his leave, Councilman Hammond also stood up. "He's right. I better get back to the office—lots of preparations are still to be completed. Let me know if any of you would like to volunteer at the information booth!"

None of us did.

After exchanging goodbyes, the councilman headed out.

"Well, I should go, too. I was just passing by and thought I'd drop in," Estella said, finishing her drink and standing, one hand on her back. "These old bones need a nap after herding the festival cats! Ellie, I'm still expecting you at the tamale making tomorrow, yes?"

"Wouldn't miss it," I called after her as she made her way out the door.

Dr. Canter remained at the counter after the others had left. His eyes followed me around the café as I cleaned up, like a cat tracking a toy.

"So, you and Landon still dating, Ellie?" he asked.

I stiffened, nearly dropping the mug I was drying. Dr. Canter's clumsy attempts at flirtation were about as subtle as an elephant at a mouse convention. "Don't even start, Anthony," I replied, meeting his gaze with a stern look I usually reserved for misbehaving kittens.

He quickly became engrossed in stirring nonexistent sugar in his almost empty coffee, mumbling something unintelligible in response. I had to bite my tongue to keep from laughing at his embarrassment.

Honestly, the man had all the romantic finesse of a hairball.

Chapter Two

I WAS COMFORTABLE IN THE PLUSH ARMCHAIR, letting my eyes drift around our weekly Friday morning coffee klatch with my two best friends. Josephine sat across from me, flailing her hands around like she was guiding a plane in for a landing while Laurie watched her with an eyebrow raised.

Which was it's usual position when Josie was telling a story.

Belladonna's second floor isolation room had become our own little soundproofed capsule for lively gossip sessions, away from the ears of any unwitting customers or volunteers. Here we could chat without fear of being overheard, and it was a welcome respite from the chaos of the cat café below.

"I'm telling you, Ellie," the lawyer said. "Charlie is going to end up passed out in a giant vat of margaritas by the end of Cinco de Mayo. You know how he gets with the tequila."

I laughed as I pictured Josie's poor husband passed out face down in a vat of frozen margarita slush. "Come on, give Charlie some credit," I said. "I'm sure he has at least an infinitesimal chance of making it through Cinco de Mayo without baptizing himself in tequila."

Josephine wasn't wrong. Poor Charlie tended to get overzealous with the margaritas, but I hoped this year, for Josie's sake, he might stay vertical.

A fool's hope perhaps, but hope nonetheless.

"Yeah, remember that time he tried to salsa dance on a table after too many margaritas?" Laurie reminded Josephine with a smirk. "Ended with a broken nose and a lifetime booze ban from Pedro's Cantina."

"You're telling me that like I could somehow forget the whole embarrassing affair?" Josie let out an exasperated sigh, throwing her hands up. "You see what I mean, though. Total liability after a few rounds of tequila. I swear, Cinco de Mayo wreaks havoc on Charlie every year."

We all laughed as we imagined the inevitable call from Josie begging us to help her rescue her plastered hubby from yet another tequila-fueled escapade. Charlie's Cinco de Mayo debauchery had become an annual tradition—at least as reliable as kids hyped up on sugar crashing after Halloween.

A sleek black streak flashed through the air, landing

on the second tier of the cat tree. The familiar glow of the magic platter flared to life as Belladonna settled atop it, halting our laughter.

"Uh oh," Laurie said with a chuckle.

"Must you hens cackle on so in my quarters?" Belladonna snapped, lashing her tail. She fixed us with an imperious glare, her golden eyes narrowing to slits. "Some of us prefer peace and quiet, not this endless stream of inane babble on things no one could possibly care this much about."

"We're just chatting, Bella," Laurie told her. "You're welcome to join us."

A flash of orange fur bounded up to join her, nudging Belladonna to one side of the enchanted metal thingamajig. "Don't be like that," Ginger said, and then his throat rumbled as he head butted her. "Let the ladies have their gossip session. Josephine was just telling a funny story about her man. Wasn't it funny?"

Belladonna let out an indignant snort, edging away from Ginger's attempt at nuzzling. She angled her body, nose turned up in a dismissive sniff. "Yes, tales of drunk, reckless men stumbling about like imbeciles. How delightfully entertaining."

Josephine rolled her eyes as Belladonna hissed at Ginger. "Well, looks like Her Royal Highness is in one of her moods again."

Ginger's ears drooped. "I just meant it's nice they feel comfortable chatting in here. This room has good energy, yeah?"

The black cat glared at us. "But must it always be so loud?"

Laurie leaned in toward Belladonna. "We don't have to keep gossiping in here if it's disturbing you, your highness. We can take all these squishy chairs right out of the place and back downstairs," she said, voice dripping with dramatic deference. "We like it because this room is soundproof, so no one can eavesdrop on our chatter. Sometimes, your contributions to our discussions are even useful."

She gave an exaggerated wink.

I bit back a smile. The vet enjoyed poking fun at Belladonna's imperious attitude. The cat stared back, nonplussed, underestimating Laurie's dedication to tweaking her when she threw an attitude.

"I don't have to let you keep using this platter for your stupid dog patients," Bella told her.

"I don't have to keep bringing you the treats you love that Ellie won't let you have because they make your poo stink like a garbage dump, either."

Belladonna fixed Laurie with an icy stare, her golden eyes narrowing.

Laurie met the cat's gaze, one eyebrow raised in challenge.

I half expected tumbleweeds to blow through the room.

Finally, Belladonna blinked and turned away with a huff, conceding this round to Laurie. "Fine. Talk."

The vet smiled. "It's the little wins in life."

Josephine smiled and then lowered her voice. "It is, and speaking of little wins... I heard Diego Gomez is back on the market." She cut her gaze toward Laurie. "You like artsy young men with a few muscles, right Laurie? Maybe you two would hit it off."

Laurie let out an exaggerated groan. "Younger men, not young—and I am not interested in Diego Gomez. The Pepto Bismal pink hair streaks? Just no. I can't take him seriously." She gave Josie a playful shove. "And 'younger men' or not, I'm pretty sure I'm old enough to be Diego's mother. Not exactly an aphrodisiac."

Belladonna let out an annoyed huff. "This is just ridiculous," she grumbled. "Since you show no signs of being done with this idle prattle, I believe I'll take my leave." She sauntered toward the door, her tail swishing behind her.

Ginger's ears drooped more as he watched her go. "Don't go yet," he called out, kneading the plate with his front paws. "We could curl up together for a nice nap, just you and me. This crystal's kind of warm."

Belladonna whirled on him, eyes narrowed. "And have you snoring in my ear all afternoon? I think not."

Belladonna streaked across the room and with a lightning quick paw, she batted him right off the magic platter and out of the cubby. Ginger tumbled to the floor with a muffled oof, looking up at her.

"Now let's go," she said, her eyes fixed on the door.

I stood up and opened it.

Belladonna leaped from her perch and went out into the hallway without a backward glance. Ginger shot me a knowing look as he slunk from the room, tail drooping, after Belladonna.

Poor Ginger, just trying to get some quality time with his persnickety paramour.

She didn't make romance easy.

Josie waved a hand. "I thought the new boyfriend would have mellowed the diva out, but I see it's a slow process." She leaned back with a twinkle in her eye. "Now, where were we? Oh yes, discussing Laurie's love life."

"Or lack thereof," I added.

"Boy, it didn't take you long to become smug about the carpenter boyfriend, now, did it?" Laurie snorted. "Just because I'm single doesn't mean my life is lacking! I have the kids, I have the dogs, I have my practice. I'm content."

"Uh huh, sure," Josie retorted. "When's the last time you had an actual date? And no, coffee with the widower from the senior center you've been volunteering your time with doesn't count."

I stifled a laugh as Laurie swatted at her.

"For your information, I go on plenty of dates," Laurie shot back. "Just last weekend, I had dinner at that new French place with a very nice veterinary pharmaceutical rep, thank you very much."

"Was that a date or a business write off?" I asked.

Josie raised an eyebrow. "Did he spend the entire night talking about doggy cholesterol meds and blood pressure data? Real romantic."

Laurie opened her mouth to retort, then deflated. "Yeah, okay, it was a pretty dull date," she admitted. "And dogs don't take statins for high cholesterol, by the way."

I raised my eyebrow. "Dogs get high cholesterol?"

"They do, indeed. Not much, though."

Josie patted Laurie's knee. "This is why you need to get back out there. Try meeting someone new, someone different—like maybe a starving artist type, with a little edge. And a pink streak. Someone totally different from your usual stable of boring divorced professionals."

"Josie, I am a boring divorced professional. And for the last time, I have zero interest in Diego Gomez. I know he and Luna broke up, but I heard he fell into someone else's bed before the drink Luna threw at him was mopped up off the floor," she said, tossing a pillow at Josie's head. "And the Pepto Bismal hair streaks are a deal breaker, even if his age and habit of hopping from woman to woman wasn't."

"Well, if you want to check him out anyway, I have to go over to the square later," I told her. "I told Estella I'd come by the market later on today and help finish the tamales."

"You? You're going to make tamales?" Josie asked.

"Probably not. The news is coming by and she wants

a bunch of women from town in the background for the shot."

"Ooh, that sounds fun," Laurie said.

I enjoyed these moments together—talking, laughing, commiserating about life and love and everything between. It reminded me how lucky I was to have such amazing friends by my side, through all the difficulties.

Difficulties that were giving us a respite, thank goodness.

The bells on the door jingled as Laurie and I entered Garcia's Corner Store. The rich scents of seasoned meat and fresh masa enveloped us. Estella had rallied the entire community today—makeshift tables were crowded with locals assembling tamales for the upcoming Cinco de Mayo festival.

A mix of Spanish and English chatter filled the store as more than a dozen women worked assembly line style, their experienced hands smearing masa and filling corn husks in smooth motions. At the center table, Estella supervised, her keen eye ensuring each tamale was perfectly formed.

"Buenas tardes, amigas," Estella called out as she noticed us. A chorus of "holas" rang out as the women looked up.

I loved the easy camaraderie between Estella and all those who showed up to help. While some bonds were forged by culture and decades of shared experiences, both joyous and sorrowful, many bonds were from right here in Tablerock as neighbors.

A decade ago, many of these women might have barely known each other, but now they chatted and joked as lifelong friends. Estella, and the Cinco de Mayo festival, had brought them together and given them a sense of singular community—Tablerock honoring a culture and a people integral to our small town.

Laurie and I edged our way toward the drinks cooler, dodging around the occupied tables. I snagged two Jarritos while Laurie grabbed a bag of Sabritas chips. Sadie Taggert smiled at us from her perch behind the counter, her weathered features creasing into a welcoming grin.

"Well, hey there, ladies," Sadie said. "Y'all here to give Estella a hand with the tamales?"

"That's the cover story." Laurie shook her head with a chuckle. "In practicality, I think we'd just get in the way." She gestured toward the bustling tables of women working in seamless unison, their motions quick and precise from years of practice. Masa and husks flew between delicate hands in smooth choreography. "We'll leave the experts to it. We'll help wrap them in foil—that I think we can handle."

Sadie nodded. "Fair enough."

I popped open my Jarrito mandarin and took a sip of the sweet, tangy soda. "I wouldn't miss this for the world, though. I just love seeing everyone come together like this. The whole town is buzzing with excitement for the festival."

"Sure is," Sadie agreed. "Gonna be the biggest one yet if Estella has her way. And Estella always gets her way."

The front door opened again and a young woman entered, microphone in hand, trailed by a man with a large video camera perched on his shoulder. I recognized the stylishly dressed reporter, her blond hair in a neat bob, from the local Austin news station. The reporter made a beeline for Estella, who had looked up from her tamale assembly with an expression of polite welcome.

Estella led the reporter to a quiet corner of the store, away from the chatter of the workers. The cameraman hoisted up his equipment and began filming as the reporter launched into her questions.

"I'm here today with Estella Garcia, owner of Garcia's Corner Store and one of the key organizers of Tablerock's annual Cinco de Mayo celebration," the reporter began in a bright tone. "Estella, can you tell our viewers a little about the history of this festival in your hometown?"

Estella smoothed her apron and smiled. "Of course. Our little town has been celebrating Cinco de Mayo for over fifty years now. It started small, just a few families getting together for food and music. But it grew over the years as more people moved to Tablerock and wanted to take part."

The reporter nodded along. "And what are some of the highlights of the festival?"

"Oh, there's so much," Estella replied, her eyes lighting up. "A parade with floats and horses, booths along Main Street with artisans and food vendors, bands, and mariachis, dances, and piñatas for the children. But my favorite is seeing our community come together, people of all cultures and backgrounds. We celebrate our Mexican heritage, yes, but everyone is welcome!"

"It sounds like so much fun," the reporter said. "What does this festival mean to you and the people of Tablerock?"

Estella considered the question. "For me, it is about honoring traditions and remembering where we come from. Cinco de Mayo commemorates a historic victory against all odds. I want to pass that pride and perseverance to the younger generations." She gestured around the store. "And look at all these women here today, working together to prepare the food. This festival is a labor of love for all of us."

"That's a beautiful thought, Mrs. Garcia, especially considering everything going on in the world today," the reporter responded. "It's clear this event has special meaning for you and everyone involved."

The old woman's face darkened at the hint of politics being mentioned. "This festival is about Tablerock," Estella told her.

"Yes, yes, of course." She paused, and her expression shifted to one of intrigue. "Now, I heard there's been some drama around the planning this year. Is there any truth to the rumors of a spat between local business owners?"

"Spats? What spats?" Estella waved her hand in dismissal. "You cannot have an event this big without some quarreling. But we don't focus on the chisme, only on celebrating our community." She leaned in with a conspiratorial sparkle in her eye. "But between you and me, the troublemaker was probably Alejandro at the feed store. He and Luis were childhood friends but had a big falling out—though I don't tell tales. We stay out of such things."

The reporter nodded, looking both amused and satisfied by the insider information. She smoothly transitioned back to her cheerful tone. "Well, it looks like everything is coming together beautifully. Please let our viewers know how they can take part in the festivities?"

"Yes, yes, everyone is welcome!" Estella said graciously. "Come to Tablerock this weekend and bring your whole family. There will be fun and food for all ages. We have so many tamales, molé poblano, barbacoa —you come in a car, you'll have to leave in a van, you eat so much! The parade starts at noon on Saturday, there are games for the kids, we have card readers. It is a wonderful time!"

"Thank you so much, Estella," the reporter concluded. "If you'd like something a little more small town than Austin's grandiose celebration, with its gourmet foods and performances by famous Mexican

Americans, join Tablerock instead for its cute little celebration!"

"It was going so well until then," Laurie said under
her breath.

I shrugged. "They're from Austin. What do you
expect?"

The cameraman lowered his bulky equipment and
gave a thumbs up. The interview wrapped. Estella and
the reporter exchanged goodbyes, and then the Austin
news team bundled up their gear and made their way to
the exit.

As the door jangled shut behind them, Estella
headed back to the hubbub of the makeshift tamale
assembly line. "Nice job representing Tablerock," I said
as Estella checked on a table of younger women.

"Oh, it was nothing," she replied, though she looked
pleased. "I want everyone to know what a special, peaceful, community-driven place our town is. Despite that
woman's naked attempts to portray us to the contrary."

Our conversation was interrupted by Cecelia
Goddard bursting through the front door, face pale with
distress. "Estella, come quick!" she cried, voice shrill and
eyes wide with panic. "I think something terrible
happened outside!"

The cheerful chatter in the store faded to tense
murmurs.

Laurie and I exchanged alarmed looks. What could
have Cecelia so undone?

After a few beats of silence, chaos erupted.

The women paused their tamale making to race to the storefront windows. Estella, Laurie and I rushed out the front door of Garcia's, nearly tripping over each other in our haste. The bright sun momentarily blinded me as we burst onto the sidewalk.

I threw up a hand to shade my eyes, squinting against the glare just as Cecelia said, "I think she's dead!"

Chapter Three

A SMALL CROWD OF ABOUT TWO DOZEN PEOPLE HAD gathered in the parking lot around one of the red and green picnic tables set up near the food tents for the Cinco de Mayo festival. Their backs were turned toward us and obstructed my view, but their hushed, urgent tones and distressed exclamations confirmed to me something troubling was happening.

The tangy sweet scent of margaritas mingled with the savory smells of chorizo wafting from the nearby tents, and a faint odor of rotten eggs hung in the air. A woman in an embroidered shawl crossed herself and murmured a prayer under her breath while holding her nose, trying to block out the putrid smell. The man with her scratched his scraggly salt-and-pepper beard, unfazed by the stench.

Their grave expressions made my pulse quicken

with dread about what horrible scene awaited us inside the circle of onlookers.

"Excuse me, pardon me," Laurie said as she nudged her way through. I trailed close behind, catching glimpses of colorful skirts and flowers woven into long, dark hair spilling over the table's edge.

With a gasp, Laurie exclaimed, "Oh my gosh, it's Luna!"

Luna Espinoza, the town's tarot card reader, splayed across the table, headfirst in a giant punchbowl filled with a viscous red liquid. Was it blood? Please don't let it be blood, I prayed.

"Is that strawberry margarita?" someone asked.

Oh, thank goodness.

"Step back and give her space!" Laurie commanded, her veterinary emergency training kicking in as she took charge of the chaotic scene.

The murmuring crowd shifted back a few reluctant steps, fraying flower crowns and poncho fringes swaying, but they continued craning their necks to gawk over each other's shoulders at the tragic scene.

A woman wearing jeans and a halter top tightened her grip on her rosary beads, her knuckles paling. "I don't think she needs any space anymore," she whispered.

"Is Luna intoxicated?" someone asked quietly.

"No, she's dead—are you blind?"

"Did you fart? What have you been eating?"

"Shove off, I did not. Wind probably blowing the paper mill smell this way. Anyway, she's always been eccentric," an older gentleman remarked with a sad shake of his head.

"What does that have to do with her face down in that bowl?"

All around us, phones and cameras were thrust into the air, their owners trying to get a clear shot of the appalling scene laid out on the pavement. The barrage of flashing and clicks only added to the morbid spectacle.

Out of the corner of my eye, I noticed Diego Gomez standing near the edge of the crowd, his shoulders hunched and expression unreadable. His dark eyes were fixed on Luna's lifeless form, one hand raking through his pink-streaked wavy black hair. He seemed... rooted in place, almost. Oddly disconnected from the tense murmurs and shuffling feet around him.

"That's enough gawking! Clear out and give us space!" Laurie said once more, her tone sharp and brooking no argument. The crowd recoiled from her commanding voice but continued peering over one another's shoulders.

With careful hands, Laurie extracted Luna's upper body from the giant scarlet punch bowl, the margarita mixture clinging in sticky strands to her dark, tangled hair. Laurie laid Luna's limp form down on the pavement. Her normally glowing, bronzed skin had taken on an ominous purplish-blue pallor underneath the tacky margarita film, and she was still.

Too still.

"Coming through! I'm a doctor!" Dr. Canter called out in an officious tone, elbowing his way through the swarm of spectators to kneel on the pavement beside Luna's body.

"Yeah, well, I'm a vet!" Laurie shot back, bristling at his interruption. "I know CPR and emergency first aid as well as any physician."

"She's not a Schnauzer. This woman needs a professional medical doctor, not a small animal vet. Move aside."

Under different circumstances, I might have chuckled at the mild territorial dispute between the two. But now was not the time for egos—Luna needed help.

Crouching, Laurie tilted Luna's head back, opened her mouth, and prepared to start CPR. Dr. Canter elbowed her aside, intent on taking charge of the resuscitation attempt.

Laurie's eyes flashed with anger. "What do you think you're doing?"

"Saving this woman's life!" Dr. Canter replied. "I'm the most qualified here."

"I beg to differ if you're going to waste time competing with me for the best seat around a dying woman," Laurie snapped. "Did you forget it's easier with two people? Take your position, doctor, and let me help. Once she's conscious, you can take all the credit."

"Since Luna's a psychic, wouldn't she know who saved her?" someone asked.

"Please!" I implored, my voice tight with emotion. "Just work together! Luna might still have a chance if you stop competing and start collaborating right now!"

With a huff, Dr. Canter made room for Laurie to help.

She began chest compressions while he alternated breaths, but after several agonizing minutes, Laurie looked up, her expression grim. "I'm not getting a steady pulse. I think she's gone," she said, defeat heavy in her voice, but she did not stop.

Diego let out a tortured, strangled cry that pierced the tense air and dropped to his knees beside Luna's lifeless body. With trembling fingers, he took her slender hand in his, cradling it as if it were the most delicate porcelain. Then, as if unable to contain the grief, Diego curved protectively over her legs as great, heaving sobs racked his frame.

A man in the crowd shouted that the county's ambulance was probably around ten minutes out.

"We have to listen to that cheater cry his crocodile tears for ten minutes?" a woman asked, her voice sharp and sarcastic.

"So, ten minutes is too long," Laurie said, continuing chest compressions. "I'm not getting a pulse, and she's not responding, but we don't have a defibrillator here. We need to get her to one. It might not be too late, but it will be if we just wait here."

The urgency of Laurie's voice was clear. We needed

help for her right away if there was any hope of ever reviving her again.

And I could tell from Laurie's expression there wasn't much hope.

Diego, his eyes glistening, said, "Here, let me carry her to my truck. I'll drive her to the local emergency tent they have set up at the end of the festival grounds, and you can continue CPR in the back bed. They have a defibrillator there already. The ambulance can meet us there."

Laurie thought about it, then nodded. "Let's do it."

"It's a good idea. You two ride with Diego and keep trying to revive her," Chief Yarbin, who appeared out of nowhere, told Laurie and Dr. Canter. "I'm going to stay back to secure the scene and get statements. Someone must have seen what happened."

We watched as Diego raced toward his dusty red pickup, Luna's limp body cradled in his straining arms. Laurie and Dr. Canter scrambled to keep pace on either side, and as soon as Diego laid Luna's body out in the truck's bed, the two resumed CPR.

They raced toward the festival's medical tent— unstaffed because the festival had not yet started—but I had little hope. Even so, I said a silent prayer for her survival. Please, please let her pull through this.

Chief Yarbin began ushering the crowd away from the table. "All right folks, clear out of this area. This is now an active investigation." Yarbin motioned for Sadie and me to move in his direction. When we reached him, he asked, "Did either of you notice anything strange or suspicious before finding Ms. Espinoza?"

We shook our heads. "No, I came running out when Sadie came in to tell us what was going on," I replied.

"And I saw her that way when I helped Ms. Jones with a cooler."

Yarbin jotted notes on a small pad, then turned his attention to the punchbowl. He circled around, sharp eyes cataloging details—the violent splashes of sticky red liquid down the sides, pools congealing on the pavement underneath.

Pulling a small testing kit from his pocket, he dipped a strip of paper into the liquid, watching for a color change. His brow furrowed at the results.

"What is it?" I asked.

"Nothing yet. I want to send this to the lab and make sure it's not contaminated."

"Oh, my gosh. You're thinking it was poison? You think someone intentionally poisoned Luna?"

"Did I say that?" Chief Yarbin's thick salt-and-pepper brows slammed together in annoyance. "I didn't say that. It's too early to make any definitive statements. But it seems to me she's too young to have had a heart attack out of the blue. But don't worry, we're going to sort this out."

The chief thinks someone killed her, I thought (with no proof) as I watched him. Then I thought back to Estella's comments about drama among the festival

vendors. Could there be a personal grudge or professional rivalry behind this tragic act? The Cinco de Mayo
celebration was supposed to bring our community
together, not provide a backdrop for violence.

Chief Yarbin sealed the punch bowl with an
evidence tag and loaded it into the back of the cruiser to
transport back to the station for analysis. Then he moved
through the crowd, notebook in hand, asking for statements from potential witnesses, but the Tablerock residents shook their heads, unable to provide any concrete
details beyond the woman's sudden tragic discovery.

It seemed no one had noticed anything amiss until
that horrifying moment when Luna was found.

After what felt like an eternity, Dr. Canter returned to
Garcia's Corner Store with Laurie. "The paramedics
managed to stabilize her enough for transport, but she's
still unresponsive," he reported. "All they can do is
monitor her condition and hope she regains conscious-
ness. The next twenty-four hours are critical."

"I have her keys," Laurie said. "The paramedics
went through her bag to see if there was a medical card
or medication and they found she was well prepared for
an accident. Like, weirdly so—she had an envelope
marked 'In Case of Accident' with her medical card,
keys, and a note that her cat, Mystico, is in her studio
and to please make sure she's fed and taken care of."

Luna lived on the second floor of Garcia's Corner Store, a weathered two-story building well over a hundred years old. A narrow wooden staircase hugged the right side, winding up past a small balcony with an intricate wrought-iron railing to Luna's front door.

The apartment took up the entire second floor. A hand painted placard swinging in the breeze on creaky chains invited curious visitors to climb the stairway and discover their fortunes inside.

Laurie and I headed up, unlocked the door, and stepped into the dimly lit room.

The scent of nag champa incense almost knocked me off my feet.

Luna had transformed one-half of the apartment into a cozy salon filled with candles, divining tools, velvet cushions, and shelves full of spiritual tomes. In the center of the room stood a round table draped with a purple paisley cloth, a crystal ball in the middle. Luna's tarot cards and candles were arranged around it.

Separated by a beaded curtain, the left side served as Luna's efficient living quarters, a snug room outfitted with kitschy, secondhand finds I knew she'd come across at estate sales. For Luna, perched above the town's cornerstone business, the charming apartment offered the ideal balance of exposure and privacy, accessibility and retreat that her unusual profession required.

The sharp click of the can opener pierced the heavy silence hanging over Luna's apartment. Laurie peeled back the metal lid, releasing the pungent aroma of fish into the air.

"Mystico? Kitty kitty, where are you?" she called into the dim space.

A low, cautious meow rumbled in response.

I scanned the room, shapes blending together in the homey area's shadows, until a gleam of turquoise caught my eye. Under the rumpled bedcovers, a pair of feline eyes peered out at us, blinking.

"There she is," I said, crouching down to seem less threatening.

The eyes narrowed and stayed fixed on us. With quiet footsteps, Laurie approached and set the food down, hoping to coax Luna's mysterious companion into the light.

A hairless sphynx cat slunk out, back arched.

"I know, I know," Laurie soothed. "We need you to come to the vet with us for a checkup. Just a quick visit."

Mystico hissed, then strutted away with her tail held high.

"Why on earth would you tell her that?" I asked her.

"What?"

"That you wanted to take her to the vet? That's the statement you thought would get her cooperation? You do know many animals dislike you, don't you?"

"Animals love me. Besides, I thought it was better than leading with the whole shelter scenario."

I looked through the studio apartment, sliding open closet doors and rummaging through the chaotic contents inside. Clothes, candles, bundles of dried herbs —Luna's belongings overflowed with her personality. Finally, tucked away under the bathroom sink, I found a worn purple cat carrier covered in stickers.

I set the carrier down, trying not to alarm her.

"Here, kitty," I called, shaking a toy mouse.

Mystico licked her paws, ignoring me.

Laurie grabbed a feather wand and began dangling it near Mystico's face.

The cat smacked at it half-heartedly, but refused to budge from Luna's bed.

"We could always just pick her up," I suggested.

"I'd rather not get shredded today," Laurie replied. She tried waving the feather wand more vigorously. Mystico took a lazy swipe, nearly toppling off the bed. She dug her claws in to steady herself, clinging stubbornly.

I moved the can of wet food and set it right in the carrier. Then, with exaggerated movements, I grabbed a cat treat container and grabbed a handful to place on top of the wet food.

Mystico lifted her nose, sniffing. Then she hopped down and crept toward the food, keeping a wary eye on us. Just as she started eating, I closed the door, trapping her inside.

Mystico let out an offended yowl.

"I know, sweetie," I said.

The cat glowered at us through the grate, radiating indignation.

"Sorry, girl, but it's for your own good," Laurie told her, lifting the carrier. Mystico grumbled deep in her throat. She turned her back to us.

We headed down the stairs, Mystico muttering the entire way at each jostle and jiggle.

Laurie and I brought Mystico's carrier up the stairs, the cantankerous feline's angry yowls echoing down the hallway of the second floor. Her cries rose in pitch and urgency with each jostling step upward, protesting her arrival at the Silver Circle Cat Rescue as well as her confinement.

"Shhh, we're almost there," I soothed, though I knew it was futile.

That cat had a lot to say, and she intended to say it as loudly as possible.

We set the carrier down just inside the isolation room. Mystico scrambled inside, her claws scraping the plastic in her urgency to escape.

As soon as Laurie unlatched the door, the hairless feline burst out in a blur of wrinkled flesh. She let out an indignant yowl, the sound fading into the sound absorbing walls.

"I don't get points for letting you out, huh?"

The cat wasted no time investigating every corner of the unfamiliar room, her pink nose twitching as it caught unfamiliar scents, while her claws clicked on the hard floor. I tapped the temperature control and raised it to ensure the cat was warm enough.

"Not up to your standards, huh?" I asked, watching the offended cat circle the small room.

Despite its jail cell-like purpose, the isolation room, with its soundproofing and high windows, was decorated with a homey feel to comfort the disquieted—it was, in fact, a very nice, very cozy room. Still, I could understand Mystico's dismay at being whisked away from her bohemian home to what must have appeared to be a sterile environment.

"Hopefully, she'll forgive us when she understands why we brought her here," I said.

Laurie didn't look convinced. "She's walking around with her claws unsheathed. She's more likely to shred our arms to ribbons first. That may be the grumpiest cat expression I've ever seen."

"It's the breed."

Well, and that the cat was furious.

Mystico finished scouting out every corner and was now staring at us with her unnerving blue-green eyes, her tail lashing back and forth.

"Okay, time to introduce her to the talker platter gizmo," I said.

"This should be entertaining."

I crouched down to Mystico's level. "I know you're mad, but we need you to talk to us. It's important."

The sleek feline twitched her ears, unimpressed by my plea.

Laurie stepped over to the second cubby hole in the carpeted cat tree, its plush interior strewn with catnip mice and feather toys thanks to Belladonna and Ginger. Reaching inside the dark recess, she extracted the ornate silver platter—the magical artifact that allowed us to communicate with animals, and them with us.

"This is the magic platter, Mystico," I explained.

The cat's unblinking blue-green eyes followed the dish, her hairless head tilting.

"If you step on it, you'll be able to talk to us. We want to let you know what's going on with Luna, but we want it to be a two-way conversation so we can be sure you're okay, and that you understand."

At the mention of her owner's name, Mystico rose to her feet. Her eyes narrowed, and she took a few cautious steps toward the platter.

"That's it," I coaxed. "Come see what this is all about."

After a few more suspicious glances thrown our way, Mystico's innate curiosity ultimately won out over caution. Her hairless form rippled with lean muscle as she took a graceful, bounding leap up onto the platter.

The crystalline inlay began emanating a soft golden glow, bathing the cat in its otherworldly illumination. She startled slightly, ears flicking upright, but the radiance didn't seem to cause alarm.

I held my breath, waiting to hear Mystico's voice for the first time.

"Well, it's about time!" the hairless cat declared

imperiously. "I've been trying to speak to you dimwitted humans for years. Honestly, I can't believe it took you this long to figure something out. You people really are brain-dead, aren't you?"

Laurie and I exchanged surprised glances.

Though we were always prepared for any personality, Mystico's abrasiveness out of the gate was... new.

"Yes, well, our apologies for the delay," I said. "I'm Ellie, and this is Dr. Laurie Gray. We're acquaintances of your human, Luna."

Mystico flicked her tail. "Yes, yes, I know who you are. Luna tells me all the gossip from town all the time—you're the cat lady shacking up with the hot carpenter, and you're the vet trying to figure out who you should shack up with."

Well.

That was blunt.

"Now, what's this about Luna? Where is she? Why did you bring me to this dreadful place?"

Laurie held up a hand. "Whoa, let's all take a beat here. I know emotions are running high and you must be worried. We want to explain everything in full, but you have to let us talk."

The hairless cat sank back on her haunches, resigned. Her piercing gaze remained fixed on us as she tucked her pink paws underneath herself, awaiting our account with flicking, impatient ears. "Well? Get to it. I haven't got all day."

"There was an incident this morning. Luna

collapsed outside your home, near her margarita competition table. We still don't know what caused it, but she
was unresponsive," I explained. "Diego rushed her to the
hospital where they were able to help stabilize her, but
she still hasn't woken up."

Mystico's eyes widened in alarm. "What?! Is she
going to be all right? What are those foolish doctors
doing for her?" Her tail lashed. "Diego took her to the
hospital? Are you people sure she made it and he didn't
just drop her in a ditch?"

I blinked.

"They're running every test they can think of to
figure out why she collapsed," Laurie reassured her.
"She's getting the best possible care. Beyond that, we
just don't have any answers yet."

"Preposterous!" Mystico spat, her tail lashing behind
her like a whip. "I should be there by Luna's side, not
trapped in this horrid little room with you imbeciles."
She started pacing the platter again, her pink paw pads
tapping against the crystal inlay as she muttered under
her breath.

"Mystico, I—"

"How could you leave my poor Luna all alone? She
needs me there to comfort her, to purr healing energies
into her soul! Her one loyal friend and confidant."

Aw. That was sweet.

"Mark my words. If any harm comes to my darling
Luna while I'm stuck in this dreadful isolation chamber,
I'll shred every piece of furniture in this place. I'll yowl all

night and day until you beg for mercy. I'll sneak into your rooms and snag threads from your nicest clothes with my claws. And then, finally, I will stripe your skin like a zebra with my claws! I'll peel you like a potato! Oh yes, you'll rue the day you crossed Mystico and her Luna!"

Okay.

Maybe not so sweet.

Laurie tried to calm the agitated feline. "I know you're worried for Luna, but the hospital is doing everything they can. The best way you can help her right now is by telling us anything you know and we'll find a way to pass it on to the doctors or police. Did Luna seem ill, or did she mention anything strange happening?"

Mystico paused her frantic pacing, tipping her head.

"Anything might help, Mystico," I told her.

"Well, she did seem more tired than usual this past week. I told her she needed to take better care of herself, but you know how she ignores me." The cat lashed her tail in frustration. "She's been so focused on that festival, running around town making preparations dawn to dusk every day."

"Did she say if there were any conflicts around the festival planning? We know there was some drama between the local businesses."

"Oh yes, Luna was stressed about all of that," Mystico said, sitting back down on the platter. "Something about the tamale shop owners bickering over who had the best recipe. Honestly, humans and their ridiculous squabbles. As if it matters! Rosa Vargas was complaining about Luna's margarita mix. As usual. Estella told Luna to ignore her."

The cat shook her head in exasperation. "She hates conflict, my poor dear. I told her not to worry so much, but she felt responsible as the unofficial town mystic and all."

Laurie jotted notes down on her pad. "Can you remember any specific threats or incidents between Luna and the other shop owners?"

Mystico's nose wrinkled in concentration. "Well, let's see... She did come home one day very upset because that wretched Blanca Cruz from Terra's Gifts was ripping her off. She was overcharging her for incense, and that woman stole Luna's Diego! Luna was quite distressed about it."

"Anything else?" Laurie prodded.

The hairless cat flicked her ears once more. "I don't know. Luna told Blanca she was charging highway robbery prices. Blanca told her to order off the internet if she wanted cheap garbage."

"Did she make any threats toward Luna or give you reason to think she meant her harm?" I asked.

"No..." Mystico said. "Just shouted inappropriate insults about her abilities and clients. Wanted to know what she saw in their readings. Luna sent her away, said she would not share personal information."

I reached out to stroke Mystico's back. She tensed,

then allowed the contact. "You've been helpful, Mystico. Thanks for sharing this with us."

The cat nodded, looking mollified by the praise. "Yes, well, I know my Luna better than anyone. You bumbling humans clearly need my help. Now, I believe I've endured this dismal room long enough. Kindly return me to my proper home at once."

Laurie and I looked at one another. "About that..."

Chapter Four

I CLEANED THE TABLES WITH A SCENTLESS CLEANER, getting rid of any paw prints left by the cats on the unused tables. Things had finally calmed down after the late midday rush, with chairs neatly arranged and empty mugs cleaned and put away. It was a moment of peace before the rush of evening commuters arrived, drawn in by the allure of aromatic coffee, delectable local pastries, and the company of adorable cats.

I glanced over at the corner table where Laurie sat, her brow furrowed, as she recounted the details of Luna's accident in a hushed voice to Landon and Waldo. Landon leaned in, his handsome face etched with concern, nodding along to her story. Their voices were too low for me to make out their words, but their somber body language conveyed the gravity of the situation.

I went over to the table.

"Can I get you all anything?" I asked, forcing brightness into my tone.

Landon scrubbed a hand across his stubbled jaw and attempted a weak smile. "We're all right, thanks, Ellie." He set his mug down, his expression turning serious as he looked at Waldo. "Have you considered canceling the Cinco de Mayo festival, Mr. Mayor?"

"Don't call me that. We've been friends too long for that kind of balderdash," he said and then rubbed his chin. "I get your question, but I don't see why. As much as Luna is an integral part of this town, there's no concern for the public. The doctors told me it was just an early heart attack."

I frowned. "Chief Yarbin seemed concerned it could be poison. That the margarita mix was poisoned," I told him. "It seems logical. I mean, who drowns in a bowl of margarita mix?"

"You only talked to him when it happened, though, right?"

I nodded once.

"Well, since then, no one's found anything of the sort."

Landon reached over and squeezed my hand, his rough, calloused palm pressing against my own in a gesture of comfort. "You know, heart attacks can happen even in young folks," he said. "It's easy to think it only affects older adults, but heart disease doesn't discriminate by age. You and Ellie should know that better than anyone."

I nodded, though Landon's attempts to reassure me didn't ease the uneasy suspicion sitting in the pit of my stomach. Sure, on the surface, Luna's situation appeared an untimely accident, but I couldn't shake the suspicion that there was more to the story. While the rest of the town seemed ready to accept the early heart attack explanation and move on, I wasn't there yet.

A deafening crash from upstairs made the whole table jump. Furious yowls and enraged hisses filtered down the stairway.

"What on earth is that?" Waldo asked.

"Cats," Laurie and I answered simultaneously.

More angry feline shrieks echoed down the stairs as thuds and scrapes reverberated.

"I'd better go check on that," I told them, and turned toward the stairs, taking them two at a time. Following the sound down the hallway, I came to a halt outside the isolation room door, now cracked open. Muffled wails and hisses greeted me from inside, along with the sound of toppling objects.

Throwing open the door, my jaw dropped.

Mystico and Belladonna were locked in a spitting, clawing fur ball of feline fury in the middle of the room. Mystico sported several thin scratches, while Bella's usually sleek-as-a-panther black fur looked like someone had taken a balloon to it.

"Ladies, stop that!" I called out in my best teacher's voice.

It was about as effective as yelling at a hurricane to

simmer down. They continued their primal tussle, a whirling dervish of fangs and claws.

I turned to Ginger, who was watching the ruckus with amusement from atop the cat tree. "How did you two even get in here?"

Ginger blinked his golden eyes at me in a bored look that clearly said 'figure it out yourself, human.'

I put my hands on my hips, pondering the mystery of Belladonna's abilities. I was convinced that cat could slip through a pinhole if she put her mind to it—and her powers of stubborn persistence? Truly unmatched.

"I said stop it!"

The cats sprang apart, fur on end, and both vaulted onto the magic platter, the only place they could verbally shred each other with me as referee. Crouched low, their tails lashed as they yowled from either side of the psychic drink tray, ears flat to their heads.

"Get off!" Belladonna let out a guttural growl and threw herself at Mystico, slamming into the other cat's side.

Mystico tumbled out of the cubby with a shriek, legs flailing. She crashed to the floor and scrambled up, hackles raised, as Belladonna postured menacingly from the entrance of the coveted hideaway.

"Stop this at once. The two of you are acting like children. I mean it! I have no problem getting the towels from the hallway to wrap you up, but I'd much rather you act like adults and stop this."

"No! You dispose of this creature at once!" Bella

spat, fixing me with her furious golden glare. "It is an aberration—a hairless monstrosity!"

"That's a terrible thing to say, Bella."

Mystico agreed, and her wrinkled face scrunched up in outrage.

The sphynx cat's ears flattened against her head as she let out a throaty snarl, the skin along her spine bristling. Muscles coiling, she launched herself into the cubby, head butting Bella's shoulder like a hairless battering ram.

Belladonna staggered, losing her footing at the entrance. She tumbled out, hitting the ground with a thud and a disgruntled yelp. She whipped around, fangs bared, ready to regain her advantage, but Mystico was already peering down at her from the cubby, having claimed the high ground.

Well...

High cubby.

Bella hissed up at her nemesis, thwarted but unwilling to concede defeat.

Mystico stared down. "You dark-furred witch! I am a Mexican Hairless, with a noble heritage! You wouldn't know dignity if it bit your ugly tail!"

Bella jumped up on a platform in front of the cubby, balancing as she stretched to place one black-velvet paw on the magic plate's crystalline surface. "My tail is sleek and stunning and fur-covered, you naked mole rat!" Bella hissed, affronted. She swiped at Mystico, who dodged her claws. "You dare insult me?"

"Okay, we need to stop this. Bella, your claws are way too long, and you could hurt Mystico," I said, moving between them. "Now, what's all this about?"

Mystico glared at Bella. "That elitist snob thinks she's better than me because she has fur! She said my owner was defective for choosing a 'freak' cat. And she told me to get out of this room!"

A black paw dropped on the crystal dish of wonder. "I wasn't being insulting. I stated the obvious. Hairless creatures are unnatural. Your owner had questionable taste."

"Why you arrogant, judgmental—" Mystico spit.

"That's enough," I said. "Every cat is unique and beautiful in their own way. Bella, it isn't kind to insult another for how they look." I stroked Mystico's soft pink skin. "Apologize, please."

Bella huffed, looking away. "Very well. I... apologize for my insensitive but totally and completely true remarks."

Well, it was an apology.

"Thank you, Bella. Mystico?"

The hairless cat grumbled. "I'm sorry, accursed witch cat."

"There, that wasn't so hard!" I was relieved their clash had reached some sort of precarious resolution. With cats, you sometimes had to lower your break-through expectations to subterranean levels. "Now, let's leave the past behind and move forward in harmony," I continued in my most optimistic, conflict-mediating voice.

The two felines turned their heads in unison to skewer me with twin gazes of disdain.

"Oh, stop. Come here, Mystico. I want to clean and treat those cuts."

Belladonna watched, perched delicately on the counter, as I cleaned Mystico's scratches. The magic plate sat right between the two cats so either could chime in if needed.

Bella tilted her head, eyes narrowed in thought. Then she stepped onto the plate, the glow suffusing her sleek fur. "Is there really a Mexican Hairless breed?" she asked, genuine curiosity coloring her tone. "I've never heard of such creatures."

"Not really." I shook my head, skeptical. "While hairless dogs have existed for centuries in Mexico, there's no Mexican Hairless cat breed."

"There is!" Mystico interrupted, tail swishing. "I'm it! Right here in front of you! Ow!" The cat winced as I cleaned a cut on her neck. "Watch it."

"Sorry about that." I raised an eyebrow, amused. "There were a few accounts over a century ago of sleek, hairless felines in New Mexico. Aztec cats, I think they called them. But today's hairless cat breeds are usually sphynx."

"I am not Egyptian!" Mystico's ears folded back.

"The sphynx does have an Egyptian name, but the

breed is from Toronto. It's sometimes called the
Canadian sphynx—."

Mystico hissed. "I'm not Canadian!"

I ignored the outburst. "Some believe the sphynx
bloodline traces back to Russian breeds like the Donskoy
and Peterbald—"

"I am not Russian!"

Bella wrinkled her nose, considering this new information. "I wouldn't dismiss that one. I've watched a lot
of Law & Orders, and the Russian women are always
obnoxious, entitled, too talkative and murderous. That
sounds like you—"

"Shut up, witch," Mystico snapped, offended.

Belladonna arched her back, affronted by the rebut-
tal. "I'm making astute observations, you arrogant
hairless—"

"Ladies, please," I interrupted wearily before their
claws came out again.

The two cats glared at each other, then looked away
with more haughty sniffs.

Evie strolled up to the counter, wisps of hair escaping
her messy bun. She wiped at a smear of cat food on her
sleeve, a souvenir from prepping upstairs.

"Afternoon, Mom," Evie said, rubbing her grum-
bling stomach. "Any chance those are almost ready?"
She nodded at the oven where plump klobasneks were

baking, their sweet bread dough rising around fillings of spiced sausage and cheddar cheese. "They're from Hanzelka's Bakery, right?"

"Yes, they are, and not quite. Patience, my dear. Good things come to those who wait."

"Ugh, fine. But my stomach might stage a coup."

"To distract your stomach, can you give me a hand getting these chairs down?" I asked.

Evie nodded and began flipping chairs off the tables while I started a pot of dark roast.

The bell above the door jangled as Josie breezed in, her usual hurricane of energy. Briefcase swinging, she headed straight for the counter. "It's Friday, ladies!" She slapped her purse down with a thwack.

I hid a smile as I passed her a steaming latte, doctored with extra foam and chocolate sprinkles—her regular.

Josie took an eager gulp, closing her eyes in bliss. "Mmm, that hits the spot. Nothing like caffeine and sugar to get the wheels spinning." She drummed her manicured nails on the counter. "So, what's the plan for Cinco de Mayo? Piñatas? Margaritas? I'm ready to par-tay!"

"It's the middle of the afternoon."

"It's closer to the evening than the morning."

"Some of us still have to work on Fridays, Josie. By the way, how's that case you're working on coming along?" I asked.

Josie sighed, smoothing a hand over her curly hair.

"You're talking about that lawsuit against the non-profit women's shelter?"

I nodded as I wiped down the gleaming counter tops.

"I'll wipe the floor with those misogynistic jerk offs. It's just hard sitting across from them and listening to them whine and complain like they're the victims in all this and not the wives hiding from them." She launched into the details of the civil case she was handling on behalf of the shelter.

The café door jingled open and Matt sauntered in, face lit up with his usual affable grin. "Afternoon, beautiful," he said, dropping a quick kiss on Evie's cheek.

She giggled, swatting at him with a dish towel.

"Hey Ellie. How's the day going?" He grabbed an apron off the hook, tying it on. "Just tell me where you need me."

The late afternoon rush seemed to hit as soon as the words left Matt's mouth.

Mrs. Applebaum settled at her usual window table, knitting needles already clicking away. Dwight and Lou bantered over chess and coffee, their good-natured bickering filling the café. Sadie breezed in, making a beeline for the counter.

"Triple shot latte for me, extra hot," she said, tapping her nails. I could swear she was already vibrating from the caffeine hit before her drink was even ready. "It's just been one of those days already."

The café cats mingled, weaving through chair legs

with arched backs and upright tails, soliciting ear scratches from their adoring fans. Purrs rumbled as fingers found the perfect spots.

Plates clattered, mugs clinked, chairs scraped. The rich aroma of coffee and sound of steamed milk blended with laughter and conversation into the comforting background noise of the cat café.

The café door chimed, cutting our conversation short. Our friend Mario—Officer Mario Lopez—strode in, nodding to customers as he made his way over.

Landon jumped up to greet him, clasping his hand in a firm shake. "Mario, good to see you. Can I get you a coffee?"

"No, not right now," Lopez replied. He turned to address the rest of us. "I wanted to let you know that Luna Espinoza passed away about half an hour ago."

He said it loud enough that many heard, and a hush fell over the café.

I found my voice first. "Do they know what happened yet?"

Lopez shook his head. "The autopsy is pending, but they've ruled out poisoning. Well, the margarita mix checked out clean, anyway. The doctors are still saying it looks like she suffered sudden cardiac arrest, even though she seemed healthy right up until her collapse. They'll dig deeper during the autopsy to pinpoint it for sure, but as of right now? There's no crime. Just a freak thing."

Matt wrapped a comforting arm around a muted

Evie. Josie stared into her coffee with a faraway look while Landon gazed out the window. The cats seemed to sense the somber mood, winding around ankles in a show of comfort and support.

The cat café, so vibrant a moment ago, carried on more subdued conversations, reminiscing about Luna and her vibrant passion for life. More customers filtered in, and we informed them in hushed tones of the loss our community had suffered. Everything took on a more solemn vibe, with patrons speaking in murmurs over their beverages.

I busied myself warming up cranberry-orange scones and remembered they were Luna's favorites. The scent of cinnamon filled the café as the scones finished baking, evoking nostalgic memories of her breezing in on busy mornings. I would miss her brightly patterned skirts swishing between tables, the tinkle of her many bracelets, the melodic lilt of her voice.

I didn't know her well, but I would miss her.

As I slid the scones from the oven, Landon cleared his throat. "I'd like to propose a toast to Luna. Her spirit shone as bright as the moon she was named for. Though she may be gone, her light will continue shining in all of us she touched with her warmth and passion. To Luna Espinoza—forever in our hearts."

"To Luna," we murmured, raising coffee mugs.

A few minutes later, I turned to Landon. "I have to tell Mystico about Luna."

His eyes searched my face, no doubt seeing the

reluctance in the pinch of my mouth and crease of my brow. "Do you want me to come with you?"

"No, but thank you. I think it's best if I do this alone."

Landon gave my shoulder a supportive squeeze, the warmth of his rough hand comforting through my shirt. I managed a smile before heading toward the stairs on feet that felt encased in concrete.

Chapter Five

I CLIMBED THE WINDING GRAND STAIRCASE OF Wardwell Manor, the colored light from the towering stained glass window splashing across the dark wood steps like a kaleidoscope. As I reached the upstairs hall-way, no sound reached me through the closed sound-proofed door to the isolation room.

I slid back the small viewing window and peered inside.

Mystico sat poised on the magic platter, peering up at the ceiling mid-chatter, her tail swishing back and forth like a metronome. She tilted her head side to side, addressing the empty air with such conviction you'd think an entire council of invisible delegates hovered overhead.

"No, no, no, I won't allow such foolishness," she protested, her whiskers twitching. "I know you would never abandon me in this dreadful place. I don't care if you did pass on to the great beyond, you'd never leave me alone with these dreary creatures. I know that."

I looked around, but I saw no one.

No humans. No other cats.

The room appeared empty.

I eased the viewing window shut, wincing as it clicked in the quiet hallway. Maybe she was just airing her worries over Luna's absence to the universe. Talking to herself? I didn't know the cat well, and this might be something she did when she was anxious—without the plate, how did we know what cats were saying when they were extra-vocal, anyway? Maybe many ranted like this when in mourning.

Though I had to admit, her spirited conviction gave me pause.

I stepped into the room and Mystico's glowing eyes darted my way, narrowing like I'd interrupted an important business meeting.

"I was just explaining to Luna why I don't blame her for dumping me in this awful place."

I blinked.

"I'm sorry, you what now?"

Mystico sighed, as if disappointed I wasn't keeping up. "Eleanor, do try to pay attention. Luna and I were just discussing the details of my care now that she's passed on. As I was saying, I refuse to remain here for very long, so you'd better get to work finding me a home with someone as equally dazzling."

I couldn't tear my eyes away from the cat, transfixed by her matter-of-fact ravings.

She looked back at me steadily.

"Mystico," I said, "I know this is a difficult time, but Luna is gone. I'm so sorry, but she can't be here talking with you now."

Mystico's eyes narrowed, her tail thrashing. "Don't be ridiculous. Of course she's here. Just because her body ceased functioning doesn't mean our connection has been severed. She was a great psychic in life and death has only honed her abilities further. Our bond transcends the physical plane."

I sank down into one of the oversized chairs, watching Mystico for any sign this was an elaborate act.

"Right, well... even if that were possible, I can't hear or see Luna. So you'll have to forgive my skepticism."

Mystico sneezed. "Just because your limited human senses can't perceive her doesn't mean she's not here. You underestimate the depth of our connection. Luna says..." Mystico tilted her head, pausing as if listening.

I swallowed, unsure of what to do.

"Luna says that she understands why you might doubt such a transcendental bond, but that you should have more faith in the unseen world, especially since you know what magic is." Mystico nodded. "Yes, Luna. You're right. Clever as always."

I stared at the cat, baffled.

By all appearances, Mystico believed she was

communicating with her deceased owner. Could it be the grief that had caused her to construct this elaborate fantasy? Or was there some mystical force at play here I couldn't comprehend?

"All right. Let's say, hypothetically, that you are talking to Luna's spirit. What have you been discussing?"

Mystico's eyes shone, thrilled to be taken seriously. "Well, as I already told you, there's no way I'm staying in this little prison without Luna. She agrees. Honestly, she should have planned for me after she first started receiving those ominous tarot readings. But does anyone listen to Mystico? Of course not."

"What ominous tarot readings?"

She licked her paw and continued, ignoring my question. "Luna says we needn't worry about such trivial matters now. She has it under control. Once the humans figure out who killed her body, she'll be free to move on from this miserable small town, too, and she'd like to know I'm in a safe place."

"You are in a safe place."

"Okay, a better safe place. With better food."

"Does Luna know how she was killed?" I asked.

Mystico paused, listening again to the invisible spirit she said she saw. "She says she has her theories about who was behind her human body's death, but does not know who committed the act itself. She sensed powerful energies stirring that day—both benevolent and sinister.

But there was too much interference to pinpoint exactly what transpired on the physical plane."

I arched an eyebrow, a wry smile tugging at the corner of my mouth. "So she saw nothing?"

"Isn't that what I just said?"

"Can you ask Luna if she recalls anything specific from that day—any strange encounters or details we should know about?"

"She can hear you." After a long moment, she replied, "Luna says she's not in the mood to talk about it, and she asks if you have any respect for the dead."

I blinked. "Of course I do. Should I not have asked that?"

"She says she knows you're not very spiritual, so it's fine. Luna also says not to judge Diego's behavior. She knows he still loved her in his own misguided way."

Diego? "Didn't they just break up?"

Mystico nodded, then stiffened, hissing at the ceiling. "Well, that was just uncalled for," she spat. After a pause, she huffed, "Honestly, so petty. Fine, we won't talk about the breakup but, honestly, since you were about to die anyway, does it matter? You can't fit a ghost for a wedding dress."

I had no idea if this astonishing interaction was real or some projection of Mystico's grief, but it was fascinating to watch.

The hairless cat turned back in a huff. "Luna insists on someone collecting my personal items from the apartment. Just because she's dead, there's no reason I should lose everything I own in the world." Mystico told me and then grumbled to herself.

How had my life taken such a bizarre turn that these were the type of situations I had to navigate now?

Just a year ago, I was living a simple life running the cat shelter, and now I'm staring at a grieving sphynx cat, trying to figure out whether she was communicating with her departed owner's ghost or having a hallucinatory mental breakdown.

I never believed in anything supernatural. I used to consider myself far too practical for flights of fancy about the mystical realm.

Yet here I sat.

I, Eleanor Rockwell, patron saint of pragmatism, was entertaining the idea that I might be listening to a cat talk to a ghost through a magic plate.

I gathered everyone into the cozy office on the first floor, the familiar aroma of well-loved books and lingering coffee filling the air. As Evie, Josie, Matt, and Mario gathered around my desk, my mind was still spinning from the bizarre encounter with Mystico.

"Mystico was in the isolation room, chatting away."

"Okay..." Mario looked confused.

"To Luna's ghost, she said."

A chorus of gasps and disbelief echoed, their voices a symphony of astonishment. Josephine clapped a hand to her mouth while Matt's eyebrows shot up, nearly disappearing beneath his shaggy hair.

"Come on, Mom," Evie said with an uneasy snicker. "I know we have a supernatural cat chat plate, but talking to ghosts? That's a stretch."

"I know how it sounds. But I'm telling you, Mystico was convinced. She kept calling out to Luna, saying she missed her, and insisting someone needed to go collect her belongings from the apartment."

Josephine's metallic shadowed eyelids fluttered like the wings of a stunned hummingbird, her usual unflappable composure momentarily scattered. "Well, slap me sideways, a ghost-whispering hairless feline. Who'd have thunk?"

Mario's thick, expressive brows furrowed as a deep frown creased his tanned face. "I try to keep an open mind considering the cat talking plate and all, but contacting spirits? This seems far-fetched, even for a tarot reader's cat."

Evie's hazel eyes darted around the room. "Yeah, I mean, Luna never claimed to contact the dead before... right?" she asked. Evie's eyes ping-ponged between us, our doubtful expressions mirrored on each tense face. An uneasy quiet descended, uncertainty thickening the air.

No one seemed to have an answer.

"Look, I'm just as skeptical as the rest of you," I said. "But I can't ignore that Mystico believes she communicated with Luna's spirit. I don't know what to make of it, and I don't know what I should do about it."

As if summoned, the office door swung open with a creak, and Landon's hulking frame lumbered through. "Howdy folks, sorry I'm late." His brown eyes crinkled. "What'd I miss?"

I recapped the situation while Landon listened.

"I'd like to say I don't believe it, but I'm beginning to wonder if just about anything's possible. A year ago, I wouldn't have thought that magic platter of yours was conceivable, but here we are."

"Okay, so, let's think about this." Evie's brows drew together as she tapped her chin, lost in contemplation. "I mean, there are lots of legends about cats having mystical powers and connections to the spirit world. So maybe Mystico did talk to Luna's ghost."

"I realize with the plate staring us in the face, it's hard to say what's possible and impossible, but contacting the dead seems... beyond the pale." Mario's words were laced with uncertainty. "If cats could talk to the dead, wouldn't we know this already? Why is it only Mystico that can talk to ghosts? Why can't Belladonna talk to Fiona? Why couldn't Honey talk to Ben? Why just this cat and this victim?"

"If she's a victim," Evie added.

"You're right. It does sound crazy," Josie agreed. "Then again, we've got a fajita platter that enables cross-species conversations. Ain't nothing normal about that, either, folks."

"What if we just go along with it?" Matt asked. "It's not going to hurt anything to pretend like we believe it and see what Mystico says about Luna's death. We could swing by Luna's and pick up some of her stuff to bring back here in case this is just a ploy to get her items. Maybe it'll give the cat some peace of mind and she'll stop making the claim."

Evie beamed at him, pride shining in her hazel eyes. "I think Mom or Laurie should go. They'll know if anything's different from when they were there before."

Josie smoothed her skirt. "Well, guess our first step is settled, then. We'll collect some of Mystico's earthly belongings from Luna's place to soothe the alleged unhappy spirit—whether that's a cat or a ghost—and the rest of us will pretend we don't think this cat is flat out nuts."

"I think we ought to keep open minds about this peculiar situation," Evie said to Josie. "I know it seems funny, but it isn't our place to judge what a mournful cat communes with, magic platter or not. If Mystico needs this to process through the grief, I say we respect that. And if she's telling the truth, we'll figure it out soon enough."

Evie's statement gave Josie pause, a flicker of wonder passing over her face, before she collected herself and granted a concurring nod. "Point taken."

Mario's fingers raked through his hair, his dubious expression mingled with reluctant acceptance. "Did she share any specific information about Luna's death that might help me know where to look?"

"Just that Luna believes she was killed," I told him. "Whether it's possible, Mystico seems convinced what she's saying is real. Oh, and she said that we shouldn't look at Diego or let what we find about Diego make us suspicious or something, because Luna was sure Diego still cared about her."

"Well, that's not very helpful. Ellie, you think maybe the cat knows something and thinks this is the only way she can pass on information and be believed?"

With a shake of my head, I dismissed the improbable idea. "Cats don't really think like that, Mario. They have pretty high expectations that they'll be believed, and their manipulations aren't that complicated."

Josie smirked. "Look at us, debating the supernatural like it's any other Friday. Never a dull moment with you folks."

Mario and Landon left to go back to work while Josie and I shuffled through the motions of our day, keeping the Silver Circle Cat Café—or lawsuits against misogynists—chugging along like a well-oiled machine. But as our eyes locked over the course of the afternoon, I could tell our minds were lost in a galaxy of thoughts.

While I brewed coffee and chatted with customers, my thoughts kept drifting back to Mystico and her supernatural abilities. Could she converse with spirits? It seemed fantastical, yet something nagged at me, a little corner of my spirit that whispered I shouldn't be so quick to dismiss.

Later that afternoon I retreated to my office, seeking refuge in mounds of paperwork. But numbers and forms blurred together as my mind wandered back to Mystico's eerie claims. In the search engine bar, I typed in "cats talking to dead people" and hit enter.

I stared at the computer screen, brows knitted.

There certainly was a lot of information.

I didn't know how long I scrolled and stared, but a sharp rap at the open door jolted me from my stupor.

"Yes?"

"Mind if we come in?" Josie's familiar voice called. "I told Laurie."

"Sure" The door cracked open, and I waved her over to the chair across from my desk. "Come on in. I'm getting zero work done, anyway."

"Figured you could use some company after the commotion this morning," she said, plopping down with a swish of her skirt.

Laurie trailed after Josie, pulling the door shut behind her. She sank into the vacant chair next to Josephine, eyes round with disbelief. "So let me get this straight," she said, leaning forward. "Ghosts? I've seen some weird stuff with that magic platter, but dialing up the deceased? That's a new one."

I took off my reading glasses and rubbed my eyes. "I

won't pretend it wasn't one of the strangest moments I've had in a while. And that's saying something around here. I keep wanting to go back up there and talk to her, but something's keeping me here." Drawing a deep breath, I exhaled. "Honestly, I'm not sure I want to know for sure."

"I know what you mean. I thought about going up there and talking to her, but you know what I thought about?" Josie let out a chuckle. "What if I go up there and my mother's found her way here? I don't know if I want to hear what Mama has to say to me from the great beyond."

"Oh, man." Laurie looked up. "My father would lecture me until next week about getting a divorce. Actually, first he'd remind me he warned me that Gary was a no good jerk that I shouldn't marry, and then he'd give me an earful about divorcing him."

"It'd almost be laughable if Mystico hadn't seemed to really believe she spoke with Luna's spirit." I leaned back. "And I can't help but thinking if she did, what does that mean? We thought we had an obligation to help because we could talk to cats—now we have ghosts, too? What's our obligation if ghosts show up here? I just can't wrap my head around it."

"Well, if anyone could reach back here from beyond the veil, it'd be that Luna Espinoza." Josie shrugged, her gold hoops swaying. "That girl always did seem to know a bit more than she should about things happening in this town."

A heavy silence settled over the office, the ticking clock suddenly deafening. Josie's gaze bounced to Laurie, one eyebrow quirked in question. Laurie chewed her lip, arms crossed, staring at the floor in contemplation.

I shifted in my seat, eyes ping-ponging between their uncertain expressions. "All kidding aside. Do you guys think it's possible?"

Josie answered with a shrug of her shoulders. "After all we've witnessed, I'd believe anything. But for the moment, it doesn't matter what I think. Point is, Mystico's convinced. Rest of us just gotta roll with the punches for the moment and things will shake out one way or another. I've seen enough weirdness around here to know better than to write anything off too fast."

Laurie nodded. "Same. I think."

"You're both right," I said. "No use getting worked up over what I can't explain. Whether it's legit, we've got a grieving cat who could use some comfort. If I concentrate on that, whatever else happens will happen."

Josie smiled. "Don't sweat the details. Yet."

With that, she hoisted herself up. "Now c'mon, enough fretting over phantoms and felines. Let's close up shop, leave Darla or Evie in charge of Elvira upstairs, and we'll go grab some drinks at the festival until Landon can join you." Landon insisted that I wait for him to go back into Luna's apartment. "Whatever else is happening, it's still party time in Tablerock. I think we could all use a margarita." Josephine's eyes glinted steel-sharp as she tapped her nails on my desk, the picture of poise. "Luna would want it that way."

Though Mystico's eerie claims still nagged at me, I knew speculating would get me nowhere and Josie's idea wasn't a bad one. Some distance was a good idea.

For the moment, I let it be.

The rest would unfold however it was meant to.

I hoped.

Chapter Six

WHEN LANDON AND I ARRIVED AT LUNA'S
apartment, I was surprised to find the space as orderly as
the last time I had been there—not what I'd expected.

I had expected the police to have combed through
the place by now, rifling through drawers and moving
furniture to look for any clues or evidence that Luna's
death wasn't natural. Seeing my expression, Landon
reminded me that in the official assessment, no crime
had been committed.

"Right," I said. "No crime, nothing to search for."

Luna's death was natural. With no suspicion of foul
play, the police had no cause to tear the apartment apart
looking for answers.

I felt a pang of frustration as I glanced around the
space. If this was a murder, the killer had been handed
more time to cover their tracks while the police sat idle.

Valuable evidence could already be lost. But without proof of a homicide, I reminded myself, the authorities' hands were tied.

"We may as well look around while we're here," I said.

Landon agreed it couldn't hurt, so we started poking around the space.

My gaze fell upon a worn leather book sitting on the coffee table and I picked it up, leafing through the pages.

"Oh, my gosh," I gasped.

"What is it?"

"Do you have any idea how many people came to Luna for readings?" Lots of prominent members of our small town came over the years to have their tarot cards read. Councilman Hammond, Doc Canter, Jessa Winthrop—even Chief Yarbin had been here. Beside each name, Luna had drawn a small symbol or image in colored pencil. I wondered what they signified. A note? An impression? "It's a lot. More than I would have thought."

I tucked it into my bag.

Landon raised his eyebrows at me. "That a cat toy?"

"Mystico might be able to make sense of it," I explained with a shrug.

As Landon and I poked through the rooms of Luna's apartment, I chatted with him about the ongoing tensions back at the cat shelter between Mystico and Belladonna.

In many ways, the two felines were cut from the same cloth. Both carried themselves with an air of entitlement and importance, demanding attention and accommodation. Neither would back down or compromise. It was like housing two insistent imperial queens under one roof.

"I just hope they can get along," I said. "All this hostility isn't helping either of them."

Landon nodded. "I'm sure they will."

Wandering into the bedroom, I paused in the doorway with a frown. The bed was made with a colorful woven blanket, the throw pillows arranged just so. But I could have sworn when I was in here before, the bedclothes were rumpled and the pillows askew, like Luna had just gotten up that morning or made the bed in a rush.

"That's strange," I murmured.

"What is it?" Landon asked from the living room.

"The bed," I called back. "It's made. But yesterday it wasn't."

Landon appeared in the doorway beside me. "Maybe Luna's ghost tidied up before she crossed over," he suggested with a playful grin.

"Hilarious." I looked around, almost hoping for a sign of her presence. Though I didn't expect to see anything supernatural, a secret part of me wished for a glimpse of her spirit, something I could see with my own eyes that suggested a visit from the great beyond. "I just find it strange, that's all."

I continued searching through Luna's bedroom for items that might bring comfort to Mystico when a drawer in the nightstand caught my eye. The handle glinted slightly in the afternoon sunlight streaming through the window, as if beckoning for me to investigate its contents.

I slid it open and found it brimming with an array of personal mementos—photographs bundled together of Luna and Diego, movie ticket stubs, receipts, little handwritten notes on scraps of paper covered in hearts.

"Hey Landon, come look at this," I called over my shoulder.

He appeared beside me and let out a low whistle. "Looks like a relationship keepsake drawer."

"I think you might be right." I began sifting through the photographs, an unexpected glimpse into Luna and Diego in happier times—kissing under fireworks, holding hands on a Ferris wheel, dressed to the nines for a black-tie benefit. "They looked so happy."

Beneath the photos were movie ticket stubs from their dates, playbills from local productions they'd seen together, and a bundle of love letters tied with a red ribbon. I untied the ribbon and unfolded one of the letters. Someone's elegant script filled the page.

"My dearest Luna, each moment with you feels like basking in the glow of a full moon. You illuminate my life with your radiance..." I refolded the letter, feeling I'd intruded on a private moment between them.

"Should we take any of this?" I asked Landon.

He considered the drawer's contents. "I don't know. You think we should?"

I selected a handful of pictures capturing Luna at her happiest, and as I tucked the bundle of love letters in my bag, a receipt fluttered out.

I glanced at it.

It was for a large order from an herbal supplier called Mother Nature's Remedies, dated two weeks before Luna's death.

"That's odd," I murmured, showing Landon the receipt.

He frowned. "Didn't Luna buy all her supplies from Terra's Gifts?"

"Mystico and Estella both mentioned Luna having issues with Blanca," I said, recalling my conversation with Mystico. "I wondered if this large order somehow tied into that. Perhaps Luna had been so upset with Blanca that she went looking for an alternative source for her herbal ingredients and spiritual supplies. Or she was stocking up in preparation to cut ties with Blanca's business altogether."

"Could be worth showing to Chief Yarbin," Landon suggested.

"Why, though? He doesn't think there's a crime."

The timing of the receipt felt significant given Luna's recent tensions over her supplier—and her ex-boyfriend. Why would a work receipt be in the keepsake drawer, after all?

For now, I slipped it into the client book to show Mystico later.

We did a last sweep of the bedroom before preparing to leave. My gaze fell on a jewelry box on the dresser. Inside, I found Luna's moonstone bracelet and silver hoop earrings. I closed the lid and placed the box in my bag, hoping Mystico would be comforted by having these keepsakes close.

I felt the weight of sadness in my bag of mementos. But if these objects could bring even a small measure of peace to the cat, it would be worth the somber errand.

Luna deserved to be remembered, especially by those who loved her most.

Landon and I emerged from the stairwell leading to Luna's apartment, our arms laden with the belongings we had gathered for Mystico.

To any outsider, we probably looked like the world's most eccentric cat sitters, lugging around toys, scratching posts, and tiny sweaters knitted for felines. I clutched a plastic bag of photos to my chest, while Landon carried a small box containing Luna's crystals, tarot cards, and the ornate silver brush that Mystico had requested—although the cat had no hair.

I hoped we could ease Mystico's grief even a fraction by surrounding her with familiar objects that still carried

Luna's scent and energy. Maybe I was being silly, projecting human emotions onto an animal. I couldn't help it. In my gut, I knew Mystico had loved Luna as dearly as any person loved any other person.

It was a beautiful spring day, with clear blue skies and a light breeze, in stark contrast to the somber task we had completed. Mother Nature didn't seem to have gotten the memo that we were in mourning—while we gathered memories, she was busy putting on a cheerful weather show, complete with bird songs and the scent of wildflowers drifting on the breeze.

Lost in thought, I nearly collided with Estella Garcia.

"Oh! Estella, I'm so sorry," I exclaimed.

The older woman waved off my apology with a warm, crinkled smile.

"No harm done, mija," she assured me. Then her dark eyes flitted over the items in our hands. "What brings you here again?"

I hesitated, unsure how to explain our strange errand. Sensing my reluctance, Landon stepped forward.

"We were just gathering some things from Luna's apartment for her cat," he stated matter-of-factly in his deep, gentle voice. "She was very attached to Luna, so we thought some familiar items might comfort her."

Estella's expression softened with understanding. "Ah, how nice. What a thoughtful thing for you to do." She shook her head. "That poor little gatita, losing her human. And Luna—so young, so young. I still can't believe she's gone."

I nodded. "We're going to take good care of Mystico. Luna clearly adored her."

"Sí, you have no idea. Those two were inseparable," Estella agreed. Then she focused her wise, crinkled eyes on me. "You have a good heart, Ellie. Luna would be glad her gata is in such caring hands."

I flushed under the unexpected praise. Before I could respond, an irritable voice interrupted.

"Estella! Estella! I need to talk to you."

Rosa Vargas emerged from the corner store with an impatient scowl that marred her otherwise attractive features. I knew Rosa had always harbored a grudge against Luna, jealous of the success of her margaritas, and their rivalry had only gotten worse this year, with Rosa filing a formal complaint against Luna's entry in the margarita cocktail competition.

A complaint that seemed pointless now.

Oblivious to the tension, Rosa breezed on. "Estella, now that our town's resident hippie witch is out of the picture, I expect you to give me the prime margarita booth spot this year." She flicked her long hair over one shoulder. "After all, with Luna gone, I'm the best mixologist around."

Estella bristled, drawing herself up to her full height of five foot two. "Rosa Emilia Vargas, shame on you!" she scolded. "That poor woman's body is barely cold, and you're already elbowing her out of the way for a margarita competition? Your mother would be ashamed of you."

Rosa rolled her eyes. "Oh, please. It's just a booth location."

"It is common decency and respect for the dead to care more about their loss than your gain," Estella retorted. Behind her, I noticed a few passersby slowing to watch the confrontation unfold.

"Fine, take her side as always," Rosa snapped, crossing her arms across her chest. "I don't know why you insist on mollycoddling that witch. Even now that she's six feet underground! She doesn't need your help anymore."

I looked at Landon and asked, "Did we miss a funeral?"

Estella drew a deep, steadying breath, as though praying for patience, and when she replied, her voice was ice cold. "Eleanor and Landon here are collecting Luna's belongings for her beloved cat. Meanwhile, you waltz over here demanding a better booth for your margaritas." She shook her head in disgust. "If I give anyone that prime spot now, it will be in Luna's memory, not to you to reward your shameful behavior."

I watched as proud, unflappable Estella Garcia scolded the middle-aged owner of Rosa's Cantina in public like a naughty child. Beside me, Landon raised his eyebrows but wisely held his tongue.

"But Estella—" Rosa interrupted, cheeks flaming in humiliation.

Estella silenced her with one withering look. "If you want to discuss this later, Rosa Emilia, you will wait until I'm not so offended by you. For now, I think you should take your selfishness out of my sight. Go!"

With as much dignity as she could muster, Rosa spun on her heel and flounced across the street toward her restaurant, head held high.

Estella watched her go, lips pursed in a tight line.

"I'm so sorry you had to witness that," she said. "This community is full of wonderful people, but some? They forget themselves." Turning back to us, the older woman pasted a smile on her face, though her eyes still flashed with irritation. "It takes all kinds, I suppose."

"No need to apologize," I assured her.

"Yes, no need, but we should really be going," Landon added. "We need to get these items back to Silver Circle. I'm sure Mystico could use one of her sweaters."

Estella's expression softened once more at the mention of Luna's cat. "Of course. Thank you again for doing this for the poor gatita." She stretched up on tiptoes and pressed a kiss to Landon's tanned cheek, then did the same for me. "You both have good hearts. I am glad my Mateo found all of you."

With an enigmatic smile, Estella turned and bustled into the corner store. As the door closed, I could hear her shouting directions to the staff inside, already moving on from her confrontation with Rosa.

"Never a dull day around here," he said, hefting the

box of Luna's belongings into the back of his pickup truck.

I laughed under my breath. "That's for sure."

As Landon and I climbed into his pickup, the sounds of a heated argument drifted from the alley behind Garcia's Corner Store. I paused with one foot on the running board, debating if I wanted to be nosy.

Okay, it wasn't much of a debate.

My nosy gene would never let this opportunity pass.

"Get in. I'm going to roll my window down," I whispered, motioning for Landon to stay quiet, and he obliged with an indulgent chuckle, knowing me too well. We both leaned toward my open window, straining to make out the muffled voices rising from the narrow passage.

"You need to back off and let it go already!" a man bellowed, his words clipped with anger.

A woman responded, her voice strained and desperate. "I'm not letting this drop until you tell me what happened that night!"

The man scoffed. "What night? Blanca, she's gone. Can you just let it drop?"

"Oh please, Diego. I know you and Luna had a deep connection."

My eyes widened after hearing the names—this was an argument between Diego Gomez and Blanca Cruz,

Luna's ex-boyfriend, and the woman Estella claimed had "swept" Luna's feet.

I still wasn't sure what that colorful Mexican turn of phrase meant and why getting your feet swept was this bad thing, but I knew it wasn't a compliment.

Diego's laughter cracked through the air. "Deep connection? We broke up weeks ago. You made sure of that. Luna made it pretty clear she wanted me out of her life after the stunt you pulled."

"Oh, get off it! I know you never stopped loving her," Blanca accused. "And she still cared for you, despite it all. If she was in trouble, she would've reached out."

"Well, she didn't, okay?" Diego snapped. "I know nothing. She never came to me about threats or conflicts or whatever you think happened."

"But the tensions around the festival... her fights with Rosa..."

"She had some petty business disagreements, that doesn't mean—" Diego caught himself mid-sentence. When he spoke again, his words were slow and deliberate. "Look, I don't know what you're getting at here, but the cops don't think anyone did anything to her. It was a tragic thing, and she's gone. Leave it at that."

I could imagine Blanca shaking her head defiantly. "Just gone? Tell me what—"

"I don't know a damn thing!" Diego yelled, making me jump. "Even if I did, what makes you think I'd tell you? She died thinking I betrayed her thanks to you!"

"I don't believe you," Blanca replied.

Diego's laughter held all the warmth of an icy gust of wind. "No? What, you think I'm the one who did it? You think I poisoned her drink or something?"

My hand flew to my mouth at his words. Diego couldn't be serious... could he?

Blanca hesitated before responding. "Why would you say that?"

"I think you were jealous and wanted revenge," Diego told her. "I think you might have slipped something into her margarita when she wasn't looking. Then you have me rush her to the hospital when she collapsed. You told me she was woozy! How would you know? She hated you! She wouldn't tell you she was feeling ill, so how would you know?"

"Stop it!" Blanca exclaimed. "That's not funny."

"Who's laughing?" Diego retorted. "Do you see me laughing? You think I murdered the only woman I've ever loved in cold blood? I couldn't live my life without her. And you knew that. And maybe that's why it happened."

Blanca was silent for several long moments. When she finally spoke, her voice was laced with uncertainty. "Even if that were true, I wouldn't—"

"If? It was true. I'm telling you it's true. You thought I would wind up with you, didn't you?" Diego asked. "You're delusional."

"Are you telling me you don't want to be with me?" Blanca asked.

When Diego responded, his voice was so quiet I

almost missed it. "You don't listen to anything anyone says, do you?"

Footsteps echoed down the passage as Diego stormed away.

"Where is she?" I whispered.

Landon shrugged. "I thought they were dating?"

"So did I."

A minute later, Blanca emerged onto the street, glancing up and down the empty sidewalk like a meerkat on sentry duty. As her gaze landed on us, her eyes narrowed and I felt like a deer frozen in headlights. I was sure she could see the guilt written on my face after eavesdropping on her oh-so-enlightening lovers' tiff.

I rearranged my features into a pleasant smile.

"Did you need something?" she asked through the open window.

The intensity of her gaze made me squirm.

"No, no, we were just leaving," I told her, and waved. Before she could respond, I said to Landon, "We should get going. Evie will wonder where we are."

Landon put the truck in gear and pulled onto the street.

As we drove off, I could almost feel the weight of Blanca's stare drilling into the back of my skull, like she was trying to telepathically convince me to spill coffee on my lap as a form of petty revenge.

"Smooth," Landon commented, with what I assumed was an attempt at reassurance.

"Was it?"

He shot me a sidelong glance, one eyebrow arched in silent commentary. "No, not really. She knows we were listening. You could see it in her expression." Landon reached over and gave my hand a comforting squeeze. "But it showed us something. What, though, I have no idea."

Chapter Seven

Zora Hillard was perched on a stool at the counter when Landon and I walked into the café, Luna's belongings in hand. She took one look at the items and let out an exaggerated wail, bursting into tears.

Landon and I froze in place, stunned into silence by Zora's dramatic reaction. She let out a shrill wail before collapsing into loud, heaving sobs, going on and on about how Luna had been her absolute guiding light in this dark world, and how she couldn't believe that Luna was gone.

I stood frozen, bewildered by Zora's extreme reaction. She pounded her fists on the counter, her words coming out in choked, uneven spurts: "How will I know when Mercury is in retrograde? How will I know when the universe has it out for me? How? How?"

With a shaky hand, she grabbed a napkin and blew her nose.

After a minute that seemed to stretch on forever, Zora seemed to regain some of her composure. She took a few deep, shaky breaths, drying her eyes on the sleeve of her blouse and sitting up ramrod straight on the stool.

"Sorry about that," she said with a sniffle. "Luna was my rock, you know? For the past five years, she's steered me through every bump in the road. Helped me make the hardest choices."

"We understand." Landon nodded, but his forehead creased and his lips formed a thin line, contradicting his claim of understanding.

Zora shook her head, fresh tears welling. "I feel like a boat with no rudder. Adrift." She crumpled the napkin in her fist. "I just don't know how I'll make it through without my spiritual lighthouse."

"I can't imagine how you feel right now," I said, setting Luna's hairbrush and tarot cards down on the counter.

Zora pursed her lips and nodded, touching her fingers to the cards like a butterfly landing on a flower. "I know, it's just awful. She was so vibrant and full of life." She emitted a shaky sigh, looking down at the hairbrush as she traced her fingers over the silver crescent moon charm dangling from the handle. "I can't believe our Luna is gone."

"It's always hard when things like this happen so unexpectedly."

Zora's expression hardened. "But maybe not so unexpected for little Miss Margarita Wannabe queen, especially considering how well Rosa seems to be making out from the death of her so-called friend," she said. "Between you and me, I don't buy this heart attack crock for a minute."

"What do you mean, Zora?" Landon asked.

She leaned in close, crooking a finger at us. "Ever since Luna died, it's like Rosa hit the jackpot. She's a shoo-in to win the margarita competition. And don't even get me started on this new restaurant deal. My inside sources tell me Rosa's about to cash out bigger than a piñata full of Benjamins. We're talking another easy half mil to the sale price thanks to her new champion margarita status."

Landon and I exchanged puzzled glances.

"What sale price?" I asked.

"Well, as you know, my husband Joe works for that restaurant acquisition group that's been buying up places around Austin," Zora said and gave a nonchalant hair flip. "And he told me they're deep in negotiations with Rosa to purchase her restaurant for a hefty sum. We're talking half a million at least. Maybe more now."

She shook her head, as if disgusted by Rosa's fortune.

Landon furrowed his brow. "I've heard nothing about Rosa's Cantina being up for sale, and Waldo would have mentioned it."

Waldo, Tablerock's mayor, was Landon's close friend. He made it his business to know about major business dealings in town—and the two men gossiped like schoolgirls, though I'm sure neither would admit it.

"I doubt the mayor knows yet." Zora gave an exaggerated shrug, waving a hand as if swatting away Waldo's awareness of anything happening in Tablerock. "It's all hush-hush for now. But trust me, the deal is as good as done. Joe recommended the place to his bosses in the first place, so he'd know."

If Rosa was cashing out and selling her beloved restaurant to some corporate giant right on the heels of Luna's untimely death, I couldn't deny the timing seemed fishier than a week-old tilapia festering in the sun.

But coincidence was also possible; this could be a morbid but accidentally fortunate twist of fate, I reminded myself.

Lately, I'd been falling into a tendency to imagine the worst possible motives behind people's actions, and I didn't want to become one of those people. You know, the meddlesome ones that saw evil intentions around every corner.

Still... my gut whispered to my sensible, open-minded head that Rosa's upcoming windfall—if it was true—could be far more than sheer lucky happenstance.

"All I'm saying is..." Zora shot a furtive glance around before continuing. "Rosa seems to be cashing in big time with Luna's unfortunate passing. That's all. Maybe it means something, maybe it doesn't." Her eyebrows raised as she sat back. "Anyway, what are you doing with Luna's stuff?"

"We went by Luna's apartment to pick up some of

her belongings for Mystico," I explained. "Cats latch onto scents and familiar items to feel secure, so having Luna's brush or scarf around will be comforting for the cat during this difficult transition."

"Of course, of course!" Zora said, leaning forward. "Luna's scent on her belongings will mean the world to Mystico right now. What did you bring her?"

I opened the tote bag and started laying out the treasures from Luna's apartment: the ornate silver hairbrush with delicate moon charms, the jewelry box, a set of amber bottles of earthy essential oils, Luna's worn tarot card deck with edges frayed from years of use. I placed a flowing embroidered purple shawl, its tasseled fringe splaying out, next to the growing collection.

"Oh Luna, Luna," Zora murmured. "I can't believe she's really gone."

Finally, I pulled out an assortment of photos and curling letters bundled with twine.

"Huh." Zora picked up a photo of Luna and Diego from happier times, staring at it with a frown. "Not sure I would have grabbed this. Mystico's more likely to scratch Diego's face off."

"Why's that? Because of the break up?"

"He's—" Zora set the photo down and dabbed at her watering eyes again with the napkin. "Oh, I'm so sorry, it's just so hard. I'm sure Mystico will appreciate having some of these familiar items to comfort her."

"We hope so," I said, wondering what she'd been about to say.

Zora nodded, dabbing at the last of her tears. As we placed Luna's belongings back into the faded tote bag, she spoke up. "I wonder... would you mind if I kept one small memento of Luna for myself? I'd love to have something to keep her memory close."

"Of course, go ahead," I said.

She selected a silver bangle bracelet from Luna's box of jewelry and slipped it onto her wrist. "There, I'll think of her every time I wear this," she whispered. "Thank you again for doing this. I know Mystico will find great solace in having Luna's things close, and I will feel her guiding me thanks to this."

With that, she gathered her things and headed out the door, the bracelet glinting on her arm.

After Zora hurried out the door, Landon shook his head with a wry smile. "Whew, that woman could win an Oscar with those theatrics. But still..." His expression turned serious. "Those were some bold accusations she was making about Rosa being behind Luna's death."

"Well, she didn't say that, precisely—"

"Were they even friends like Zora claimed?" Evie asked.

I turned to her. "Who are you talking about?"

"Luna and Rosa," she clarified. "Zora called Rosa Luna's so-called friend. Were they actually friends?"

I frowned as I thought back to our tense encounter with Rosa and Estella at the festival earlier. "Estella seemed angry at Rosa for focusing on getting Luna's booth and best margarita title before Luna was even in the ground," I said slowly. "From what I saw, it didn't seem like Luna and Rosa were close friends—I mean, Estella accused Rosa of capitalizing on Luna's death, and I don't think the accusation was that far-fetched. If the two were friends, Rosa hid any grief well in that exchange."

"I think it's all just gossip for now," Landon said.

"Well, not what we heard. That's not gossip. We heard things."

"True, but the rest of it? Mostly gossip."

He was right.

It was all mostly gossip.

But after the wild mysteries and crimes we'd unraveled in this small town over the past year, it seemed Tablerock had a penchant for turning mundane events into convoluted, dangerous sagas.

A part of me almost hoped Zora's gossip about Rosa was just idle chatter, for the town's sake... but my sixth sense persisted that in a place like Tablerock, you couldn't count on anything to stay uncomplicated for long.

As Landon and I entered the quiet isolation room, the hairless sphynx perked up when she saw us, her luminous eyes zeroing in on the canvas bag of Luna's belongings I lugged in.

"Good evening, Mystico," I said.

Her ears swiveled forward, and she voiced a tiny "mrrup" of curiosity, padding over to inspect the bag.

"I brought some things from Luna's apartment for you," I said, placing the bag on the floor and sitting down. Mystico peeked inside, her eyes widening when she spotted the familiar hairbrush and Luna's favorite scarf.

Mystico leaped up into the magic platter cubby, her pink paw pads landing on the smooth surface. "Oh, thank you, thank you! It warms my heart to have these pieces of my Luna close to me again."

I returned Mystico's smile, then pulled out the leather-bound book. "I also found this book. It appears to be a record of Luna's tarot readings," I explained, opening the cover to reveal page after page filled with neat handwritten notes—clients' names, appointment dates, and Luna's mysterious symbols. "Can you tell me what these symbols mean?"

Mystico's warm, curious gaze shifted to a stern, wary glare. Her eyes narrowed, pupils constricting to slim lines, and her tail gave an agitated flick.

"Luna says she does not want that book in your hands," the cat stated bluntly.

"Are you sure that's what Luna says?" I asked. "Because it sounds like that's what you say, Mystico. And that's okay if you have an opinion and you want to tell me that opinion, you know. We care about what you want."

Mystico let out an exasperated sigh, as if

explaining something obvious to a stubborn child. "Why should I bother sharing my own thoughts and opinions? You don't listen," she said. "Just because Luna's physical body has passed on does not mean her spirit has vanished. She remains here, watching over me always. And she insists I inform you her client book is private—you should not be rifling through that."

The cat finished her lecture with a reproachful look, flicking her tail in annoyance at my intrusion into Luna's confidential records.

I exchanged a glance with Landon.

It was clear Mystico still believed she could communicate with Luna's watchful spirit. And if that was the case, I could understand why this spectral version of Luna wanted privacy around her personal client records.

But our investigative instincts couldn't be ignored, either.

As much as I wanted to honor Mystico's (or Luna's) desire for secrecy, this book could hold valuable clues and my desire to confirm the truth about Luna's death outweighed the temptation to respect the phantom Luna's demands that I set this potential evidence aside unchecked.

I took a deep breath, bracing myself for Mystico's indignant reaction to my pragmatic decision.

"Mystico, death means Luna can't control physical things anymore," I said. "I understand your desire to keep Luna's information private. I really do. But we need to look through her stuff, including this book, to figure out if someone hurt her."

"It's Luna's book." Mystico lashed her tail in agitation. "You don't understand. The spirits remain. You just can't see them. Luna says the book should go to Diego. He'll know what to do with it. It's her book. She would know where it should go."

Now it was my turn to bristle.

"Interesting you suggest Diego," I said. "Landon and I overheard an argument between Diego and Blanca today, and it was quite suspicious—"

Mystico's eyes blazed with fury, her skin bristling. "Don't you dare accuse Diego of anything!" she spat. "He loved Luna with every fiber of his being—he would rather die himself than ever cause her harm!" She dug her claws into the glowing platter, bald tail lashing in outrage at the implied accusation against Luna's ex-boyfriend.

Her grief over Luna had transformed into a ferocious protectiveness over Diego's name and reputation.

Which was... weird.

I raised my hands in a gentle, reassuring gesture, hoping to soothe her anger. "I'm not accusing anyone of anything. But we can't ignore that the two fought, and it sounded heated, and it sounded like it was about Luna. What happened between the three of them, Mystico?"

Mystico turned away, radiating anger, her sleek skin rippling as her muscles tensed beneath. She stared at the wall, pointedly avoiding eye contact with me.

"Mystico..."

The tips of her tail flicked back and forth, like an agitated metronome. I could almost feel the waves of indignation coming off her.

"I can wait here all night, you know. I live here, too."

After a long, tense moment, she spoke again, her voice low. "Luna says I should tell you their quarrel was just a lovers' tiff. Diego wanted her to move in with him, but she wasn't ready. He was hurt when she refused." Mystico faced me again. "They both said some harsh things, but Luna knew Diego would never hurt her. He demanded she commit. She broke up with him to teach him a lesson." The cat hissed. "Then Blanca moved in like a tornado."

If Luna felt secure that Diego's devotion and care for her outweighed his occasional storms of passion, then maybe I owed it to her not to make unfair assumptions.

I resolved to keep a more open mind—

Wait.

Was I really basing my judgments about a possible murder investigation on alleged messages from beyond the grave, delivered by a cat?

When I put it like that, it seemed downright absurd.

Factual.

But absurd.

"I understand. Thank you for explaining, Mystico," I said. "And you have my word. I'll keep an open mind about Diego. But I'd still like to look at this book on the off chance it holds vital information."

Mystico bowed her head.

I flipped through the delicate pages, scanning each entry for any clues that stood out. Some held brief notes about the client, the cards drawn, and Luna's mystical interpretations of their meaning. Those symbols by names, but beyond that, nothing too unusual jumped out.

But then I landed on a page dated two weeks before Luna's untimely death. This log had only a single name —Rosa Vargas—and below it a chilling label in Luna's graceful script: Death.

I stared at the word, a creeping chill running down my spine.

"Mystico, can you tell me about this?" I asked.

The sleek cat had cocooned herself in Luna's flowing purple scarf, nearly disappearing within its soft folds. She purred, nuzzling her face against the scarf and breathing in Luna's comforting scent, ignoring my words. Lost in her own world of memories and solace, she had drifted far from our conversation.

I sighed, but didn't have the heart to disrupt her peaceful moment.

Questions could wait; for now, I just let her be.

"What is it?" Landon asked.

I showed him.

This ominous notation could mean nothing.

Or... it could mean everything.

But one thing was certain—this was no ordinary reading about romance or money. Maybe Luna had uncovered something dark in Rosa's future. The question was... had that sinister shadow fallen across her own fate as well?

Downstairs, the café was empty except for Josephine and Darla. Josephine sat tapping away on her laptop, likely putting the final edits on some brilliant legal brief. Darla lounged next to her, aimlessly scrolling through her phone.

Looking up from her screen, Darla perked up when she saw me. "Oh, hey Ellie! Everything's closed up. We're all still heading over to Cinco de Mayo tonight, right?"

I nodded. "I'd like to hear what secrets get spilled once the margaritas flow."

Darla chuckled, giving me a thumbs up.

Josephine glanced up from her laptop, pushing her red cat-eye glasses up her nose. "I'm in, too. Gotta take a break from this case at some point!" She looked around. "This place sure cleared out fast once closing time hit."

"I imagine everyone's eager for the festival weekend," I said. "Which reminds me, I've got some new info to share from chatting with Mystico earlier."

"Ooh, do tell!" Darla said, setting her phone down. "I feel like I've been out of the loop on this whole thing."

I filled them in on my latest chat with Mystico, including her continued claim of contacting Luna's spirit. I relayed how Luna allegedly insisted we speak to Diego.

Josie tapped her chin, pondering the possibilities. "If Luna's spirit is guiding Mystico, we should follow where those clues lead. I'm open to reconsidering Diego if there's any chance it helps us uncover the truth."

Just then, the mantrap front gate creaked open, and Laurie breezed in, her canvas tote bag slung over her shoulder.

"Sorry I'm late, got held up at the clinic," she told us as she joined us. Her eyes glinted with curiosity as she took in the scene. "So what did I miss? Give me all the latest scoops."

I caught Laurie up on the conversation. She nodded along as I explained and gestured to the book on the table. Then Josie gave her the big picture on Zora's claims.

"Interesting stuff if some developer really is moving into town," she remarked. "Definitely worth monitoring Rosa and her plans. There has to be some way we can confirm that."

"I think so," Josie agreed.

"So what's our next move, detectives?"

Before anyone could answer, the front door swung open, the cheerful bell jingling, as Evie breezed in, her boyfriend Matt following behind. He lugged a large white pastry box.

"Hey Mom, we're back from Estella's with tomorrow's fresh baked goods!" Evie announced, setting her own box on the counter.

I smiled at them. "You two are lifesavers. Thank you so much for picking those up."

"No problem. Happy I could help," Matt replied, his kind eyes crinkling at the corners as he returned my smile. "So, what are you all working on in here? Catch me up to speed on the case."

Once more, we took turns explaining all the developments and leads we had gathered so far in the investigation. Matt listened, his sharp private detective's mind absorbing each additional detail. We were midway through the exhaustive rehash when Landon came tromping down the stairs, red metal toolbox in hand.

"Well hey folks, sorry I'm late to the party," he greeted us, giving me a quick kiss on the cheek before setting his toolbox on the floor. "What'd I miss? Fill me in."

Josephine groaned. "We need to schedule regular meetings for this. I think the information has been etched into my brain at this point."

"You didn't miss anything, Landon," I told him. "I was just telling them what the cat said upstairs."

"Right. I think that's some interesting stuff with this developer idea," he said. "If Rosa's really trying to sell, anyway."

Just then, Darla piped up from her spot at the counter. "As interesting as this all is, if we don't get a move on, we're going to be late for the Cinco de Mayo festival opening tonight."

Laurie nodded. "Oh, let's not be late for that. We can observe people in their natural boozed up habitat and keep our eyes and ears out for anything suspicious."

Margaritas might be the unlikely keys to cracking this mystery wide open. And not just because the victim was an award-winning mixologist found in a vat of margarita mix—though that connection was weird enough.

No, it was the liberating effects of the drinks themselves that would unlock tongues and secrets tonight.

In vino veritas, after all.

Or in this case, in margarita veritas.

Under the bright paper lanterns and fueled by the best Mexican tequilas, intimate truths would emerge from even the tightest lips.

I hoped.

Chapter Eight

THE TANTALIZING AROMAS OF SIZZLING FAJITAS AND sweet churros filled the air as Landon, Evie, Matt, Josephine, Laurie, Darla, and I walked through the crowded Cinco de Mayo festival. Vibrant decorations and banners adorned the buildings surrounding the town square, where makeshift booths and stages had been set up for the weekend's festivities. Mariachi music mixed with lively chatter and laughter, resulting in an upbeat atmosphere.

We were excited to begin the celebration, but we also knew we needed to keep an eye out for any clues regarding Luna's mysterious death.

"Welcome, amigos and amigas, to our annual Cinco de Mayo festival!" Waldo's voice echoed from the central stage as we passed under a papel picado-adorned archway, and cheers erupted from the crowd as our mayor gestured, the glittering lights casting dramatic shadows across his face. "I want to give a very special thanks to our very own Estella Garcia for all her hard work in organizing this event!"

More applause followed as Estella waved from where she stood near the stage, beaming with pride.

"I'd be remiss if I didn't mention the loss our community has suffered this week and to remind everyone that we should celebrate the spirited life of our dear friend, Luna Espinoza..."

As Waldo talked about Luna's mysterious, eccentric nature and lasting impact on the town, I noticed Diego shift his weight from one foot to the other, glancing down with a pained expression. The mention of her name clearly triggered complex emotions in him, feelings he seemed desperate to conceal from the public eye.

"And now, it's my honor to officially kick off these festivities!" Waldo declared. "Let the music play and the margaritas flow!"

As the mariachi band's festive ranchera melody filled the air, Matt flashed a playful grin and swept Evie into an impromptu dance, twirling her around. Her laughter rang out, joy lighting up her face and deepening the dimples in her cheeks. Watching my daughter's carefree moment of happiness made my heart swell.

I lived for these simple times when Evie could feel so unburdened, especially given her health struggles, when she was just a woman enjoying the vibrance of a festival with no dark mysteries or danger in sight.

Well.

Except for the potential murderer in our midst.

Matt dipped Evie dramatically, eliciting another bubbly laugh, before pulling her into a sweet embrace.

"Ah, young love, so untroubled and full of possibility. Shall we get some grub? Romance isn't the only appetite that needs satisfying tonight." Josephine said, eyeing the sizzling food stalls.

"Is there a sincere romantic bone in your body?" Laurie asked her.

"That's a romantic bone," she responded, pointing to a plate of ribs.

The savory aroma of sizzling carne asada and sweet churros enveloped us as we made our way through the crowd. My gaze shifted from face to face, looking for anyone who stood out among the happy families and friends.

The tempting smells made my stomach grumble and my mouth water with anticipation, but I forced myself to concentrate on what I came here to observe.

I didn't come to indulge.

Well, much.

I came here to see what I could...

There.

A brooding Blanca Cruz weaved through people, a deep scowl marring her striking features. She seemed to search for someone, her gaze combing the area near the stage where Diego stood, surrounded by admirers.

I wondered if she really did suspect Diego of being involved in Luna's death like she'd had accused him of. It seemed ridiculous to be so attached to someone you thought capable of such a heinous act.

Laurie stopped to chat with the local Xolo Club, a group dedicated to appreciating the sleek, hairless Mexican dogs. This left the rest of us loitering in front of Rosa's garish margarita booth as she hawked her drinks with smug superiority, occasionally throwing shade-filled glances at Estella's modest stall next door.

I pivoted in her direction, eager to question her about the secret sale of her restaurant to Austin developers, but Landon's sturdy arm gently held me back.

"Patience, grasshopper," he murmured, a teasing glint in his eye. "We'll hop over for a chat once she's not so busy playing bartender. There's a lot of people around her, and I doubt you'll get any answers now."

I exhaled, letting him steer me toward the alluring scent of fried dough and spices wafting from a nearby puffy taco stand.

He was right.

Rosa's interroga—er, chat would have to wait.

"Rosa's strutting around like she's already won the margarita contest," Darla said under her breath as we waited in line for tacos. "You'd think she could at least pretend some modesty and respect for the dead."

"Come on, we're celebrating Cinco de Mayo. It's a party," Josephine said. "You can't expect Rosa to set up a shrine and withdraw from the contest out of respect for Luna or something. I seriously doubt those two women were friends."

Laurie leaned in. "Seriously. But I do want to know about this sale. If this development thing is legit, she might have a serious motive. If it's just gossip, the actual killer could have started the rumor to deflect suspicion."

"You raise a good point," Josephine said with a thoughtful nod. "I'll do some digging into property and permit records. That paperwork might shed light on whether Rosa was considering selling her place."

I waved my hand. "Or we could skip the paperwork and just go straight to the source. A chat with Rosa herself would get us answers pronto."

"In the middle of all this?" Josephine said. "Sneaky is better."

The sprawling oak cast dancing shadows across our faces as we sat beneath its branches, plates piled high with tacos al pastor and elotes dripping with cream. Laughter and steady mariachi music carried on the breeze as we chatted, making small talk about the warm May weather.

Yet despite our carefree guise, I could see each of us kept one eye surveying the crowd, ever vigilant for anything amiss beneath the fiesta lights.

While devouring the tacos, I cocked an ear to eavesdrop on the conversation at the neighboring table, my eyes darting over to observe a conveniently positioned couple gossiping discreetly.

Or so they thought.

A man leaned across the table, his shoulders hunched as he lowered his voice to a conspiratorial whisper. "Did you see Diego earlier? The poor guy looks grief stricken."

The woman seated opposite him nodded, her eyes wide. "I know, it's just heartbreaking. I ran into Blanca today and she told me Diego and Luna were this close to getting back together." She held up her hand, pinching her thumb and forefinger together. "That girl is consumed by jealousy over Luna, even now. Get this —she's livid that Diego is auctioning off those beautiful custom tarot paintings he made in Luna's honor. All proceeds go to the youth arts program, but oh no, Blanca won't stand for him memorializing her. How insecure do you have to be to be intimidated by a dead woman?"

The man shook his head, sighing. "Honey, when a woman tries to stop a man's grieving, you know she's bad news..."

"Can you imagine?" the woman whispered. "Being so spiteful and resentful over a man doing something nice to honor someone he cared for? It's disgusting. She won. She's still alive, while poor Luna is dead."

If Blanca was still simmering with bitterness over Luna even after her death, it wouldn't take much imagination to envision her brewing up the perfect murderous revenge against her perceived rival.

Jealousy did strange things to people.

"Seems to me all we've got are maybes," I said out of nowhere, popping a stray chunk of avocado into my mouth. "Blanca boiling over with jealousy, Rosa seething about her restaurant, Diego drowning in heartache." I shrugged, letting the implications sink in.

"Doesn't narrow down our suspect list," Josephine muttered.

Darla sighed, scooping up shredded napkin bits into a little pile. "We need more to go on than hunches about folks' hurt feelings if we wanna solve this thing."

"I don't think Diego killed her," Laurie said. "I mean, everyone says how much he loved her. Their relationship seemed complex, and they were in a bad spot, but it looks to me like he cared for her."

"It wouldn't be the first time someone killed someone they loved," Landon pointed out, his deep voice low and solemn. "Maybe his sadness is guilt masquerading as grief."

"You don't even know if she was killed. Goodness, you people really are dark, you know that?" Josephine said.

"Dark, maybe, but he's not wrong," I said. As much as we all wanted to believe Diego was innocent, we couldn't rule him out based on emotion alone. "Who wants to go to an art auction?"

The art center hummed with energy.

Vibrant paper flowers and banners draped the stark white walls and hung from the ceilings, infusing pops of fiesta color into the otherwise minimalist space. Upbeat music blended with the cheerful chatter of families, couples, and friends browsing the galleries, and children's giggles echoed through the halls as they dove into a hands on art project, finger-painting designs onto small clay pots.

I sipped my margarita and ventured with the group into the gallery's Día de Los Muertos exhibit where vibrant paintings covered every inch of the white walls— La Catrinas (skeletal figures dressed in elegant hats and dresses associated with the holiday) grinned under festive floral hats while marigolds and sugar skulls stared back at us.

I paused at an abstract skull rendered in hypnotic swirls of fuchsia, gold, and turquoise, feeling its empty eye sockets follow me as I walked.

"That one's creepy," I muttered to Landon. "I think it just winked at me."

He studied the painting. "Nah, it just thinks you look cute tonight."

I stuck my tongue out at him. "You don't look so bad yourself."

We turned a corner and stepped into a room bursting with vivid tarot paintings. Diego's intricate brushstrokes brought the major and minor arcana to life in his signature dreamlike style.

"Wow," Josephine breathed, her eyes wide.

I lingered at the painting of The High Priestess, transfixed by the image of Mystico perched atop a crescent moon, her all-knowing gaze peering out from the canvas. The accompanying booklet noted the card represented intuitive powers, inner voice, and hidden truths, but the cat's mysterious stare seemed to convey secrets beyond the written words.

At the back of the room, an enormous portrait depicted Mystico dozing on a swath of vivid tarot cards, her wrinkled skin and spindly limbs splayed across the canvas. Diego had perfectly immortalized the sphynx in bold strokes and vibrant hues.

I edged closer, taking in the ornate details.

Beneath the slumbering cat lay The Empress, the woman in the card cradling a heart as birds encircled her with outstretched wings. Nearby was The Magician, one hand raised to the heavens.

"Beautiful, isn't it?" Diego said, materializing beside me. "That was the last piece we created together. We photographed Mystico for hours trying to get the perfect shot for reference." His lips curved into a bittersweet smile. "It was hard to get that cat to sit."

"I can imagine. And yes, it's incredible," I replied. "You really brought Mystico to life on the canvas."

"She's with your shelter?"

I nodded.

"I figured." Diego nodded, gazing at the painting. "I'm glad you took her in," he said after a pause. "That cat was Luna's entire world. She'd be relieved to know Mystico is being cared for."

"Of course, it's what we're here for," I said.

Diego's gaze dropped to his shuffling feet as he reminisced. "Luna got Mystico as a tiny hairless kitten. She'd carry that little wrinkled alien-looking thing everywhere." His lips curled into a faint, wistful smile. "I'll never forget Mystico's first night home, how she squeezed under the covers and curled right up on Luna's chest, purring like a motorboat. After that, we couldn't pry that cat off us at bedtime. She'd wiggle her way between us and konk out."

The eccentric looking artist blinked back tears.

"When Luna did readings, that curious kitten would bat and pounce on the tarot cards spread out on the table. She sent the cards flying more than once. Drove Luna crazy, but she'd just sigh and scoop Mystico up. I grew attached to that cat over the years. She was Luna's furry little shadow."

Diego's gaze lingered on the portrait of Mystico, his eyes glistening. I could see the deep bond he still felt with Luna's beloved companion.

Why hadn't he come to the shelter?

"Would you like to come see her?"

Diego exhaled, a wistful look in his eyes. "I know Mystico probably won't want anything to do with me now. Not after how things ended with Luna and I."

I offered a comforting glance. "What happened between you two? If you don't mind me asking."

Diego leaned against the wall, gazing up at the painting. "It was stupid. We got into this huge fight over me spending too much time focused on my art. Luna said I was neglecting her. So I suggested we move in together, and she exploded. Said proximity would not fix the problem."

As he recounted the details of their fight, his voice strained with emotion. I could see how heavily the guilt weighed on him.

"Instead of talking through it, I stormed off to Blanca's shop. I was angry. She'd been flirting with me for months, Blanca, always asking me to paint her portrait, dropping hints we'd be better together." Diego sighed. "I went out drinking with her that night, knowing it would upset Luna. Nothing happened between us, but still, it was childish. Vengeful.

"It upset her, all right." He lowered his eyes. "Luna and I didn't speak for over a month. Then, the day before..." His voice broke, and he trailed off, wiping a stray tear with his palm.

I stayed silent, watching him.

Waiting.

What happened the day before Luna died?

"Anyway—"

No.

Not "anyway."

What was he about to say?

"I never got to make things right. She died thinking I didn't care anymore. But I loved her more than anything." Diego gazed up at the painting, his eyes glistening. "Now she'll never know how sorry I am."

It drove me crazy when people opened their mouths,

only to abruptly stop short right when it gets interesting. Why even bother saying anything?

The mystery hung thick in the air between us, Diego's unfinished sentence frustrating me.

He took a shaky breath, composing himself before turning to me. "Promise you'll take care of Mystico, Ms. Rockwell. She meant the world to Luna."

"You have my word," I told him.

Diego managed a small, grateful smile.

"If you want to see her, please come by anytime. We live at the shelter, so we're always around. I think she'd like it more than you'd think."

Diego opened his mouth to reply, but quickly closed it, averting his eyes.

⚜

Leaving the art center, Landon held open the heavy wooden door, its faded paint peeling around the edges. I stepped out into the buzzing Cinco de Mayo night, the lights from the festival tents casting a warm glow.

"That was a nice tribute Diego put together for Luna," I said.

Landon nodded. "You don't think he did it, do you?"

"I don't know that's it, exactly. I think... I don't want him to have done it."

The two of us strolled down the sidewalk, the others having split off to enjoy the festivities, past laughing families carrying prizes from game booths. As we neared a sprawling oak tree, Landon halted, squinting into the shadows beneath its branches.

"Isn't that Josie's husband over there?" he asked, motioning with his chin.

I followed his gaze to see Charlie Reynolds hunkered against the trunk, one hand braced on the bark as he retched into the bushes. His normally tidy hair was mussed and sweat plastered his shirt to his back, the fabric clinging to him like a second skin.

"Oh dear," I murmured. "It looks like Charlie's gotten himself into some trouble."

Landon and I hurried over.

Charlie flinched when Landon clasped his shoulder, peering up at us with red-rimmed eyes.

"Hey there, buddy. You all right?" Landon asked.

Charlie flinched at the contact, then looked up blearily. "Oh, hey folks," he slurred, staggering. "Don't mind me, just... enjoying the sunshine. Beautiful day, huh?" He gestured sloppily above us.

"It's nighttime," Landon told him and pointed. "That's a streetlight."

Noting his unfocused eyes and the potent scent of alcohol emanating from him, I said, "Do you need us to call Josie?" I realized it was a foolish suggestion as soon as the words left my lips, and Charlie's panicked reaction confirmed it.

"No!" He recoiled, terror flashing across his face. "No, no, I'm fine." He grabbed my arm, pleading.

"Please, whatever you do, do not tell Josie about this. She'll kill me."

I extracted my arm from his clammy grasp, exchanging an amused look with Landon.

"What happened, Charlie?" Landon asked. "How on earth did you let yourself get this drunk?"

Charlie doubled over with a pained moan, one hand clutching his stomach while the other braced against the rough bark of the oak tree. "It wasn't my fault," he insisted. "That mango drink tricked me. It looked so harmless, just sitting there, all orange and fruity. It had sorbet in it. And mangos! I mean, who could be afraid of that? But the red on it... that red... it burned. Son of a monkey, it burned!"

The empty plastic cup lay discarded in the grass beside him, the last dregs of the drink spilled out as evidence of his folly.

I had to press my lips together to keep from smiling. It seemed Charlie had run afoul of a chamango—those blended mango drinks were deceptively potent, often catching people off guard with their hefty doses of tequila and spicy chili-lime salt.

"Let's get you home and sobered up before Josie finds out," I suggested, taking one of Charlie's arms while Landon supported the other.

Charlie staggered between us as we guided him down the street, his shoes scuffing on the pavement. "This was a set up," he slurred, gesticulating with his free arm. "That mango monstrosity seduced me with its sweet tang and promises of vitamin C. But it betrayed me! It was spicy! Then I had to drink more to put out the fire!"

He shot an accusatory glare at a peach tree as if it were to blame for his predicament, and I had to bite my lip to keep from laughing at his impassioned tirade against the devious fruit.

"Please don't tell Josie," he implored, giving me his best puppy dog look, which was only somewhat diminished by his disheveled appearance. "I know I promised her no margaritas this year, but that sinister mangonada duped me! But I kept my promise. It wasn't a real margarita. It had mangos in it!"

He said "mangos" with such indignation, as if the presence of fruit absolved him of any wrongdoing.

"I don't think your wife was referring to the specific ingredients when she asked you to refrain from drinking. It's the alcohol content of the drinks and your ability to handle it that concerns her." I paused, eyeing his disheveled state. "One drink did this to you?"

"Yes, just one, but it did it four times!"

"What do you mean, four times?" I looked at him. "You mean four drinks?"

"Yes, but my mouth was on fire! It was so spicy!" Charlie grimaced, shivering at the memory. "I'm telling you, those festival beverages have it out for me. It's a conspiracy!"

As we continued guiding Charlie's wavering steps

down the lamplit street, he rambled aloud about his day, the alcohol greasing the gears of his tongue.

"Before that duplicitous mangonada, I met some real eager beaver developer types," he remarked. "The three of 'em mentioned they're looking to invest in Tablerock, eyeing up properties around the square. Even mentioned making an offer on Rosa's place." Charlie threw his arms wide, nearly clipping me in the process. "Our little town is moving on up, Ellie! Pretty soon we'll give Austin a run for its money."

We were not in any danger of giving Austin a run for its money, but his enthusiasm for Tablerock was rather endearing, even if it was chemically enhanced.

That wasn't what caught my attention, though.

"Did you say they want to buy Rosa's restaurant?"

"Yep, seemed real keen on scooping it up," Charlie said. "Of course, I didn't tell them about... you know." He tapped the side of his nose.

Landon looked confused. "Her cocaine business?"

"What? No! That they're probably going to have to pony up more cash because she's going to win the margarita contest now that Luna's out of the picture."

Josie's husband was a commercial attorney, so if he was aware of it and felt comfortable discussing it, it was most likely not a secret.

Well...

That, or he was so drunk he forgot about his oath to keep his trap shut regarding his client's business. Charlie, as a court officer, had certain ethical obligations regarding confidentiality—which he may have violated.

"Are these people your clients, Charlie?" I asked.

"No," Charlie replied with a vigorous shake of his head.

It nearly caused him to lose balance.

"How about Rosa?" I pressed further. "Does attorney-client privilege apply here? Has she ever hired you for anything?"

"No," he said again, though with less conviction. "Oh, wait. Should I be talking about this?" He thought, then shook his head. "Yeah, doesn't matter."

"So, how do you know about this?"

Charlie gave a vague, noncommittal shrug in response. "I hear things. You're not going to tell Josephine about this, are you?"

"Don't worry, Charlie. Your secret's safe with us."

At that, some color returned to his pallid face. "Oh, thank heavens. Josie would have my hide if she found out." He mimed a whip cracking.

"Let's just focus on getting you home in one piece," Landon said, guiding him around a curb.

Charlie belched, then made the sign of the cross. "Bless you for this, both of you. You're doing God's work."

I doubted that.

We continued on, supporting the stumbling attorney through the quiet streets until his house was blessedly, finally in view.

Chapter Nine

LANDON AND I STROLLED HAND IN HAND BACK toward the lively sounds of the Cinco de Mayo festival, leaving our tipsy friend Charlie in the capable hands of his live-in housekeeper, Alice Sanchez. The night air was warm with a gentle breeze, and strings of festive lights lit our path along the sidewalk.

I wasn't too worried about Josie's husband—Charlie wasn't normally one to overindulge these days and after the Pedro's Cantina incident last year, he'd sworn off liquor cold turkey and seemed to mean it.

But fruity drinks at Cinco de Mayo were his weakness, and this year they proved too tempting to resist. I knew Alice would brew him a pot of strong coffee and get some food in his stomach once we left.

She might even keep his secret from Josephine.

As we walked, Landon swung our hands between us. "You know, Ellie, there's something I've been meaning to talk to you about," he began, a touch of nervousness in his tone.

I glanced up at him. "What is it?"

Landon tread cautiously. "I hope I'm not overstepping, but I'm curious why you've been hesitant about my suggestion that we move in together."

I treasured these quiet moments alone with Landon. I felt a deep connection—one unlike anything I had experienced before. Landon was a true gentleman, tender and devoted. Simply holding his hand made my heart flutter.

But when he brought up us moving in together, I tensed. As much as I cared for him, that was a big step I wasn't sure I was ready to take.

Seeing my reaction, he added, "Ellie, there's no pressure," he said, his voice low and soothing. "I know this is all new for you. For both of us."

"Landon, you know how much I love spending time with you. You're the kind of man I wish I had met when I was younger, instead of the jerk I ended up with. But because I did find a jerk, it's not easy for me to be vulnerable."

Landon nodded in understanding. "I would never want you to do anything you aren't comfortable with, Ellie."

His sincere words touched my heart. After years of distrust and heartache, it was still hard for me to believe a man as wonderful as Landon could care for me. I searched his face, looking for any hint of deception, but found only earnest affection shining in his kind eyes.

"I know," I said. "You've never given me any reason not to trust you." I hesitated, hating to even ask, but my old doubts crept in and it ran out of my mouth before I had the chance to stop it. "Have you?"

"Of course not!" Landon said, startled that I would even ask. "I would never do anything to hurt you, Ellie. I hope you know that."

Landon had proven time and again, through loving acts both big and small, that he appreciated me. Even with proof, though, I had doubts.

"I'm sorry," I told him, squeezing his arm. "It's not about you, Landon. It's just... I know I've said this before, but I never thought I would be in a relationship again. I'm an overweight, middle-aged mother to a bunch of cats and a disabled daughter. Who would be crazy enough to take me on?" I gave a small, self-deprecating laugh.

Landon stopped and turned to face me, his hands coming up to rest on my shoulders. "I would," he said.

After years of keeping my heart locked away, here was this wonderful man saying he wanted me—insecurities and all. I searched his eyes, struck by the sincerity and tenderness I saw shining there.

Before I could react, he drew me close and wrapped his muscular arms around me in a warm, comforting embrace. I melted against him, laying my head on his broad chest to listen to the steady beat of his heart.

I felt cherished, secure.

After a long moment, he pulled back just enough to look into my eyes. "Ellie, you are an amazing woman," he said, intensity etched in every word. "So beautiful, inside and out. Your kindness and strength take my breath away. Being with you makes me feel like the luckiest man alive."

His thumbs caressed my cheeks, his expression so full of warmth and adoration it made my heart ache.

I started to protest, but his lips descending on mine silenced any objections. The kiss was chaste yet full of tenderness, and when we broke apart, Landon kept his arms around me, his fingers tracing soft circles on my back.

"Please never question the depth of my feelings or my patience," he said. "We can take this as slow as you need. Just know that when you're ready, I'll be right here."

I laid my palm against Landon's stubbled cheek, overcome with emotion. "Thank you for being so patient with me," I whispered, my voice catching.

As I searched his kind, steadfast gaze, it hit me— Landon truly cared for me, flaws and all. After so many years of hurt and distrust, I had nearly given up on finding this kind of unconditional acceptance. But Landon saw me, insecurities laid bare, and still he looked at me with such unwavering devotion.

I felt a fragile flutter of hope awakening inside me.

Landon made me feel seen—and maybe, just maybe, I deserved to be loved exactly as I was.

We returned to the festival, the air between us calm and assured. As we approached the town square, raucous music and the savory scents of grilled meat greeted us once more, as strands of twinkling lights illuminated crowded tables and a throng of people dancing in the street.

Near the main stage, I noticed Police Chief Yarbin conferring with one of his officers. He caught my eye and nodded in greeting before returning to his conversation. I wondered if they had learned anything new about Luna's death.

Landon and I made our way through the boisterous crowd to an empty picnic table. As we walked, I recognized familiar faces from around town—the woman who ran the bakery, one of Evie and Darla's friends, and the shipping clerk from a postal store off the square.

Tablerock may be small, but its community spirit was always evident at events like this.

Settling onto the bench across from Landon, I took in the scene. On the stage, a mariachi band decked out in ornate charro suits belted out a fast-paced song, to the crowd's delight. Nearby, a long line had formed at Rosa's food stand; she rushed to fill orders, her signature scowl firmly in place.

Why does that woman always look so unhappy?

"Some party, huh?" Landon commented with amusement, his eyes roving over the merry chaos.

"It's great to see everyone enjoying themselves," I said. Though Luna's absence cast a bittersweet pall, people seemed determined not to let tragedy derail the tradition she cherished so much. Taking Landon's hand again, I said, "About what you asked before... yes, moving in together is something I'm willing to consider. But I meant it when I said we needed to go slowly. I have a lot to consider, including the shelter and how Evie would take it."

Landon's face brightened with a smile. "There's no rush at all," he said. "I'm just happy being with you, Ellie." He raised my hand and pressed a kiss to my knuckles, his gaze never leaving mine. "I hope you don't blame me for wanting more time with you."

Before I could respond, Evie and Matt found us watching the musical performance. My daughter approached with a mischievous grin, her boyfriend in tow.

"What? What is that expression?"

"You'll never guess who we were just chatting with," Evie said. "Go on. Guess."

I raised an eyebrow. "Just tell me."

"Oh, just the three sharpest dressed city slickers this small town gal has ever laid eyes on," my daughter replied, laying the Texas twang on thick.

"You were raised in Austin."

"Well, these guys breezed in from the big city of Austin for some 'business.'" She made air quotes around "business," and rolled her eyes, a wry smile playing on her lips. "They looked as out of place as a vegetarian at a steakhouse."

Landon and I exchanged a glance.

"Did they say what kind of business?" he asked.

"They're investors or developers or something like that. Called themselves 'Town Prosperity Investments.' They mentioned they knew Charlie, Josephine's husband, so I figured he invited them."

With a rueful shake of his head, Landon disagreed. "I don't think Charlie invited those men. We just walked Mr. Reynolds home, and he'd just met those three. Said they were interested in buying some properties in town."

"Including Rosa's," I added.

Evie nodded. "Must be the same people. The three partners—Bobby, Bill, and Dan—said they were in town for the weekend, and I didn't think it was for the margaritas."

"What did you say their name was?" I asked.

"Town Prosperity Investments."

A chill ran through me as I recalled the ominous articles I'd read about Town Prosperity Investments.

The predatory company had gained notoriety for swooping into charming small towns, snatching up beloved community landmarks and local businesses for a song. With ruthless efficiency, they'd bulldoze decades of history and replace it with cold high-rises and glitzy chains catering to the rich.

Families and older residents soon found themselves priced out of their lifelong homes. Within a few short years, the unique character of these towns had been stripped away and replaced with soulless gentrification.

I shared what I remembered from the article with the others.

"Oh, man, I remember that article—and it makes sense." My daughter said, launching into an animated account of her conversation with the men. "That Bobby guy did most of the talking. Slick as anything in his fancy suit and tie, going on about the opportunities they saw here."

"Let me guess—opportunities that involve demolishing things," I said.

"They didn't say it outright, but it was pretty obvious."

Matt picked up the story. "Bobby said they'd had great success revitalizing communities in Houston and Dallas." He made air quotes with his fingers around "revitalizing."

"More like ravaging," I muttered.

"He started bragging about how they'd bought up Nut Ranch Grove outside of Houston and made a fortune."

"That development displaced dozens of elderly residents."

"Wait, I think I know what you're talking about. They evicted all those seniors who'd lived there for decades and tore down the affordable houses," Landon said, disgust in his tone. "Replaced them with million-dollar McMansions, right?"

"Yep. Almost as bad as what they did in Dallas," Evie said. "Buying up all those historic buildings just to bulldoze them."

I remembered seeing a news segment about the callous demolition of those century-old architectural treasures.

Landon shook his head. "Predators and vultures, the lot of them."

"No kidding," Matt agreed. "The way Bobby boasted about the profits they've reaped by forcing out 'decaying' neighborhoods and businesses..." He trailed off, looking around the square. "I wonder if that's what they think of this town."

My gaze met Evie's. "That's their plan for Tablerock, too?"

She nodded. "I think so. They as much as said so. Kept going on about 'underutilized properties' and 'modernization.'"

I pictured the cozy downtown square replaced by cold, gleaming high-rises and choked traffic. The charming family-owned shops giving way to upscale chains.

My skin crawled.

"Did they mention any particular properties or

businesses?" Landon asked. I knew he was thinking of what Charlie said about the men and Rosa's restaurant.

"They didn't name names," Matt replied. "But did say they'd already been scoping out redevelopment sites around town."

Evie gave me a knowing look. "They did seem very curious when I mentioned I lived at the cat rescue in Wardwell Manor, Mom."

My jaw tightened.

Vultures.

I met Landon's eyes, seeing my own anger reflected there.

Tablerock was our home, not their playground.

"Well, they won't get Wardwell Manor," he said.

I nodded in agreement, a surge of determination rising within me.

"They said nothing about Rosa's place?" I asked.

Evie pursed her lips. "Bobby did make a point of complimenting the restaurant's location. Called it 'prime real estate.'"

A heavy silence fell over our group as we absorbed the gravity of the developers' plans. But then the boisterous blare of trumpets cut through the gloom as the band struck up a fast-paced tune.

Despite myself, I felt my foot tap along to the lively beat as I scanned the crowd and took in the smiling faces and spinning couples bathed in the golden lights. Watching my friends and neighbors sway and laugh to the infectious music, my dark worries momentarily lifted.

Tablerock still pulsed with life tonight.

And the town aimed to keep it that way.

I stood, holding out a hand to Landon. "Come on. We can't let those scoundrels ruin our fun. Let's show them what genuine community looks like."

With a grin, he let me pull him to his feet and I laughed as Landon twirled me around. The music flowed through me, buoying my spirit.

Tablerock wasn't lost yet.

The dance floor swelled with smiling, spinning bodies—young and old, lifelong residents and newcomers alike.

I doubted those developers had a clue what this town was about, and it certainly wasn't for sale. Our little community's unique character meant nothing to them—they just wanted to sweep in like vultures and pick our bones clean in the name of their bottom line, make this place some faceless extension of Austin.

Well, this town was our sanctuary, not their capitalist chessboard. Tablerock's heart still beat strong beneath the surface—in places like the cat shelter, Estella's store, and the shops around the square.

We wouldn't hand it over it quietly.

Like a magpie drawn to sparkly trinkets, Jessa Winthrop flocks to gossip and scandal faster than you can say "bleached bouffant." She'll hover unseen in the background, eavesdropping with her bejeweled ear to the ground, waiting for that opportune moment to swoop in and insert herself into the action.

Subtle as a fireworks show, that one.

So I can't say I was surprised when Jessa sidled up to the picnic table where Landon and I were sitting and plopped herself down beside us, uninvited as always.

"Well, hey there, you two! Fancy running into y'all here!" Jessa drawled with an exaggerated accent I was sure she practiced in a mirror.

We greeted her politely, but without enthusiasm.

She leaned back, listening to the mariachi music filling the square. "The bands sure were livelier last year when I was mayor. We had double the performers and rides back then, too." She examined her long red nails. "Of course, the town's budget was less tight in those days."

I could see Landon bite his tongue to avoid a sarcastic retort about how Jessa's lavish overspending while in office had nearly bankrupted the city.

"Yes, well, I'm just enjoying my retirement these days," Jessa continued with a dismissive wave of her adorned hand—although no one had asked her a darn thing. "So much free time now for my philanthropy work. Turns out having the right social connections can accomplish more than just holding some political title."

She gave a knowing wink. "All those folks who used to try manipulating me? Well now, I'm one of them."

Jessa's coy, Cheshire cat smile made me wonder if she was implying what I suspected—that she had somehow brought that shifty development company, TPI, to town. Before I could voice the accusation brewing in my mind, Jessa steamrolled ahead, her heavily lined eyes scanning the festival crowds like a vulture seeking carrion.

"Shame about all the changes happening around here," she remarked with faux concern, her talon-like nails clicking against the picnic table. "Why, I remember when Cinco de Mayo meant rodeos and street dances that went on till dawn! Now it's all about 'historical preservation' and 'protecting tradition.'" She emphasized these words with exaggerated air quotes.

"Well, progress always comes with some trade-offs," Landon responded. "The trick is balancing new growth with preserving what makes this town special."

Jessa let out an incredulous laugh. "Oh please, Tablerock's been preserved to death! What we need is more youth, more money, more pizzazz! This place is just collecting dust. It's time for some fresh blood, I say!"

Her words raised my hackles, but I tried to keep my tone neutral.

"Many longtime residents disagree. They don't want to see Tablerock turned into just another gentrified Austin suburb full of condos and overpriced cafés. We need a measured approach."

"Longtime residents? Did you just move here a few years ago?" Jessa eyed the humble booths around the square with disdain. "Measured approach? That's code for stagnation. Back in my day, we had grand events at the Winthrop Ranch, not these pitiful little street fairs. The Winthrops helped build this town, but the town itself seems determined to destroy our legacy."

I bit my tongue, resisting the urge to remind Jessa about the shady land deals and cronyism associated with her family's so-called legacy.

"Now I'm not saying those lovely TPI folks who just came to town had anything to do with my views." Jessa continued to examine her blood-red nails. "But progress is important, even if it means a few ruffled feathers. Change is inevitable."

"What do you know about TPI?" I asked.

Jessa's plucked eyebrows shot up, her expression oozing exaggerated shock like a bad soap opera actress. "My goodness, whatever makes you ask that?" she gasped, pressing a glittery hand to her ample chest.

We all engaged in a silent battle of wills, Jessa's shadowed eyes wide with pretend affront while Landon and I tried to stare her down.

"Y'all are just too much!" Jessa let out a girlish titter, fussing to smooth out her gaudy floral dress. "A lady like me would never gossip about such things." Chin tilted skyward with unmistakable superiority, Jessa rose from the picnic table like a beauty queen ascending her throne.

"Now I simply must be going. So lovely catching up, darlings!" she proclaimed with an exaggerated drawl.

With a dramatic flourish, she produced a small bottle of silver polish from her oversized designer handbag and placed it in front of me with a coy wink.

"A little gift for you, hon. That thing you pretend you don't have must be getting tarnished by now."

Chapter Ten

THE FOLLOWING MORNING, THE SLEEPY
tranquility of the near-empty café was shattered by the
loud bang of the front door swinging open. Josephine
came barreling in, the tails of her navy blazer flapping
behind her like wings as she marched across the floor. I
looked up from wiping down tables, startled by the
dramatic entrance.

Marching up to me, Josephine jabbed an accusatory
finger in my direction. "Eleanor Rockwell, how dare you
not tell me about my husband's little mangonada
escapade last night!" she exclaimed, placing her hands
on her hips in an authoritative stance. Her emerald eyes
blazed with irritation behind her cat-eye glasses. "I'd
expect that kind of bro code nonsense from your significant other, but you? I should tear up your sisterhood
card."

What mystical small town information network did

she have that kept her constantly updated on everyone's business?

"Now, Josie, I'm sure it was just—" I started, but she cut me off.

"That man got himself so drunk he practically face-planted into a mangonada cart in the town square. I cannot believe you didn't give me the 411 the minute it happened!"

"Landon and I weren't there when what you just described happened." I gave her an apologetic look. "I'm sorry. I probably should have told you, but Charlie just seemed so embarrassed, and he begged us not to say anything. We got him home. Isn't that what's important?"

Josephine rolled her eyes. "Well, la-di-dah, aren't you just the perfect loyal friend to that drunken lout? Look, Ellie, I don't need you covering up for my ridiculous husband. He does the crime, he needs to own up to it."

"Fair point. I'm sorry."

"That boneheaded husband of mine is lucky you two came along to scrape him off the pavement," she huffed, blowing an errant auburn curl off her forehead. "I swear, that man struggles to dress himself without me there to supervise. You'd think after thirty years he'd have learned not to test my patience with his harebrained antics." She shook her head, her expression a mix of annoyance and amusement.

"Are you worried that he's got a drinking problem?"

"Oh, I know he has a drinking problem. The problem is he can't drink without face planting into the nearest cart, garden, or potted plant. He does know that, and he rarely drinks, but Charlie gets around a boozy smoothie and all memories of logic flies out of the man's head."

At that moment, the bells above the front door jangled as Landon sauntered in, jostling his trucker hat to sit just so atop his salt-and-pepper waves.

Josephine's eyes lit up as she whirled toward me, one eyebrow raised. She pressed a finger to her lips. "Not one peep out of you, missy. You owe me that after staying mum about my rummy hubby's latest stunt."

I nodded, lips zipped.

"Well, speak of the devil! Landon Rogers, just the man I wanted to see," Josie called out in a singsong voice, smoothing the front of her blazer.

Landon's brows shot up as he ambled over, his worn work boots scuffing along the floor. "What can I do for you ladies this fine morning?" he asked with an affable grin, though his eyes held a glint of wariness.

"Oh, I think you know exactly what's going on. A little tweety bird told me all about a certain someone's tequila-fueled tango with a mangonada cart last night."

Landon tugged at his collar, suddenly finding the floorboards fascinating. "Uh, not sure what you mean, Josie."

"Oh, please, enough with the innocent act," Josephine told him. "I already got the skinny on how

Charlie took a nosedive right into Senor Mangonada's boozie slushie stand and tried to slurp his way to the bottom. Left quite a mess under that big oak if I heard right." She leaned in, lowering her voice. "And you just happened to have a front row seat. And didn't tell me."

Landon shifted his weight, glancing between Josie's knowing look and me. I gave a slight shake of my head and he cleared his throat. "Now, Josie, a gentleman doesn't betray a brother. What happens at the Cinco de Mayo festival stays at the festival." He touched the brim of his hat, as if taking a vow. "At least until we take it home and put it to bed. Which we did."

"You had a responsibility to tell me." She waved a finger at him.

Landon threw his hands up at Josephine's scolding. "There's a sacred bro code, Josie, and you know it," he insisted, eyes twinkling. "You can waggle that finger at me all day long, but sorry—some secrets aren't mine to tell, no matter how hard you cross-examine."

"Honestly, the tales I could tell about that man..." She trailed off, shaking her head. "Bro code. What nonsense."

"If you and Ellie went out, and she drank a little too much, would you tell me?"

"That's different."

Landon chuckled. "Only in your mind. Charlie means well."

"Oh, of course," Josephine sighed. "He's lucky he's cute. And that I've gotten used to his harebrained annual drunken wagon dives after thirty-some years." A wry smile crossed her face. "To tell you the truth, he keeps life interesting. Never a dull moment with that one."

Her momentary annoyance with us seemed to have passed, and I knew she could never stay angry with her hapless husband for long. The two shared a fiery, theatrical relationship—bickering and bantering with melodramatic flair, then collapsing into laughter moments later.

An agreeable silence settled over the three of us.

But leave it to Josie to break it with an unexpected subject change.

"Well, since we're all here, there's something that occurred to me last night when we were looking at the art," she said, plopping her large tote bag on the counter with a thud. She rummaged through it for a moment before pulling out a flat wooden board painted with letters, numbers, and symbols. "If we're going to be involved in magic and tarot cards and all that, might as well go all the way."

Landon and I exchanged bewildered looks as Josephine thunked a Ouija board down on the counter with a dramatic flourish.

She eyed us and clucked her tongue. "Oh, don't give me those skeptical sideways glances, you two. This place is emptier than a ghost town today." She paused, chuckling at her own joke. "Get it? Ghost town? Because we're trying to talk to one?"

"Josie—" Landon warned.

Josephine waved a hand. "Lighten up. With all the recovering revelers sleeping off their hangovers, we've practically got this place to ourselves. So why not take the opportunity to settle this whole 'talking to spirits' hullabaloo and see if Luna's ghost is hanging around here?" She waggled her fingers over the Ouija board and winked.

"I saw a horror flick once that painted those things in a pretty sinister light," Landon said, eyeing the Ouija board like it might bite. "Said they were like sending up a flashing neon invitation asking any old spirit to come on by and stir up trouble. Even if it does work, we don't know enough about those contraptions to use one safely. Seems to me like we'd be sticking our hands in a hornet's nest, and I don't fancy getting stung by whatever might come buzzing out."

"I'm with Landon. That's playing with forces we don't understand."

Josie waved a hand again as if shooing away a fly buzzing around her head. "Oh hush, it's just a little harmless fun. What better way to understand whether Luna's spirit is still hanging around than by asking her? Do you trust the information we're getting through the cat?"

"I don't know, Josie," Landon said, shifting his weight. "Messing around with one of those Ouija contraptions seems like we'd be asking for a heap of trouble. Especially in a place like this. We could end up stirring up forces better left alone."

"Wait a minute. A place like what?" I asked, looking around the cozy café interior in confusion. "What's wrong with this place?"

Landon rubbed the back of his neck. "Wardwell Manor is old, Ellie. This is an old place, with old stories. I figure it can't help but soak up vibes over the years, and I'm sure that platter isn't its only secret."

I looked around the cozy café that had become a home taking in the cheerful walls, warm lighting, and rows of colorful cat toys and treats. This welcoming space, normally filled with regulars chatting over lattes and cats lounging in patches of sun, was about as far from an eerie, haunted mansion as could be. I could not imagine any dark forces lurking within these friendly walls.

And yet...

"You two are no fun at all," she huffed. "But suit yourselves. I'll just conduct my séance solo." She started clearing a space on the counter.

"Are you kidding me?" I stopped her. "Don't you dare try to do this here," I hissed in a loud whisper. "Anyone could walk in and see."

Josie rolled her eyes again but relented, shoving the Ouija board back into her overstuffed bag.

"Fine, fine, you're the boss," she sighed. "Isolation room?"

Despite the protests of Landon and myself just moments earlier, we found ourselves huddled around a Ouija board in the isolation room. Josephine Reynolds had a remarkable way of steamrolling over any disagreement until she got her way, ignoring all logic and reason. Once she set her mind on something, there was no stopping her, no matter our misgivings.

I watched as she placed the planchette in the center of the board, her eyes glinting with excitement.

"Are you sure this is a good idea?" I asked, skepticism heavy.

She leaned back in her chair. "Back in my college days, I was part of a Wiccan coven. We used to have séances and spirit circles all the time." A faraway look crossed her face. "I'll never forget the night we made contact with Ol' Gunny, the ghost of a Confederate soldier. Why, his messages knocked our socks clean off!"

Josephine refocused on us, her expression smug. "Then in law school, my roomies and I had a regular date with the spirit world every Saturday night. Had to relax somehow between all that case study, you know. So believe me, I know how to handle these things. This cat's got nine lives of experience." Josephine glanced up, her green eyes flashing. "Don't you want to know what happened to Luna?"

I wanted answers, but contacting the dead through a board game seemed outlandishly dangerous at worst.

"I still don't like it," Landon said, shaking his head as he studied the Ouija board. "This seems like a mighty risky business to me. A door that's better left unopened. Nothing good ever came from meddling with forces we don't understand."

Josie stared at Landon. "I guess you've never heard of physics."

"I've heard of poltergeists."

Josephine rolled her eyes. "Oh, please, you're being so dramatic. What are you afraid of, some chain-rattling specter emerging in a puff of smoke?"

From the plush magic platter cubby, Mystico watched us, her pink nose twitching. "What are you doing?" she asked, her voice tinged with suspicion.

Josephine looked up. "We're going to contact Luna's spirit using this Ouija board."

"But I already talk to Luna. I can sense her presence all the time."

Landon raised his eyebrow at Josephine. "See? We don't need to do this."

"That cat is grieving. I'm not saying what she says is incorrect, but she could be imagining things and passing on information that comes from her own psyche. We need real, concrete answers." She patted the seat beside her. "This might get it for us—and it could also confirm what Mystico is saying. Come on, it'll be quick."

Reluctantly, I sat down.

"Okay, you two, fingers on here like so," Josephine directed, placing her manicured fingertips atop the planchette. She glanced up at Landon. "You, too, big man. Come on now, don't be shy. Time's a wastin'."

Landon hesitated, eyeing the Ouija board as if it might nip at his fingers. After a moment, he sat down and reluctantly added his calloused fingertips to the planchette.

I followed, the smooth plastic piece feeling oddly cool beneath my hands.

Josephine nodded, then closed her eyes, back ramrod straight as she took a deep, dramatic breath. I stifled a chuckle—even communing with spirits had to be a theatrical production with Josie.

"We don't want to speak with any nasty spirits!" Josephine bellowed, making Mystico startle and nearly topple off her perch. "Hear me, spirit world? Only good spirits that mean no harm!"

I stared at her. "That's your magical protection technique? Yelling at ghosts?"

"It's about intent. Intent is powerful."

"I'm sure Luna didn't intend to get murdered."

Josephine's eyes snapped open as she turned to me. "I suppose you have a better spirit warding method, Miss Skeptic?" Without waiting for me to answer, Josephine closed her eyes once more. "Spirit world, you have been warned! Only friendly ghosts allowed in this séance! So mote it be and yadda yadda!"

"Well, I, for one, feel much safer now," Landon said, his voice dripping with sarcasm. "Yelling at ghosts seems like a rock-solid defense against malevolent spirits. I bet all those nasty poltergeists are quaking in their boots after getting an earful from you, Josie. Makes me wonder why I ever got a concealed carry permit when I can just shout real loud at bad guys and tell 'em to stop their shenanigans."

Josephine cracked one eye open to level a withering glare at Landon. "Put those fingers back on the planchette, doubting Thomas."

With a resigned sigh, Landon scooted his chair closer to mine and returned his fingertips to the plastic piece. I felt his sturdy arm brush against mine, oddly reassuring in the strange situation I found myself in.

Josie closed her eyes once more, face serene yet determined. "Luna Espinoza, if you are here with us, please give us a sign."

We waited, the silence heavy.

Nothing happened.

Mystico scoffed at us from her cubby. "This is foolishness."

"Well, we tried," I said, beginning to withdraw my hands from the planchette.

Josephine's eyes flew open, and she grabbed my wrist in a vice-like grip.

"Stop. Didn't you feel that?" she whispered, eyes wide with excitement.

"Feel what?"

"It moved!" Josephine insisted. "Just a slight vibration, but it was there! Luna must be trying to come through."

I studied the smooth wooden surface. The

planchette hadn't so much as budged an inch from its starting position at the center of the board.

"I don't think so, Josie."

She leaned forward, gaze intense. "I'm telling you, there was a definite quiver. We have to try again." Her hand remained clasped around my wrist, as if worried I might flee.

I looked at Landon.

He shrugged.

Had there been a movement that I hadn't perceived? Or was Josephine's overeager mind playing tricks on her?

With a mix of hesitation and curiosity, I placed my fingertips back on the planchette's smooth plastic surface. Josephine did the same, while Landon followed reluctantly, brow still shadowed by unease.

Josephine closed her eyes again, concentrating. "Luna, we need your help. Did you die of a heart attack or did someone kill you? Assuming you know. Which, I mean, you're dead. I assume you know more than any of us here now."

I focused on feeling the planchette beneath my fingers, wondering what unseen forces might change its trajectory. Landon waited alongside me, his eyes fixed upon the board.

"I felt that," Josie whispered. "Did you feel that?"

"I don't think so." I sat, awaiting any sign of other-worldly movement. "What am I supposed to—"

"Shhh!" Josephine squeezed her eyes shut tighter.

I was growing annoyed, ready to withdraw my hands

again, when the planchette jerked hard beneath my fingers.

"Whoa!" I yelped, yanking my hands back in shock.

"It moved! Did you feel that?"

I stared down at the board, stunned. The planchette now rested askew, having slid a few inches across the letters. The hairs on my arm stood at attention.

"I—I think so," I stammered, stunned.

Landon, too, had recoiled, looking bewildered and examining his fingertips as if expecting to find burn marks.

"Let's try again," Josephine urged. She replaced her fingers on the planchette.

Hesitantly, I followed suit.

"Luna, if you're here, can you tell us if you died of a heart attack?" Josephine asked.

The planchette glided across the board as if guided by an invisible hand. It stopped with an audible tap on the letter N.

Josephine gasped, gripping the table edge. "It's spelling something out!"

Thank you, Captain Obvious, I thought.

Before I could react, the planchette moved again, sliding down to land on O. It continued to H, then A.

"Noha," Josephine breathed, brow furrowing. "Who on earth is Noha? Is there someone by that name here in town?"

The planchette didn't pause, still sliding over the letters. B-A-D-G-A-S.

"Noha Badgas?" Josephine muttered, shaking her head in confusion. "What kind of name is that?"

"Wait, not Noha," I said aloud as understanding hit me. "It's spelling N-O H-A. No heart attack. I think."

The planchette's movements had been so smooth, so deliberate. But had Luna's ghost delivered these hints about the manner of her death? Or was Josephine's subconscious toying with us to serve her need to be right?

"Badgas is bad gas? I know some gas can be dangerous if it accumulates in an enclosed space and displaces oxygen, but how would that happen outside?"

"It can't, right? People on the sidewalk would have fallen ill," I said.

Mystico sniffed. "Luna did not say any of this to me."

"Can you see Luna here now?"

"She's always with me." Mystico sniffed. "Always."

"Did you see her move that planchette?"

"Why should I help you? You're not listening to me."

I stared down at the Ouija board.

Had we really just communicated with Luna's spirit?

Or was this all some strange trick of the mind?

I wasn't sure what to believe.

"I don't know what to think," Landon said, echoing my thoughts.

I nodded, still trying to process what had occurred.

The planchette had seemed to move of its own volition, spelling out a message denying Luna died of natural causes. Yet the rest of it—the cryptic mention of "bad gas"—made little sense.

"All right, whether that was Luna, I think we can agree that was... odd." I said. "But not entirely implausible. I mean, there are documented cases of spirits communicating through Ouija boards and mediums."

Josephine nodded. "As I said."

I shifted. "I think we should be cautious about jumping to conclusions. There are a lot of unanswered questions." I ticked them off on my fingers. "Who moved the planchette if not us? Was it Luna's spirit or something—someone—else? And if so, why would she give such cryptic clues instead of straightforward answers?"

Mystico flicked her tail in agreement. "Sensible questions. You should listen to Ellie, glitter woman."

Josephine shot Mystico an annoyed look before turning back to me. "There is more to this world than science and logic can explain, Ellie. But I do think we need to start with bad gas."

As we descended the stairs from the second floor, I stopped on the small landing and touched Landon's muscular arm. I could feel the warmth of his skin through the worn fabric of his plaid shirt.

"Remember when I said I wanted to wait before you moved in?" I asked.

Landon paused, one foot on the step below, and turned to face me. The fading sunlight filtering through the circular window at the landing caught on his salt-and-pepper waves, illuminating his rugged, thoughtful face. "Sure, I recall that conversation," he said after a moment, his brow furrowing. His bright blue eyes studied me with a hint of curiosity. "I believe it was just last night, so hard to forget in that short of time."

"Well, I've been thinking more about it, and I've changed my mind," I told him, running my hands over the smooth wooden railing. "I was wondering if maybe you'd like to stay over with me tonight?"

As soon as the question left my lips, I felt a nervous flutter in my stomach.

Landon regarded me. "This change of heart wouldn't have anything to do with that spooky Ouija board session putting you on edge, would it?"

I looked down. I wanted to say no. I really did.

I wanted to tell him I thought about it and realized I was being silly, and that's the only thing I thought about.

But I also didn't want to start this off with a lie.

Landon placed a hand under my chin, guiding my eyes back to his. "It's okay if it did unsettle you some," he said, his voice reassuring. "I didn't like it much myself, and I know how seriously you've been taking this investigation into Luna's passing. I have no problem with the fact that you'd like to have a friendly face around tonight. And tomorrow. And maybe the day after that."

I reached out and took his rough, calloused hands in mine. They engulfed my own. "It's not just that," I said.

"No?"

"The truth is, I'm keeping barriers up between us for no good reason. Evie and I are adults—she loves you, and I doubt she'd have an issue with it. I have no doubt you and I can handle sharing space. My choice to delay is really about making you pay for mistakes I made in my past with other relationships, and it's not fair." I looked down. "And, yes, okay, maybe that bizarre Ouija encounter did freak me out a little. Having you around would make me feel less nervous."

Landon regarded me for a long moment, his piercing blue eyes searching my face. Then his expression softened into a crinkly-eyed smile.

"Well, in that case, I'd be happy to provide some comfort and protection tonight and any night you wish to have it, ma'am," he said, giving my hands a gentle, reassuring squeeze. "I'll take any excuse to fall asleep beside you, Ellie Rockwell—it's my favorite place to be."

I smiled back, my nerves dissolving.

As long as I had this steady man by my side, ghosts and ghouls didn't stand a chance.

Landon tucked a strand of hair behind my ear, his rough fingers grazing my cheek and sending a shiver through me. He leaned down and kissed me, the familiar scent of leather and timber enveloping me.

"I love you, you know," I whispered.

"I love you, too." He pulled back, keeping his forehead rested against mine. "Let me just swing home to pick up a few things, then I'll be back to banish any lingering evil spirits. We can make more permanent move in plans after the festival."

We continued downstairs hand in hand, both smiling, and I realized this wasn't just about convenience or post-séance jitters.

Deep down, I knew Landon belonged here with me.

Chapter Eleven

I STOOD BEHIND THE POLISHED OAK COUNTER, IDLY running a rag over its already spotless surface. The cheerful jingle of bells above the door remained silent, no customers bustling in.

I glanced at the clock, its steady ticking seeming to echo through the vacant space. Only 1:30 p.m. On a normal Saturday, the café would just be hitting its busy afternoon period, chairs filled with chatting regulars and the rich aroma of coffee permeating the air.

But of course, today the Cinco de Mayo festival was still in full swing down on Main Street. I pictured the crowds congregating around the taco stands and margarita carts, laughter and music spilling from the park where children frolicked beneath the piñatas strung between two trees. Everyone was caught up in the revelry of the annual celebration.

Meanwhile, my cat café sat forgotten, a ghost town of empty tables, idle machines, and bored cats.

I was contemplating flipping the sign to "Closed" and calling it a day when the ringing of the café's doorbell snapped me out of my thoughts. I looked up to see Laurie entering, free from her afternoon of veterinary appointments.

"Hey there," I greeted her. "How were the patients today?"

"Oh, a special array of upset tummies," she replied, stifling a yawn. "You wouldn't believe how many tiny dogs seem to have a knack for finding half drunk margarita cups sitting on the ground in the square."

"Well, hopefully we can perk you up with a nice cup of coffee," I said, already grabbing a mug and starting up the espresso machine. "Josie's on her way back over here, and Matt and Evie are upstairs. Once Landon gets back, we can all sit down and talk about Luna's case."

Laurie's eyebrows shot up in surprise as she settled onto a stool at the counter. "Is there new news?"

"Josie brought a Ouija board here."

"A what?"

"A Ouija board. A wooden board with a bunch of letters for talking to the dead? She thinks we talked to Luna."

Laurie's eyes went wide. "You're joking. Please tell me you're joking."

"I wish I was. Josie insisted we try it, and I'm not sure what to make of it, honestly. The planchette moved

—she says it moved on its own. I think she believes it, but I don't know what to believe."

Laurie dragged a hand over her face. "That woman, I swear..."

"By the way," I said. "Landon's moving in."

"Finally!" Laurie exclaimed, tossing her hands up in dramatic exasperation. Her eyes widened with excitement. "I swear, Ellie, you really made that man run the gauntlet."

I felt my cheeks flush. "What gauntlet?" I asked. "We just took things slow."

Laurie let out a chuckle. "That's what I mean! The gauntlet of 'taking things slow.'" She emphasized the words with air quotes. "The poor guy has been waiting months for you to finally let him move in. I saw the way his face lit up every time he brought it up, only to fall when you said you weren't ready yet."

I pictured Landon's expression morphing from hopeful to crestfallen, like a puppy denied a treat. "I don't think that's true."

"Think what you want. You made him jump through all kinds of hoops," Laurie continued, counting them off on her fingers. "He had to get along with Evie, he had to help at the shelter, he had to be nice to Bella... not to mention waiting months before you'd even call him your boyfriend. You put that man through a very gentle but very persistent wringer. But I'm glad you came around."

I rolled my eyes.

But... maybe she had a point. I hadn't made things easy for poor Landon. But the fact that he'd stuck it out, respecting each of my hangups and boundaries, just proved how right this was.

"Yeah, yeah, okay," I conceded with a smirk. "I guess I did put him through a bit of a gauntlet. But he passed with flying colors."

"No doubt about it. Now let's celebrate him reaching the finish line!" She lifted her coffee mug in a toast.

With a contented smile, I clinked my own mug against hers.

Three unfamiliar men entered the café, their polished leather shoes squeaking against the worn hardwood floors, expensive watches glinting under the warm glow of the bulbs overhead as they walked through in their tailored suits, peering at the furnishings and local artwork adorning the walls.

Everything about them, from their slick haircuts to their briefcases, screamed out-of-towner—and the guarded way they scanned the surroundings told me they were here for more than just coffee and scones.

"Welcome to the Silver Circle," I greeted them with a polite smile. "What can I get started for you gentlemen this afternoon?"

The man in front flashed me a wide, toothy smile

that didn't quite reach his sharp eyes. He was tall and lean, with neatly parted sandy brown hair. "Three coffees, please. Just regular old drip for me and my associates," he said.

His voice was friendly and casual, but something in his assessing gaze as it swept over the café's interior set me on edge.

I rang up the order, the register chiming in the quiet café. "Coming right up. Can I get a name for the order?"

"Bill," the man replied, straightening his crisp slate blue tie. He jerked his thumb over his shoulder at the two impeccably dressed men behind him. "This is Bobby, and that's Dan. We're just visiting your quaint little town for a bit of business."

The developers.

As I poured their coffees, Bobby craned his neck, taking in the surroundings. "This is a charming little spot you've got here," he remarked. "Great way to preserve the history of an old place like this."

"Thank you," I said. "It's one of the oldest buildings in town. The contractor that renovated the place, Landon, worked very hard to keep its character intact."

Bill's sharp gaze roamed, seeming to appraise and catalog each item like a shrewd auctioneer. "I can see that. He did a wonderful job."

"I'll tell him you said so." I felt the hairs on my arms prickle, uneasy with his clinical cataloging of my beloved café's charm.

Just then, the front door swung open, and Landon

appeared, his brow furrowed. As he passed through the man trap and saw the three men, his shoulders tensed and his eyes narrowed almost imperceptibly. I could tell by his guarded body language and the way his jaw clenched that he sensed something was amiss the moment he laid eyes on the crisp suits.

"Afternoon, hon," he said, kissing my cheek. "Who do we have here?"

I performed hasty introductions. Landon shook their hands, his expression unreadable.

"You've done some incredible work on this place," Bobby said to Landon, admiring the hand-carved moldings. "Really top-notch craftsmanship. That wainscoting must've taken ages."

"A labor of love," Landon replied.

I could tell he was sizing them up as much as they were analyzing every inch of the café.

The three men continued complimenting the construction details, asking about types of wood and restoration methods. Landon answered, but without offering much. I busied myself wiping down the espresso machine, half listening.

After exhausting the topic of carpentry, Bill redirected the conversation. "So, Eleanor—you run this place on your own?"

"My daughter and some staff help," I explained. "But I oversee the operations, yes."

Bill nodded, taking a sip of coffee. "It seems like a real gem for this town. A cat shelter, a coffee shop. I noticed you even have a vet office off the front. You must have built up quite a loyal customer base by now."

"We have our regulars, and I like to think we created a space for the community to come together."

From my peripheral vision, I caught the almost invisible tightening of Landon's shoulders.

Again.

"Of course, of course," he said again in his smooth voice. Bill leaned back, and he regarded me with an appraising look. "But a place like this, in a historic building with so much character—why, I imagine you've had some offers over the years."

He let the implication hang in the air between us, as thick and cloying as the aroma of a ripe litter box. I busied my hands wiping down the chrome espresso machine, avoiding his probing gaze.

"Actually, I just inherited this place a year ago," I explained after a pause, hoping he wouldn't pry further into the complicated circumstances of the inheritance.

"Oh?" Bill's forehead creased as his eyebrows lifted, his eyes glinting.

I hesitated, unsure how much to reveal to these strangers who had appeared so suddenly in my café. "It belonged to a distant relative," I said at last, keeping my words vague. "She left it to me in her will when she passed."

It resembled the truth, if not the whole truth.

I was Bella's guardian, and Fiona had been Bella's human mom. Fiona felt like family now. I certainly wasn't about to get into the details of Fiona Blackwell's murder with these unfamiliar men. Let them assume what they wanted about long lost relatives and surprise inheritances.

"Even so, I bet you get offers all the time."

"Not really."

"No?"

"Now and then, someone that isn't familiar with us asks if we'd consider selling," I said. "But Silver Circle Café is part of the fabric of Tablerock, and this home has become a place of refuge and healing for cats and humans alike. I couldn't imagine being anywhere else, and"—I looked him in the eye—"I definitely couldn't imagine handing those keys over to just anyone."

I hoped the not-so-subtle emphasis on "just anyone" would convey that they fell into that category, but Bill seemed undeterred.

"Yes, of course," he said. "But from a business perspective—everyone has their number, right? You'd have to consider an offer if it was substantial enough."

"I'd have to?" I repeated, bristling at his presumptuous assumption. I straightened up, leveling a stern gaze at Bill. Just who did this slick stranger think he was, waltzing into my café as if he owned the place and insinuating I could be bought out like some commodity? Out of the corner of my eye, I noticed Landon shift his stance, ready to intervene. The easygoing atmosphere of the café evaporated, replaced by crackling tension. "I don't believe there's much in life I have to do."

Bill held up his hands in a conciliatory gesture, though his eyes remained calculating. "No offense meant, of course," he backpedaled. "Just speculation during a friendly chat, that's all."

The nerve of this man.

"I think you fellas are barking up the wrong tree," Landon told him, an unmistakable edge in his tone as he crossed his thick arms over his broad chest. The fabric of his plaid shirt strained against his biceps. "Wardwell Manor isn't for sale. Not now, not ever. Not for any price."

Bobby and Dan shifted their feet, averting their gazes. But Bill maintained his genial facade, an oily smile plastered across his face.

"Like I said—just making casual conversation here, Mr. Rogers," he replied, though his darting eyes betrayed his unease. "Can't blame a guy for asking about a real gem like this."

"I can blame a guy for not taking no for an answer."

"Fair point, Mr. Rogers. Fair point."

We endured a few more agonizing minutes of stilted small talk before the men finished their coffees.

"Well, it was a pleasure to meet you both," Bill said. He pulled out a business card and placed it on the counter next to a hundred dollar bill. "That should cover the coffees, a donation to your little shelter, and my phone number in case you ever change your mind and decide to explore options."

I stared at the card without picking it up.

Bill chuckled. "Well, it was worth a try. You folks have a nice day now."

"What a bunch of snakes," I muttered through gritted teeth as the door chimed shut behind the departing men.

"Sorry if I overstepped by saying you would never sell Wardwell Manor," he said. "I should have asked you first or just kept my mouth shut. I figured even if you would sell someday, it wouldn't be to men like them."

"You were right," I told Landon while sweeping Bill's business card into the trash can. "But just out of curiosity, why were you so sure I wouldn't sell to them?"

"Not a one of them pet a single cat while they were here."

As if on cue, Digby wound between my ankles, purring as I reached down to scratch between his ears. "I think Landon knows what we value pretty well, huh, Digs?"

Digby meowed in agreement.

"Well, it's about time," Josie said as she plopped down on the sofa next to me, setting her coffee mug on the low table with a clink. "I was wondering if Landon was going to be stuck living out of that tiny box of his forever."

Landon's tiny house stood tucked behind his wood shop nestled against a grove of live oaks. He had built the compact dwelling himself from reclaimed lumber and salvaged windows with clever design details like a sloped metal roof angled just so to collect rainwater and a salvaged barn door on rustic metal rails serving as the entrance. It had incredible handcrafted charm, and I loved it.

But Josephine wasn't wrong.

It was tiny.

Landon walked by with a cardboard box balanced on his broad shoulder. "Don't you be knockin' my tiny house, Josephine," he said, shooting her a mock stern look. "I love that place. She saw me through many a long night out under the stars."

"Oh, please, that decrepit box of yours is hardly bigger than an outhouse." She waved a hand. "I'm surprised you didn't get a crick in your neck from stooping over just to walk through the door."

"You're a very negative woman, you know that?"

"I have high standards. Are you going to keep the thing there or sell it?"

"For now, I'll keep it there."

"You know, Luna suggested once that we build tiny houses on the property here so people could sleep near the catios..." I trailed off, thoughts drifting back to our ongoing investigation into her shocking death. Shaking my head, I turned back to Laurie with a smile. "Anyway, I'm just so glad he's moving in. It feels right."

Matt hustled in toting a heavy box overflowing with Landon's books. "Where do you want these, Ellie?" he called over to me. "Downstairs or upstairs in the living area?"

"Oh, just set them next to the counter for now," I told him. "We'll get everything organized later."

Matt deposited the box with a thud. "Well, that was the last one," he proclaimed, wiping his brow. "Landon is a hundred percent moved out of the tiny house and into your place."

"Thank goodness," my daughter said as she emerged from the back room. "I was thinking you two would just keep dancing around the subject forever."

Laurie turned toward Evie. "Now hold on there. Landon didn't dance around anything. He's been ready for this for ages. It was your dear mother over here who kept two-stepping away whenever he brought it up."

Josephine nodded, the gold hoop earrings dangling from her ears swaying with the motion. "Laurie's right, hon," she said, fixing me with her piercing gaze. "All the dancing was done by you, Eleanor. That man has been nothing but open and willing."

With friends like these...

"Hey now, cut Ellie some slack," Matt chided Laurie and Josephine, an amused grin spreading across his boyish face. He sauntered over to where Evie stood and grasped her shoulders, his muscular arms protective. "This is a big step for both of them after their first marriages. A step I'm pretty sure neither one of you has ever taken—Laurie, you're still single, and Josephine, you've never been divorced."

"Not yet, but the weekend's not over—and listen to you, pretending like you belong at the adults' table," Josephine told Matt. "You're just sucking up to your future mother-in-law.

"Stop, all of you," I said, but I could feel myself blushing.

"But really, Mom," Evie said, unable to keep a smile from tugging at her lips. "It's about time. We couldn't be happier for you two."

After my divorce, I'd sworn off romance for good. The long string of disappointing dates over the years that followed only affirmed that. But then Landon Rogers had sauntered into my life with his serene confidence and boyish charm, and to my immense surprise, I'd fallen for him.

Hard.

Even after we'd started dating, I was wary of rushing into anything too quickly. The sting of my failed marriage had made me cautious, afraid to get hurt again —but Landon had been patient and understanding. He never pushed, just made it clear he would wait for me for as long as it took.

Over time, my walls came down, and here we were, moving in together.

It was a little terrifying, but also thrilling.

Landon grinned down at me, his eyes crinkling at the corners. "You have no idea how happy it makes me to be here, Ellie," he said. "I've been ready for a long time, but I wanted you to get there in your own time. I'm not going anywhere now though, so you're stuck with me!" He planted a kiss on top of my head, then turned to address the room. "I want to thank y'all for helping me move all my worldly possessions. I couldn't have done it without my trusty moving crew!"

Callie (the calico cat with patches of black, orange, and white fur who had been shadowing Landon's footsteps for months) climbed up his pant leg and leaped onto the counter in front of him. She nuzzled her face against his elbow and let out a low, rumbling purr of contentment.

Landon chuckled and scratched behind her ears, eliciting louder purrs.

I chuckled. "I told you that cat would be yours." I made a mental note to take Callie off the website's adoptable list.

Well, to tell Evie to do it.

She—Callie—obviously wasn't going anywhere.

Chapter Twelve

ONLY A FEW CUSTOMERS REMAINED AT THE scattered tables. My imagination was filled with the distant thrum of Latin music and laughter from the annual Cinco de Mayo celebration as if I could hear it through the open windows and sliding doors leading to the catio. Which I could not—the festival was too far away for me to hear anything.

The front bell sounded and I perked up, ready to greet a potential coffee-drinking adopter—but the brisk clack of high heels had my eyes widening as I recognized the woman entering.

It was none other than Blanca Cruz.

What was she doing here?

As far as I could recall, Blanca had never set foot in the cat café before.

She paused just inside the entrance, sharp eyes scanning like a sentry on night watch. After a long moment, she headed straight for the counter where Evie was chatting with Darla, her heels clicking on the wood floor.

A dozen questions whirled through my mind.

What was she doing here? What was that intense look in her eye? Was she here because of the conversation I overheard between her and Diego? Should I swoop in and intercept her, or hang back and see what unfolded?

My protective maternal instincts flared, wary of this unfamiliar potential threat encroaching on my daughter —but I held myself in check, pulse quickening. The place had few people in it, but there were still people. She wasn't likely to do anything with five witnesses; I told myself. For now, I would observe—and hope to glean some understanding of Blanca's motives.

I watched and listened, obscured from plain view.

"Hello, sorry to interrupt," Blanca said as she approached them. "Is the cat shelter closed today?"

Evie smiled. "No, it's open. Just a little quiet since so many people are at the festival."

Blanca nodded. "I see. Is Mystico here, by any chance? The cat that belonged to Luna Espinoza, the tarot card reader?"

"She is, but she's still in isolation since she's only been here a few days," Evie explained. "No one can visit with her for about another week."

A flicker of frustration passed over her face, but was quickly smothered.

An imperious meow pierced the café's calm, catching our attention. The three women turned to see Belladonna perched on the second floor banister, staring down at Blanca with suspicion. Her melodic meow had commanded the room like a royal trumpet announcing royalty.

Blanca's stare did not waver, holding the cat's scrutiny with a cool expression. "I see. Well, that is unfortunate timing. When do you think I might be able to come see Mystico?"

"Like I said, early next week, once she's out of isolation," Evie told her.

Belladonna continued watching a moment more, before turning with a flick of her tail and leaping from her perch.

Darla piped up cheerfully, "We've got fresh coffee and snacks if you'd like to sit and chat for a bit! There are plenty of other cats that would love to spend time with you."

I had to admire Darla's friendly overture, though I doubted Blanca was here for casual conversation over lattes. Still, Darla's bubbly nature could draw out even the most taciturn.

We might uncover clues if she could get Blanca to linger.

Blanca gave her a thin smile. "No, but thank you. I should be going." She turned her focus back to Evie. "One more thing—I heard you were dating Matt Garcia? Estella's grandson, correct?"

Evie blinked in surprise, but nodded. "Yes, that's right."

"I don't know him well, but Estella is a dear woman," Blanca mused. Then her expression turned shrewd. "Speaking of Estella, I'm curious... why was your mother meeting with those developers earlier today?"

Wait... what?

How did those two things correlate?

I puzzled over how Blanca could have known about the earlier meeting—it had ended over an hour ago. There was no way she could have spotted those investors leaving Wardwell Manor from the street unless she was parked on the stretch of road in front of our place, watching.

What interest could she have in those investors that would compel her to lurk around staking out the manor?

Evie looked confused. "Just a friendly chat, I think. This is a café."

"Hmm, I see," Blanca murmured, though she didn't seem satisfied. Her dark eyes flicked between Evie and Darla. After an awkward beat, she said, "Well, I should be off."

No more information—and more oddities.

I filed away Blanca's behavior as another piece of the puzzle surrounding Luna's death that made my hair stand on end. It was a puzzle I hoped would start making sense soon, because I was tired of feeling like I was fumbling in the dark.

"Please let me know when I can come back to see Mystico."

"As I said, in about a—"

Without waiting for Evie to finish, Blanca pivoted on her heel and strode out the door without so much as a goodbye, leaving Darla and Evie staring after her departing figure.

"Rude," Evie said.

"Rude and weird," Darla added, voicing my own thoughts. "What interest could she have in those developers?"

"And how did she know they were here?" Evie wondered. "Do you think she was, like, spying on the place or something, Mom?"

I stepped out from behind the large cat tree, glancing at the two remaining customers lingering at a corner table across the room. "I don't think we should talk about this here," I said in a low voice, leaning in close to Evie and Darla. "Let's continue this conversation somewhere more private."

As we slipped through the doorway into the back hallway, the cozy coffee scents gave way to cooler, sterile air that carried a subtle undertone of antiseptic.

"I think there was more to Blanca's visit than just checking on Mystico, but I don't want to jump to conclusions," I told Evie and Darla. "I didn't get enough from anything she said or did to hazard a guess what she's up to."

"I'm hearing you, but what was with the investor questions?" Evie asked.

Darla gave a casual shrug. "Maybe we should ask around, see if anyone knows why Blanca would be so interested in those investors visiting here." She craned her neck to peer back into the café, where the only two remaining customers were gathering their things to leave. "Oops, I'd better get back out there. Looks like they need their check."

"I guess that's our cue too," I said, turning back to Evie. I tilted my head toward the front of the café in a 'let's go' gesture. "We won't know anything until we poke around some more."

We went back in the café and found Darla already flitting between tables toward the two customers, flashing her bright smile as the front door chimed.

Laurie and Josie breezed in mid-laugh with their heads bent together. Their bubbly chatter filled the somber air left in Blanca's wake, lifting the gloom like sunshine burning away morning mist.

"Well, don't you two look like you're having fun?" I leaned on the counter.

"We just watched the tomato toss competition," Josie explained with a grin. "It was hilarious. You should've seen Charlie out there. Looked like a tomato exploded on his face at one point."

"Poor guy," Evie chuckled. "He's not having a great festival."

"Oh, he loved it," Laurie assured us. "By the way,

did we miss anything exciting here while we were gone?"

"Not too much," I said. "We did have a visitor asking about Mystico, though—Blanca Cruz. I was so surprised when she walked in, my face almost hit the floor."

Josie and Laurie exchanged a look. "What did she want?"

"Asked after Mystico and when she could see her," I told them. "She also seemed very interested in those developers that came by—and somehow she knew they had been here, which was odd. Evie and I think she may have been watching the manor for a while before coming inside."

"I think she has a hearing problem," Evie added. "I told her she couldn't see Mystico for a week, and I think she asked twice more after that. I'm not sure if she was trying to catch me in a lie or poke until she got the answer she wanted. But it was weird."

"Huh, that is weird," Laurie agreed. "And we have no idea why she'd be so interested in them?"

I shook my head. "No clue. Unless she owns the building Terra's Gifts is in, and she's involved in this whole developer sale thing, too."

Laurie nodded. "We can do some friendly neighborhood gossip gathering when we head back to the festival tonight. I think Cecelia is going to be there, and if anyone knows who owns what in this town, it's her."

I glanced around the vacant café, noting the spotless tables and lack of customers. "You guys go on back.

I need to close up shop here, but it shouldn't take long." I held up a hand when Laurie opened her mouth to offer help. "It's okay, I've got it. With business being so slow today, there's hardly any cleanup to do."

Josephine was already heading toward the back.

Laurie rolled her eyes. "Holler if you change your mind. I can always lend a hand."

"I appreciate it, but really, I won't even break a sweat getting this place squared away." I made a shooing motion toward the back room. "Now go on and get plotting back there. I'll join you all as soon as I've turned off the lights and locked the front door."

Once I had closed up shop, I removed my apron and went on to the rear of the café. As I headed to the back room, Josephine's emphatic voice grew louder with each step.

"...can't rule him out just because Mystico said so! He had the best opportunity to slip something into her drink."

As I reached the door, Matt's bewildered response was audible. "But why would Diego kill the ex-girlfriend he still loved? That makes no sense."

I took that as my cue to enter.

Six heads—Josephine, Laurie, Matt, Evie, Darla, and Landon—swiveled toward me as I stepped into the room and slid the door closed behind me. "So, what did I miss?" I asked, settling into an open armchair.

Josephine threw her hands up. "Your future son-in-law is too romantic to be suspicious. We keep debating whether Diego is innocent, but we're just talking in circles at this point."

Laurie patted Josie's hand. "I understand why you're convinced Diego could be the culprit, but we can't disregard what Mystico told Ellie. The cat was certain Diego wasn't involved."

"I know this is kind of our thing, but how can we take the word of a cat over what's obvious?" Josie argued, her voice rising with conviction. "Mystico could be mistaken or even covering for Diego. We can't take her testimony as absolute truth. And anyway, our focus should be on this 'bad gas' clue instead. That's the actual key here."

"You want to ignore the cat's lead and cling to a vague statement from a toy? Be reasonable—we have no solid proof linking Diego to Luna's death yet. It's all conjecture."

Josie stared at Evie, her expression sharper than the mangonada chili salt that'd knocked Charlie on his butt. "When did we say you could sit at the adult table with that tone?"

I winced, bracing for the clash I could see coming between Josie's signature bluntness and my daughter's unyielding conviction. At the same time, I had to admire Evie's spine as she coolly returned Josie's stare.

"No one had to tell me," Evie said without missing a beat. "Strong women grab a chair and take their own seat. They don't need anyone's permission."

After a tense moment, Josie cracked the barest hint of a smile and patted Evie's knee. "Good girl," she said, her tone holding a hint of grudging respect.

Josie admired those who stood up to her, though she'd never admit it. She was like a grizzly bear poking at someone to see if they'd run in fear or push back.

In her book, if you had a backbone, you were worthy of her esteem.

"I like Diego as a person, but I think Josephine makes a fair point. We shouldn't dismiss him as a suspect just yet," I said. "As much as I want to believe in his innocence, we don't have definitive proof of it. However, continuing to debate Diego's guilt could lead us in circles. Let's shift our focus to some of the other leads we have."

I leaned forward. "I'm growing more concerned about the dispute between Blanca and Luna. Especially after Blanca's odd visit here this afternoon. In my opinion, that rift hasn't gotten the attention it deserves. I think we need to probe deeper into whether they were once friends and what was behind their falling out two weeks ago."

Evie frowned. "Diego and Blanca dating, I thought?"

"According to Diego, that was a month ago. And according to Mystico, Blanca and Luna fought about Blanca ripping her off—not about Diego. That tension coupled with Blanca's strange behavior today is too suspicious to ignore. That and the claim that Diego was about to go back to Luna."

"If the rumors are true, and Diego wanted to reconcile with Luna? That could have motivated Blanca to get rid of her rival," Matt proposed. "Crimes of passion happen all the time—people kill for love or money. This situation might involve both."

Laurie's brow furrowed. "Hold on, who said Diego was trying to get back together with Luna?"

"Diego," Landon and I responded in unison.

Laurie looked taken aback for a moment before nodding. "Well, in that case, I see Matt's logic here."

"But," Landon said, "that doesn't explain why Blanca sounded like she was accusing Diego when we heard them arguing."

Josephine perked up. "I think I should chat with her when we rejoin the Cinco de Mayo celebrations tonight. It'll be reconnaissance. But with margaritas."

I inevitably smiled to myself as Josie's eyes lit up at the prospect of being sent on a "clandestine mission" to gather intel. Nevermind that said mission involved casually chatting with our neighbors at a small town festival.

"What about that other woman Mystico mentioned?" Evie asked. "The one who fought with Luna about incense prices or something?"

Landon looked up from his laptop. "That's Blanca. Same woman."

"Blanca sold Luna incense for years and then two

weeks ago, Luna suddenly bought from another vendor. Blanca is obsessed with Diego, Luna's ex-boyfriend." I tapped my fingers against my chin. "And she was the woman Estella accused of, er, sweeping Luna's feet. That's a lot of links and problematic coincidences."

"That's also a simple answer. If Blanca was jealous of Diego trying to get Luna back, she could have decided to get rid of the competition with bad gas," Josephine said. "Let's not forget that's what Luna said—she died of bad gas."

"What does that mean?" Matt asked. "Is it a gas leak, car exhaust, a chemical weapon, a poisoning that caused bloating?"

"Well, I can't do everything," Josephine told him. "I got us the clue. It's up to you people to help figure out what it means."

Matt chuckled. "All right, Evie, Darla, and I will try to engage Blanca in conversation this evening at the festival," he said. "We'll see if we can get her to open up about the relationships between herself, Luna, and Diego. With any luck, she may let slip some revealing details."

"Now wait just a minute," Josephine said. "I thought I was going to be the one to speak with Blanca?"

Matt gave her an apologetic look. "No offense, Mrs. Reynolds, but your interrogation style can come across a bit... intense at times. I think our more easygoing approach may get Blanca to lower her guard more."

He made a valid point.

Matt's friendly demeanor and the fact that the kids are all close in age may let him coax Blanca into sharing candid insights she would never share with the rest of us old fogies.

"I agree," Landon said. "In the meantime, there's also the matter of this mysterious developer, TPI, that's poking around about buying up property in town. Starting with Rosa Vargas's restaurant."

"I still think we should just do some more digging into public records, see if we can find any concrete plans or purchase offers between Rosa and TPI first," Josephine suggested. "There has to be a paper trail somewhere."

I nodded. "While that's a good idea, I think Landon and I should hang around her margarita table—which was Luna's margarita table—and see what she tells us and what we can spot around the area."

"Hold on, I wasn't volunteering—I'm not staying back here on a computer while you all go on a taco-infused Mission Impossible," Josie said.

Laurie grabbed her arm. "You can hang out with me. We can walk around, compliment all the dogs, and ask everyone for the latest gossip. Maybe we can turn something up we haven't considered."

"That sounds like a great idea." I stood, stretching out the kinks in my back. "I think that's enough scheming for one day. Why don't we head back up and get ready for the evening? Sounds like we all have things to do."

Landon and I went upstairs to shower and prepare for the Cinco de Mayo festival. When we entered the bedroom, I found Belladonna and Mystico curled up on the bed, watching us with curiosity as we gathered our clothes.

As Landon and I bustled about the bedroom gathering our outfits and accessories for the evening, we bumped into each other more than once in the confined space. Each accidental collision came with a muted "oops!" and an awkward chuckle as we side-stepped around one another.

It reminded me just how unfamiliar this whole cohabitation thing was.

After so many years on my own, I had my routines down pat; now, it was like an ungraceful dance trying to navigate around another person in my private spaces.

Not that I minded sharing with Landon, but old habits die hard.

Case in point: when it came time to change, I reflexively ducked into the walk-in closet, closing the door most of the way.

"You know you can change out here in the bedroom, right?" Landon called through the door. "No need to barricade yourself in the closet on my account."

I poked my head out. "Oh, I know. But this is just what I've always done. My closet has always been my little sanctuary. When Evie was young, she never knew the meaning of knocking before entering a room. I couldn't risk the emotional scars of her walking in on me indecent!"

Landon chuckled, his eyes crinkling at the corners in that sweet way I adored. "Well, in that case, who am I to disrupt your routine? Although just know that should you ever decide to change out in the open, I swear to keep my eyes averted like a gentleman."

"I appreciate the offer, kind sir," I said in an exaggerated formal tone. "I shall keep that in mind for the future. I'm just not a flaunt-my-bits kind of girl."

After contorting myself to get the maxi dress on in the closet, I stepped out to find Landon buttoning up a sharp guayabera shirt, the vibrant blue fabric offsetting his warm tan.

"Well, don't you look sharp," I said, walking over to straighten his collar. "You'll be the most dashing man at the festival tonight."

"Only because I'll have the most beautiful woman on my arm," he replied, slipping an arm around my waist. I rolled my eyes, but couldn't suppress a smile. His charm was relentless, and my heart fluttered.

Get it together, Ellie, I chided myself.

This was hardly new territory; we'd been dating for months. But somehow, seeing him all spiffed up reignited that pulse of nervous excitement, like I was glimpsing my date through the front door peephole for the first time.

The man did cut a fine figure in that shirt.

We regarded our reflections standing together in the full length mirror. I realized again how natural it felt having him here. Any awkwardness was only because it was still so new.

"It's kind of nice, isn't it?" I said after a moment. "Having someone to get ready with for things like this."

Landon smiled, giving my waist a little squeeze. "It is. I'll admit, I was nervous about how this would go... moving in together. I know you value your space and routines. But I'm happy we took this step."

I leaned into him, feeling that same happiness rising in my chest. "Me too. I think we're finding our way pretty well so far. Though I apologize in advance if I get territorial about the kitchen or bathroom. When it comes to my organizational systems, I can get a bit rigid."

"Duly noted," Landon laughed. "I will tread lightly around your kitchen and bathroom shelves. And you just tell me if I'm ever invading your space too much. I want you to be comfortable."

His patience and consideration never failed to warm my heart.

After years of getting it wrong, I finally found a partner who understood and respected my needs. Landon never pushed, never demanded more than I could give. He let our relationship blossom at its own pace.

I turned in his arms to face him, sliding my hands up his chest. "You're wonderful, you know that? I don't tell you enough." I shook my head, feeling a swell of emotion. "After my ex... I put up so many walls. I didn't think I could trust like this again. But you've been so patient and kind. I'm still getting used to it."

Landon cradled my face in his hands, brushing his thumbs over my cheeks. "You deserve to be treated with kindness and patience, Ellie. I know it takes time to rebuild trust after you've been hurt. I'm just grateful you've given me the chance to show you how a relationship should be."

"I love you," I whispered.

"I love you, too," he murmured.

At that moment, it felt like we were the only two people in the world. The nerves I'd been carrying about this new step melted away.

All that mattered was that we were together.

The rest we would figure out.

Chapter Thirteen

THE EVENING AIR WAS ALIVE WITH MUSIC AND laughter as we arrived at the town square for the Cinco de Mayo festivities, sending my senses into overdrive once more.

Our group took in the lively atmosphere.

Matt glanced around, then pointed toward a corner of the square, saying, "There's Blanca. Evie, Darla, and I will go chat her up and see what info we can get. You guys enjoy the festival and we'll meet back in a bit to compare notes."

I hoped the kids' youthful charm would persuade the reticent Blanca to open up—given her glare at me, I was confident they'd do better than I would have. I sensed it would take more than charm and small talk to penetrate through that steel exterior.

Matt gestured for Darla and Evie to follow as he wound through the boisterous crowd. They squeezed between an exuberant toddler shaking a glow stick and a group of teenagers laughing while nibbling on churros.

I kept my eyes trained on the trio as they made their way across the square toward Blanca, who sat poised on the edge of the bench, back rod-straight like she was about to be served tea by the queen. Her scrutinizing gaze scanned the crowd as she took dainty sips from her margarita.

"Well, looks like it's just us for now," Josephine said. "Come on, Laurie, let's you and me do a lap around this place. Maybe we'll catch a juicy tidbit or two if we keep our ears open."

Laurie hooked her arm through Josephine's. "I'll follow your lead, secret agent Josie. Just point me where you need me."

The two ambled off, Laurie oohing and ahhing at the decorations while Josephine shushed her, whispering, "Focus up, agent! We're on a mission."

"I think Laurie may have pre-gamed. Or pre-loaded. Or whatever the kids are calling it when you drink before going out." Landon slipped his arm around my waist. "Well darlin', anywhere you'd like to start?"

"Why don't we just wander for a bit? I'm sure we'll—"

"Evening, folks," a familiar voice interrupted.

We turned to see Mario Lopez approaching us, looking casual in his jeans and t-shirt. "Feels like I've barely seen you all week," he said with a smile. It was a little odd seeing him out of his police uniform—I assumed he'd be working all weekend.

"Hey, Lopez, nice to see you," Landon greeted him, shaking his hand. "Been busy, I take it?"

"Finally off duty so I can unwind tonight with the family," Mario said, running a hand through his hair. "Man, you wouldn't believe the crazy calls we've gotten about the festival so far. Couple of rowdy drunks tried doing a human pyramid near the taco carts—can you imagine? They're lucky they didn't break their necks."

Landon chuckled.

"But anyway, I'm glad to clock out and just try to enjoy the festival with my folks, you know?" Mario smiled and shook his head, though it seemed strained, his eyes not matching the casual tone. "I just hope Cecelia doesn't max out our credit card buying up folk art. She has a thing for blankets I'm not allowed to use as a blanket."

"Is everything okay with you and your wife, Mario?" I asked.

"Oh, yeah, everything's fine." He brushed his fingers through his dark locks and gave an awkward cough. "In fact, it's good news about Luna's case. The coroner was able to confirm she died of natural causes—some sort of heart issue, it seems. So at least we know there was no foul play involved."

Landon and I exchanged surprised looks.

"They did this in a day?" I asked.

Mario shrugged. "I guess so."

"Well, that is fortunate," Landon said. "And a little surprising. I thought there were some suspicious circumstances surrounding her collapse."

"So did I, but apparently, she'd felt ill that morning while setting up," Mario explained with a casual shrug. "Rosa Vargas mentioned Luna had some dizziness and shortness of breath. The coroner concluded those symptoms indicated a heart issue, either from an illness or heart problem."

I understood the whole Texas independence thing—I really did. We were Texans, and we did things in our own way. Most people liked it like that.

But the lack of centralization—like with coroners and medical death investigation, which was county based—seemed like a recipe for disaster. Counties with less than a million residents weren't even required to have one at all—and in a huge state like Texas, that was most counties.

I understood clinging to independence and resisting overreach, but when it came to practical matters like death investigations, some centralized coordination could improve things. People's lives were at stake.

Well, okay, maybe not at that point.

"Hold up," Josie's voice rang out as she and Laurie rejoined us. "Did you say the coroner thinks it was just an illness that killed her?"

Mario nodded. "That's right."

"That's not what the spirit board said. It spelled out—"

Laurie abruptly linked her arm through Josie's and gave it a warning squeeze.

"—that there were suspicious circumstances," Josie finished.

Mario's brow furrowed, his head tilting like a puzzled puppy. "Spirit board, did you say?" He blinked, eyes wide, like he couldn't quite process those two words together.

"Well, yes, we—"

"Hold on. Let's just slow down a minute," he said, crossing himself. "You folks were messing around with one of those supernatural Ouija boards?" He shook his head in dismay. "Madre de Dios, as if talking cats weren't enough! Now you want to invite the devil over for tea and cookies with those occult games?"

"Oh, don't be silly, Mario," Josephine said. "Satan would want whiskey."

Mario dragged a hand down his face, looking disturbed. "Listen, we got enough real world problems to handle without dabbling in the occult, yeah? Those boards are nothing but trouble. So do yourself a favor and stick to more wholesome activities—like knitting or bingo night at the community center."

Uh oh.

Laurie put her hands on her hips, eyes narrowing into a fiery glare that could burn through steel. "Well, if that wasn't as offensive as all get out. Now you listen here," she said, jabbing a finger at Mario's chest. "We're not a bridge club of little old ladies."

Josephine leaned in closer, lips pursed. "We are grown, discerning adults exploring spiritual matters with thoughtful diligence, okay? This is serious business, not some horror movie Ouija board nonsense."

"I mean, yeah, we had some wine and cheese first to set the mood," I joked, shooting Josie a look to zip it. "But still, very serious spiritual scholars over here."

Josephine caught my eye, one brow raised.

An awkward silence descended, punctuated only by the distant sounds of mariachi music and laughter floating on the breeze. Mario shifted his weight, clearing his throat as he looked at Landon expectantly.

I could almost see the thought bubble above Mario's head thinking, "Well? Aren't you going to talk some sense into these silly ladies?"

Men always seemed to default to seeking another man's opinion.

Laurie, Josie and I swiveled our heads in unison toward Landon like spectators at a tennis match awaiting the decisive serve.

Landon took a half step back, palms raised toward Mario. "Your look, friend, seems to ask me a question I'm almost sure I'd be better off not answering. In fact, I'd like to stay out of this discussion," he said with an awkward chuckle. "I'm just going to nod and smile here and say it's a beautiful night here in Tablerock. Don't you think?"

"Ay dios mío," he muttered under his breath. Mario tipped his hat to us and said, "You folks enjoy the rest of your night." He then scurried away into the crowd as if wanting to escape the dark forces he thought we were involved with.

"Well, you can't blame the guy," Laurie murmured. "Have you met his parents? They're very religious."

"Information is information." Josephine turned to us, arms crossed. "And I think what he said is a bunch of bull. That coroner doesn't know bupkis—Luna said someone killed her, and she died from bad gas. I'm not walking away from what she said."

Oh, boy.

I hoped no one at this crowded festival overheard that.

"Yes, I remember the... message," I said. "But we can't ignore an official determination."

"Have you met the county coroner?" Josie asked. "Of course we can. And we frequently do."

Landon nodded. "Ellie's right, we should keep open minds. No use jumping to conclusions either way until we get all the facts. In the meantime, why don't we—"

"Hey guys!" Matt's voice called out.

"You'll never believe what we found out," Evie said, her eyes bright with excitement as she, Matt, and Darla joined our group again.

"It took some friendly persuading, but we got Blanca talking," Matt explained. "And she revealed some pretty crazy stuff about Luna accusing her of making people sick with her essential oil misters."

My eyebrows shot up in surprise. "What? How so?"

Evie jumped in, always one to relish spilling fresh gossip. "Okay, so get this—according to Blanca, about two weeks before she died, Luna started claiming that the essential oil misters Blanca provided for Luna's business were making people nauseous and lightheaded."

"That's why they argued about the incense," I realized aloud. "It wasn't about the price at all."

Evie nodded. "Exactly! Luna told the vendors to stop using the misters and brought back the ones she'd bought from Blanca. When Blanca refused to investigate, Luna told people that Blanca had tampered with the oils to make people ill."

"But why would she think Blanca would do that?" Laurie asked with a frown.

"Blanca claims she has no idea—she swore up and down the oils were safe and she'd never distribute anything dangerous," Matt answered. "But Luna was convinced she'd messed with them to cause problems and get Luna blamed because of their little love triangle with Diego."

Mario, who was walking by arm in arm with Cecelia, did a sudden double take as he overheard us, his head whipping back around so fast I worried he'd get whiplash. He stepped back over, reluctance written all over his face that screamed, "I don't want to get dragged into another occult discussion."

"Did this woman just confess to you all that she was accused of poisoning people?" he asked, eyes wide.

Matt's eyes widened. "Oh, no, no, it wasn't a confession. We just overheard Blanca venting about the situation to someone else nearby. We didn't talk to her."

"Hmm, I see," Mario murmured, though he still seemed puzzled by this new information. "This is the first I'm hearing about any of this. I'll be sure to pass along any relevant info to the chief."

Josie chuckled. "You guys did a bang up investigative job, huh?"

Mario ignored her.

"There's more," Evie added. "When we were eavesdr—I mean, overheard this conversation, guess who showed up and started arguing with Blanca again?"

"Let me guess—Diego?" Josie said.

"Bingo! Those two were going at it." Evie shook her head. "It was hard to make out everything with them talking over each other, but we heard Diego accuse her of killing Luna over jealousy and Blanca yelling back that she wasn't a murderer."

"Apparently, Diego only found out about the oil mister fight this weekend," Matt explained. "Estella told him Luna had come to the store upset over her argument with Blanca before she died. After hearing that, Diego said it made him wonder if Blanca did slip something toxic into Luna's drink that day if she could poison essential oil misters."

"Whoa," Laurie murmured. "So this confirms Diego

was trying to reconcile with Luna and gives Blanca a potential motive if she was angry over Luna stealing her boyfriend back."

Josephine cocked her head. "Back that taco truck up. How exactly does a chat with Estella confirm this whole Diego reconciliation theory?" She waved her hands as if trying to grasp invisible threads of logic hanging in the air. "Did I miss something, or did you make an Olympic-level leap there, honey?"

Laurie pursed her lips, staring down into the remnants of her margarita as though the answers might be swirling in its depths. "Actually, I don't know." She looked down at her glass. "Maybe my margarita-fueled detective skills aren't as sharp as I thought."

People drifting past began shooting sidelong glances in our direction, heads leaning together to whisper as they took in the bizarre scene—seven adults huddled in serious discussion beside a mouthwatering spread of tacos and margaritas, periodically making dramatic hand gestures or exaggerated facial expressions.

I couldn't blame them—we probably looked like some community theater troupe rehearsing an avant-garde street performance.

Mario held up a hand. "I think maybe you all drank a bit too much. You're jumping the shark here. There's no murder suspects or motives—the coroner determined Ms. Espinoza died of natural causes. There's been no homicide."

Mario seemed satisfied by this definitive conclusion

and turned to head off into the crowd again to catch up with his wife, Cecelia.

But after only a few steps, he paused and turned back.

"Rose Vargas," he said to me.

"Rosa Vargas," I repeated. "We know she had tensions with Luna. That's not in dispute—in fact, almost everyone knew about it. My question based on what you told us would be this: what if she caused Luna's death through this 'bad gas' somehow, then explained away Luna's health issues to the authorities to cover? It would steer suspicion away from her."

"Rosa does seem pretty cutthroat," Matt said, rubbing his chin. "And I think we said she had the most to gain from Luna being out of the picture from a monetary standpoint."

"Now hold on, let's not go throwing around wild accusations," Mario cautioned, holding up his hands. "I understand you all have your suspicions, but it's best to stick to the facts for now. Ms. Vargas is not a suspect, and there is no homicide investigation pending. Those are the facts."

"You're right, of course," I said. "Like I said earlier, we shouldn't rush to any conclusions."

"Exactly."

"Without proof." I offered what I hoped was a reassuring smile.

"Exactly." Mario nodded, satisfied again. "Okay then."

"Okay, then," Josephine repeated.

"I'll let you get back to your evening. Stay safe."

He looked back once, and then again once more, and strolled back into the crowd, leaving our group to ponder this newest information.

Josephine rolled her eyes. "He doesn't know if he's in or out, does he?"

"Forget about him for now. Where do we go from here?" Laurie asked.

"Search Luna's apartment?" I asked. "I don't know. What do you all think we should do next?"

The others frowned. I could see the gears turning behind their eyes, each mulling over potential angles.

Finally, Matt spoke up. "Here's what I'm thinking—"

Before Matt could tell us what he was thinking, the lively music filling the square was interrupted by feedback screeching through the speakers. We winced at the sharp noise as Mayor Waldo tapped the microphone and leaned in.

"Good evening, folks!"

His amplified voice boomed out, echoing off the buildings and making people jerk back. Scattered, disoriented applause rose from the crowd at his greeting.

Waldo enthused over the details of the town's upcoming bake sale and bingo night before moving on to the main event—announcing the winner of the annual margarita competition. "Now for the moment you've all been waiting for," he proclaimed, pausing as if about to announce the Oscar winner for Best Picture. "Who has concocted the margarita that will take home Tablerock's coveted 'Best Of' award this year?"

"I'm on pins and needles," Josephine deadpanned under her breath.

"And the winner is... Rosa Vargas, for her mango chili margarita!"

Rosa let out a shriek of excitement and rushed onto the stage, nearly toppling Waldo with an exuberant hug. The crowd cheered and whistled as a few flashes popped from people snapping photos with their phones.

"Rosa will hold the coveted Margarita Queen title, and her signature recipe will be featured at next year's Cinco de Mayo festival!" Waldo concluded. "The tangy mango margarita is available in limited quantities now, so ya'll better grab it while you can!" Waldo advised. "In fact, looks like the line is already wrapping around the square!"

I scanned the crowd, expecting to see hordes mobbing Rosa's booth. Instead, just a handful of people meandered that way.

Waldo always did tend to exaggerate.

"I won't keep you any longer. Have a great rest of your night!" Waldo concluded. "Pro tip—grab some tacos to soak up that margarita!" He mimed chugging from a giant margarita glass, then pretended to stumble tipsily, drawing scattered chuckles from the crowd. "Stay on the right side of sober, folks, and have a good night."

Rosa beamed as she stepped across the stage, her cowboy boots clicking against the wooden boards with each step. The band struck up a dramatic fanfare befitting a champion, and with one last dazzling grin and wave to the cheering crowd, she descended the stairs clutching her trophy.

"Make way, make way for the Tablerock Margarita Queen!" she shouted, twirling in a circle once she reached the asphalt, breathless and flushed with victory. She shimmied her hips from side to side, causing her curvaceous figure to sway. "Finally, I'm recognized as the best margarita maker in the whole town!"

A few onlookers whistled and cheered.

Others looked appalled by her performance.

Rosa sashayed off toward her booth, calling over her shoulder, "Come get a taste of sweet victory, folks!" before disappearing into the crowd with the margarita trophy held aloft like a boxing championship belt.

"Tasteless," Laurie said.

"Tone deaf," I added.

"Well," Josephine said, her words dripping with sarcasm. "Tact has never been Rosa's strong suit."

Chapter Fourteen

WE JOINED THE ENDLESS CONGA LINE OF MARGARITA pilgrims snaking toward Rosa's booth, all desperate to get their lips around her award-winning mango nectar before supplies ran dry. As we shuffled along at a pace that would impress an arthritic tortoise, I spotted the three sharp-dressed sharks from earlier—Bill, Bobby, and Dan—in front of us.

With rather unbecoming resentment, I noticed that despite the humidity, they somehow managed to look as crisp and polished as department store mannequins.

"How do they do it?" I muttered.

I smelled money-grubbing schemes brewing beneath those polished smiles, and I didn't trust these out-of-town hotshots as far as I could throw them in kitten heels —which, for the record, would not be far.

My inherent clumsiness and weak ankles were why I now only wore flats.

Landon noticed my apprehension and slipped a reassuring arm around my shoulder. Leaning close, he murmured, "Don't let them spoil the festival or distract you from why we're here." His calm presence eased my nerves. "They're just a bunch of city folk that are going to be surprised how fast this small town shows 'em the door. And if Tablerock ain't smart enough to do that, me and Waldo can always just challenge 'em to a fight."

I smiled at Landon.

Meanwhile, Josephine was growing more impatient by the second as our line crawled along. "Good gracious, we're moving slower than Christmas in quicksand," Josie grumbled, scowling like she'd sucked a lemon wedge. "At this rate, I'll be celebrating Cinco de Mayo with a walker and a Life Alert button by the time we get our drinks."

I chuckled. That woman had less patience than a sugared-up toddler.

"You are a paragon of poise and restraint," Laurie chirped back. "Never stooping to complaining or immature foot-stomping."

Josie scowled in response.

As we inched along, snippets of the men's conversation began floating back to us in the sticky night air.

"...valuable location..."

"...prime real estate..."

I strained to catch more. Were they discussing making an offer on Rosa's place? I pressed closer, smooshing my face into Landon's shoulder in my eagerness to snoop.

Landon noticed my nosy behavior and whispered, "Reckon those fellows are mapping out all the places they're planning on bulldozing?"

"It sounds like it," I whispered back.

Up ahead, Bobby remarked, "If only there was somcone in town we could make a bulk offer to. Pick up multiple properties in one go."

"Now that would be ideal," Bill agreed. "A package deal of sorts."

Landon gave a low whistle. "Well, ain't that interesting," he murmured. "Seems their ambitions stretch beyond a few strip malls."

As the line moved forward again, Landon tapped Bill on the shoulder. "Pardon me, fellas, couldn't help but overhear you discussing business opportunities you perceive are waiting for you in our fine town."

Bill turned, recognition flashing across his face when he spotted us. "Well, hello again! Fancy seeing you two here," he said smoothly. If he was surprised Landon had been eavesdropping, he didn't show it. "Enjoying the festivities?"

"Sure are," Landon replied with an easy grin. "And I gotta say, I'm real intrigued by this talk of possible investment plans."

"You didn't seem so before, Mr. Rogers."

"Well, now, that's true, that's true. I think Ellie and I might have been a little hasty—I mean, we don't want to sell our place, but some fresh blood in town in other places might not be so bad for our café, if you get my drift. Anything you'd care to share with a couple of interested locals?"

Landon charmed those out-of-towners with his good ol' boy act, buttering them up like biscuits at a church picnic. On the surface, Landon was all Southern gentility wrapped up in rugged denim—which I normally admired. But as I watched his deception flow with such ease, his slyness surprised me.

What was that man up to?

Bill chuckled. "Straight to the point—I appreciate that. Let's just say we've had our eye on this charming little town for a while now. Real potential for the right developer to come in and... enhance things."

Bobby nodded. "Revitalize, if you will. There's value here, but it requires a certain vision to unlock it."

"What did you have in mind?" I asked.

Dan cleared his throat, shooting Bill a questioning look.

Bill waved a hand, unconcerned. "No harm in sharing high level details with potential partners, Dan," he said smoothly. "As I mentioned, we're interested in a more extensive investment—purchasing multiple properties throughout downtown Tablerock to redevelop. Create more of a... unified aesthetic, let's say."

Code words for bulldozing the town square's character and replacing it with cookie-cutter uniformity, no doubt.

"I've heard tell you're interested in Rosa's restaurant, too," Landon pressed. "You looking to purchase that as part of this grand vision? It's not very close to the town square."

"Oh, Rosa's is on our radar," Bill conceded. "Ideal location with the highway going right by it. We're exploring all options. Of course, we'd need a willing seller."

"And Rosa's not?"

Dan chuckled. "I think Ms. Vargas has been too busy focusing on that trophy."

Just then, Josie piped up from behind us. "So let me get this straight—you boys are aiming to snatch up half the town?"

Bill gave her an indulgent smile. "Truth be told, more than half. But, yes. We feel Tablerock has untapped potential as a suburb and we'd like to take it to the next level. They're building the toll road out here. By the time it gets here, we'd like to make sure Tablerock offers the sophistication people in Austin expect."

"Did he just call us a suburb?" Laurie asked Josie.

"More like an exurb on a bullet train to becoming a bona fide suburban sprawl-ville," Bobby answered, straightening his tie with a smug flick of his wrist. "We've engaged in some preliminary pillow talk, if you catch my drift. Nothing set in stone yet, but the mayor seems open to getting between the sheets with deep-pocketed partners, so to speak. All in the name of bene-fiting the good people of Tablerock, naturally."

Um.

Ew?

"Waldo?" Landon asked, surprised.

"Oh, no, the previous mayor," Dan chimed in, waving a hand as if discussing weekend plans rather than shady backroom deals. "You know how elections go —the winds of change blow through, ruffling feathers and shaking things up."

Landon crossed his arms, eyeing them. "What would the former mayor have to do with current town business partnerships?"

The men exchanged strained smiles like naughty schoolboys caught raiding the cookie jar.

"Well, you know what they say about old habits," Bobby offered with an awkward chuckle.

Thankfully, we all reached the booth before I gave in to the impulse to punch any of them in the nose.

As Landon handed us our margaritas, I shook my head. "Well, unfortunately, that didn't tell us much we didn't already know. But at least now we can confirm they're aiming to buy up a sizable chunk of downtown, and Jessa's behind the push."

Josephine eyed her margarita. "Think it's safe to drink?"

"I'm sure it's fine," Laurie said.

Josie shrugged and took a gulp. Her eyes widened. "Okay, Rosa may be morally questionable and possibly even a murderer, but the lady knows how to make a mean margarita."

Old Carl came stomping out of the dispersing crowd looking about as cheerful as Eeyore at a rained-out picnic. His craggy features were fixed in his permanent scowl, and the tails of his shabby brown jacket flapped behind him like angry wings as he hurried over to our group, gesticulating wildly.

Carl approaching with fire in his eyes usually meant someone was about to get an earful. It looked like tonight that would be us.

"Evening, Carl," I said. "Did you have an enjoyable time at the festival tonight?"

"Enjoyable?" He huffed. "How could anyone have a pleasant time with that awful stench fouling up the air?"

Carl was known for complaining anytime he made a public appearance about anything he could think of, so opening with a complaint was pretty on brand for the old man.

"What smell are you talking about?" Josephine asked.

Carl's scowl deepened, carving furrows across his weathered forehead. "Your sniffer must be broken, because it reeks out here! Smells like someone egged the market and then left the eggs in the Texas summer sun." He swiveled his head from side to side. "Can't any of the rest of you smell it? It's downright nauseating."

Laurie sniffed the air. "I'm not noticing anything too offensive. Just the usual festival smells—food, drink, sweaty people." She gave an unconcerned shrug. "Seems fine to me."

"It most certainly is not fine!" Carl insisted, his face reddening. "In fact, I was just on my way to lodge a formal complaint with the mayor about this unbearable stench."

I hid a smile.

Only Carl would try to chew out the mayor over a phantom odor ruining his evening.

"Here now, I'll prove it to you all," he declared. "Come on, it's this way."

"You go," Josie said. "Laurie and I need to pee."

Laurie looked confused. "I don't."

"I do, and I need someone to accompany me since my husband isn't allowed to come to the festival at night anymore."

Before I could object to chasing imaginary smells or bathroom breaks, Carl marched off one way down the street and Laurie and Josie left, heading the opposite direction. With a sigh, Landon and I followed behind him.

Humoring Carl's outrage might at least provide some entertainment.

We trailed behind Carl as he led us around the corner, leaving the lively music and laughter of the festival behind. Our footsteps echoed on the side street, a stark contrast to the buzzing crowds just a block away.

"There! Can't you smell that now?" Carl demanded.

We were standing in almost the exact spot Luna had

been sitting just yesterday when she was found after her untimely collapse. No one had cleared away the small, weathered folding table set up along the curb. Next to it, a single creaky metal folding chair lay on its side like a felled soldier, adding to the overall air of abandonment.

I inhaled, steeling myself for the noxious odor that had Carl so riled up. But I detected only faint traces of spilled margarita mix and stale tamales lingering in the air. Certainly nothing that warranted Carl's dramatic gagging display.

"I can't say I'm finding smells to be bothersome myself," I said. "At least, nothing out of the ordinary."

"I don't smell anything unpleasant either," Landon agreed. "Just the usual outside smells."

"Are you people daft?" Carl asked. "It's right there, clear as day! A rotten, eggy stench. It's not as strong as it was, but it's there. It's there."

I glanced at Landon, who shook his head—he wasn't catching any foul odors, either.

Carl threw up his hands in exasperation. "You're all hopeless! But mark my words, something foul is afoot here! That smell ain't right."

With that, he shuffled off down the street.

"I know Carl likes to tell stories, but it's odd that he would take us to this spot, don't you think?" I wondered aloud. "Maybe he is picking up on something." I tilted my head toward Luna's table.

Landon looked thoughtful. "Why don't you and I take a quick look around?"

I looked at the area around the table and found my attention drawn to a dingy gray trailer parked a few feet away at the curb. It was a weathered old thing—the kind used for hauling equipment or storage—plain and unmarked.

It was the lack of a company name that caught my attention.

"Any idea what this might be?" he asked, following my eyes.

"I mean, it could belong to any of these vendors. The whole downtown is crawling with trailers right now." I leaned in, peering closer at the back of the dingy metal trailer, searching for some identifying mark.

As I drew near, a powerfully foul stench slammed into my nostrils, making me reel back in disgust.

"Oh! That is definitely a rotten smell," I gasped, fanning the stagnant air from my face. The noxious odor smelled like a wretched mix of sulfur, rotten eggs, and moldy cheese left to fester in the sun. It stung my eyes and coated the inside of my nose, so pungent I could almost taste the putrid fumes.

Landon leaned forward, inhaled, and then coughed and sputtered, nose scrunched against the fumes. "Reckon you're right. This must be what Old Carl was raving about." He waved his hand in front of his face. "That's one heck of a stench."

"What could be inside?" I wondered.

"Well, there's no label or markings. We got no way of knowing where this shipment came from unless we trace the license plate. I'll text it to Mario, but I have to say, Ellie, I find it mighty peculiar there's something foul-smelling materials right by where Luna fell ill yesterday."

"You don't think Josie's right about this bad gas thing, do you?"

"I don't know." Landon checked his watch. "Suppose we should head home, anyway. I think we've poked around enough back here this evening. I'm going to text Mario and let him know about this—just in case this smell is dangerous."

As we left, I paused, squinting at the area again.

For a moment, I thought I glimpsed a figure hovering in the flickering evening lights. But when I looked closer, there was nothing—just shadows playing tricks on my eyes.

With a sigh, I turned away and fell into step beside Landon.

⁂

"Okay, Mario texted me back, and he's going to send some officers by during the overnight to investigate that nasty smelling trailer," Landon said, setting his phone down on the dresser by the bed. "He'll look into tracking down the license plate number and ownership, too," he added. "With any luck, we'll have some solid leads by morning and know whether this is all just a coincidence."

"I don't think it is," I told Landon. "I just remembered something—I could swear that I smelled something similar when we found Luna."

"Are you sure?"

"It was faint, but people were commenting on it." A puzzled frown crossed my face. "Do you really think there could be a connection between that trailer and Luna's death? It seems such an odd coincidence it was right there."

"I think it's a good question. Hard to say for sure just yet if it's related or just a strange happenstance," Landon replied. "But I don't believe in coincidences myself. That smell by her table raises some questions in my mind—especially if that stench was there when she passed away."

I plopped down on the edge of the bed and slipped off my shoes, groaning in sweet relief as my aching arches met freedom. After being upright on my feet all day, sitting felt akin to a gift straight from the heavens.

Landon chuckled as he removed his own boots. "Now you see why I prefer a sturdy pair of boots over those flimsy little flats you insist on wearing."

I shot him a wry look and tossed one sequined ballet flat in his direction.

He snagged the projectile shoe out of the air and set it aside, still grinning. "I do love how those shoes look on you, though," he added with an exaggerated wink. "Really shows off those cute little feet."

"My feet are anything but little."

I felt my cheeks flush warm at the flirtatious compliment, still not used to this romantic banter even after months of dating. Like a nervous schoolgirl with her first crush, the slightest compliment from Landon could turn me into a blushing, giggling mess. I was a grown woman, yet his casual flirtations melted my composure faster than a popsicle in July.

Maybe I was just out of practice after so many years alone. Or maybe it was the effect of a kind, attractive man genuinely appreciating me.

Either way, I couldn't stop the giddy butterflies that took flight in my belly under Landon's admiring gaze. All I could do was duck my head and continue getting ready for bed, praying my burning cheeks would cool before I spontaneously combusted.

We continued preparing for bed, moving around each other in our new domestic dance of a couple's evening routine. As I wiped off my makeup, I saw Landon's reflection glance my way in the mirror.

"You know, I meant what I said earlier about not believing in coincidences," he said. "The bad gas, the rotten egg smell... it all seems hinky to me."

I set down my makeup wipe and turned to face him. "I was thinking the same. I think Josie's right. I think there's more to Luna's death than natural causes."

Landon paused in unbuttoning his shirt, his expression growing serious. "You really suspect foul play could be involved?"

"I don't want to make any wild accusations," I said.

"But a few things don't sit quite right with me and it hasn't from the beginning. That mysterious smell we found tonight being so close to where she was sitting when she died? That's just the latest thing. It all just doesn't seem right."

I moved to sit on the bed, brow furrowed in thought. "I know I noticed a faint trace of that same stench around Luna's body yesterday after she collapsed. At the time, I assumed it was something a vendor spilled at the festival, something spoiling in the hot sun, but now..."

I trailed off, looking up at Landon.

"You're certain?" he asked. "You clearly remember noticing that same odor around Luna when she died?"

I nodded. "The more I think about it, the more sure I am. It was very subtle, but that sickly sweet, rotten scent was there." I rubbed at the tension knot in my neck. "I just can't fathom how something like that could be connected to her death. She was outside when she died."

Landon sank down beside me on the mattress. "Unless she wasn't."

"Maybe." I nodded, stifling a yawn.

My mind still churned with questions, but exhaustion had settled deep into my bones. Further investigation could wait until dawn.

We finished preparing for bed and soon were tucked beneath the covers with Mystico, Belladonna, and Ginger curled up asleep at our feet.

"How do they keep getting out of the isolation room?" Landon asked.

"You're the carpenter. You tell me."

As I switched off the bedside lamp, Landon drew me close and pressed a soft kiss to my lips. "Sleep well, my dear. Tomorrow is a new day, and we'll get this mystery sorted out."

"The cats breaking out or Luna?"

He chuckled. "Both."

I nestled against his chest, comforted by his steady heartbeat under my ear. "Good night," I whispered back. "And if I haven't mentioned it, I'm glad you moved in."

"Me, too."

"Love you."

"Love you, too."

As I drifted off, my last hazy thoughts were of Luna. Justice would prevail in the end.

It had to.

Didn't it?

Chapter Fifteen

THE NEXT MORNING I WALLOWED IN THAT TIMELESS limbo between sleep and wakefulness, thoughts sluggish as molasses dripping from a jar on a cold winter morning. Beside me, Landon's soft snores rumbled.

I smiled and rolled over to face him.

His features were relaxed, lips parted as he slept. I reached out and brushed a stray lock of hair off his forehead before nestling closer, hoping to absorb some of his zen-like calm before the day demanded action.

"Mornin' beautiful," Landon mumbled, voice still husky with sleep.

"Good morning," I whispered back.

My mind geared up quickly, already starting to buzz with swirling thoughts, questions, and theories about the mysteries surrounding Luna's death like someone turned on a light switch; I wished I could quiet my endless mental chatter and exist in each tranquil moment as

Landon seemed to do—and as much as I wanted to try, my rumbling stomach reminded me it was time for breakfast.

My phone vibrated on the nightstand, the screen lighting up with a new text. I grabbed it, Evie's name flashing across the top. Swiping it open, I read, "Having breakfast with Matt. See you later."

My thumbs hovered over the keyboard before pecking out a reply. "Okay, see you later." I glanced at Landon, then added. "Try to remember to knock."

"Evie?"

"Yes." I stretched and sat up. "She's having breakfast with Matt, so it's just us. I'll go start the coffee. You might want to check your phone and see if we have any texts from Mario about that trailer."

Landon yawned and nodded. "Good idea. I'll be out in a minute."

I shuffled to the bathroom to freshen up, then headed into the main living area of my wing in my pajamas. As I emerged, three sets of impatient meows sounded as Belladonna, Ginger, and Mystico trailed after my heels, their plaintive cries and figure-eight leg rubs making it clear it was breakfast time.

"All right, all right, keep your fur on," I told them as I scooped food into their bowls. "You'd eat faster if you stayed in the isolation room, you know. The volunteers were here an hour ago."

Done with the cats, I filled the glass carafe with water and scooped fresh grounds into the basket, the rich aroma already sparking anticipation of my morning coffee. I flipped the switch; the machine gurgling to life, the drips and trickles signaling caffeine was on its way.

Not fast enough, frankly.

As the dark, fragrant brew filled the pot, I checked my phone. The screen showed no missed calls or new messages. My shoulders slumped a bit in disappointment. I had hoped to see some update from Mario about the suspicious trailer, but my notifications were empty. I sent him a quick text asking if there were any fresh developments.

Just then, Landon came out. I turned to greet him, only to catch myself staring. He hadn't bothered with a shirt, just slipped on a pair of jeans that hugged his muscular thighs. I found myself distracted by the sight of his broad, sturdy chest and sculpted torso, the morning light accentuating every ripple and contour of muscle.

Landon flashed a crooked grin. "See something you like, darlin'?"

I blushed and busied myself grabbing mugs. "I was just, um, still wondering if you got any texts from Mario. I got nothing during the night."

"Well, I'm a little disappointed that's all that's on your mind," he chuckled. He came up behind me, slipped his arms around my waist, and nuzzled my neck. "To answer your question, no new messages yet."

I leaned back, nestling into Landon's sturdy frame. It was a strange feeling, and I realized I was hyper-aware of every point where our bodies met and pressed together.

My shoulders settled against the solid wall of his chest, his brawny arms encircling my waist. We began to sway in unison to the delicate melody of birdsong drifting in through the open window.

For a moment, we existed together, needing no words to communicate the connection we felt.

It was nice.

The coffee maker beeped, breaking the tranquil spell that had fallen over the kitchen. I tipped my head back and placed a quick peck on Landon's cheek before pulling away. "Coffee's ready. I'll get started on breakfast."

I moved to the counter and cracked several brown eggs into a glass mixing bowl with a series of crisp taps while Landon rummaged through the fridge, the jars and bottles clinking as he searched.

"Where do we keep the butter?" he asked.

My heart beat faster.

He said "we."

"Bottom drawer in the fridge, behind the cheese."

More rummaging sounds. "Honey? Jam?"

I smiled to myself. We were still figuring out the choreography of living together. "Top shelf, door to the left."

Landon made a small noise of success finding the items.

As I mixed up eggs and milk for scrambled eggs, he popped bread into the toaster, the two of us working side by side cooking breakfast. Landon hummed as he set the table, and I recognized the melody of one of his favorite songs we'd danced to on one of our first dates.

Once the food was ready, we sat down to eat. Landon devoured his eggs and toast with his usual hearty appetite that I envied, especially when stress killed my own desire to eat. I picked at my food, too preoccupied wondering about the trailer to have much of an appetite—and fine with skipping breakfast, anyway. I could stand to lose a few pounds.

"You all right?" Landon asked. "You've barely touched your plate."

I sighed. "Just anxious to hear from Mario."

Landon reached over and gave my hand a reassuring squeeze. "I know. But Mario will handle it properly. He'll get to the bottom of it."

Belladonna let out an insistent meow, her green eyes fixed on Mystico as her tail swished back and forth. Mystico tilted her head, considering Bella's cry, and then offered a returned meow of her own. Their vocal exchange sounded almost conversational to my ears.

"What's got your fur in a bunch this morning, Bella?" I asked.

She swished her tail and turned up her nose with a little "hmph," unwilling to dignify my question with a response.

We finished breakfast and cleaned up together. As I was washing dishes, Landon's phone pinged with a new message.

"It's Mario," he said.

I hurried over, hands still dripping soapy water. Landon angled the screen so I could read the text:

Found trailer. Smell gone. No hazardous materials inside. Ran plates—registered to a Marco Jimenez, Austin guy that owns a party store. Makes sense. Festival rental. Will keep you updated if anything changes.

"Well, shoot." I sagged in disappointment. "So much for that lead."

"Maybe." Landon stared down at his coffee, brow furrowed. After a moment, he met my gaze, his eyes clouded with uncertainty. "My well-fed gut says we shouldn't dismiss it outright." One hand rubbed the back of his neck as he chose his next words. "Between you, me, and the wall, I'll admit the local police have over-looked a clue or two in their time."

"That's a polite way of putting it."

Just then, the landline rang.

I hit the speakerphone button and said hello. "Morning, Ellie! Josie and I are doing coffee and gossip at the café. You two want to come downstairs and join in on the fun?"

"Sure," Landon said. "We'll be right down."

"In a minute." I looked at him, brows raised.

"What?"

"Aren't you forgetting something?"

I hoped the man would take the hint that it wasn't exactly proper to greet my friends shirtless on a Sunday morning in the middle of my café. While I appreciated the view, I doubted Laurie and Josephine would be as receptive to glimpsing Landon's chiseled physique over coffee and scones at our newly cohabitating residence— well, at least not without teasing me relentlessly about it.

I had the appearance of propriety to maintain, after all.

"What?" he asked, genuinely oblivious.

Oh, bless his heart.

For all his many charms, subtle social cues occasionally slipped past Landon unnoticed like a feather floating through the air—gone before you realized it was there.

"Don't you think you should at least put on a shirt?" I asked.

"Oh my. What did I interrupt here?" Laurie joked, her melodic voice echoing through the speaker in a singsong tease.

I felt a flush creeping up my cheeks.

So much for propriety.

Landon and I made our way downstairs to the café, where I spotted Josephine and Laurie seated at a table near the front windows. I gave a cheerful wave and smiled as we walked over to join them.

"Morning ladies," Landon greeted them.

"Well, good morning to you, too, handsome," Laurie said, giving him an exaggerated wink. "I'm a little disappointed in the shirt."

Landon blushed, but laughed it off.

We pulled out the wooden chairs across from them and settled in for our usual Sunday morning chat. I poured Landon and me some more coffee from the carafe on the table.

"So, did you two lovebirds get Mario's update about the stinky trailer?" Josephine asked, spooning some sugar into her mug.

"We did. Sounds like it was a bit of a dead end." I relayed what Mario had texted Landon about the trailer being registered to a party rental place in Austin and containing no hazardous materials.

I hadn't noticed Old Carl perched on his usual stool at the counter just a few feet away, but that cantankerous man had the ears of a hawk. He'd already zeroed in on our arrival, listened to our report, and was poised to swoop in with his unsolicited opinions at the first opportunity.

"The police wouldn't know hazardous material if it jumped up and punched them in the nose. Of course, that's what they would say," Tablerock's resident grumpy gadfly complained from his usual spot at the counter. "Those nimrods couldn't recognize a suspicious smell if it up and bit 'em on the rear end."

"Now, Carl, I'm sure Mario is doing his best with the information he has," Landon said, defending his friend. "We don't know the complete story, so let's not judge—"

"Not judge?" Old Carl charged in, guns blazing,

propriety be damned. "His best ain't good enough! Why, when Landon and Ellie here took me over to that spot last night, the whole dadgum street was choked with a foul effluvium smelling of putrid eggs! Made my eyes burn something fierce. Darn near gassed me right outta my boots!"

We didn't take him over there.

He took us over there.

But, anyway.

"Effluvium?" Josie chuckled.

"Please, tell us how you really feel," Laurie said under her breath.

"I heard that! It was malodorous as a dozen rotten eggs baking in the sun!" He rapped his knuckles on the counter for emphasis. "You tell me—how can a smell that godawful just up and vanish overnight?"

"Airflow distribution?" Laurie guessed.

"Normal circulation?" Josie added.

Old Carl glared at them. "Don't make a lick of sense. Something real fishy is going on around here, I'll tell you what."

Carl lurked around the café daily like a curmudgeon vulture waiting to peck apart any opinionated conversation within earshot—and he intruded without invitation. Because of this, I'd grown used to nodding politely while ignoring what he said.

But...

Carl did have a point.

The stench Landon and I noticed had been powerful. It seemed odd it would have dissipated entirely by the time Mario went to investigate.

"He's not wrong," Landon leaned forward, lowering his voice. "When Ellie and I were over there last night, that stench nearly knocked me flat on my backside. Burned my eyes a bit." He hesitated, shooting Josephine an uncertain look, as if reluctant to give voice to his next thought. "If I was a betting man, I'd wager it was some sort of... noxious emission."

Josephine's sculpted eyebrows shot up. "Noxious emission, you say?"

"I knew she was gonna start," Landon told me. "I almost didn't say anything."

The lawyer leaned in, dropping her voice to a conspiratorial stage whisper. "Why, Landon Rogers, do you mean to imply..." She paused, eyes darting around before whispering, "...you smelled bad gas?"

Laurie waved a hand. "Oh, come on. Maybe it was just the remnants of a stink bomb some hoodlums set off. Or a smell from the sewer, the paper mill, a piled up trash can. I mean, there's not all that many things that smell like rotten eggs. Actually, there's just one thing I know of—hydrogen sulfide."

"Which is..." Josephine stared at Laurie.

"A gas, but—"

"A ha!" she exclaimed, pointing a manicured finger at Laurie in triumph. "You admit it's a gas!"

"Yes, it's a gas—a colorless gas with a distinctly rotten odor, similar to rotten eggs. It's often found in natural settings like volcanoes, hot springs, and swamps due to geological processes," Laurie explained. "It can also be present in industrial settings like sewers, petroleum refineries, tanneries, and mines where organic matter breaks down without oxygen—but you're not going to find dangerous concentrations of hydrogen sulfide wafting around the town square in Tablerock on a quiet Saturday night."

Josephine shook her head, waving a hand. "Says who? And how do you know so much about this?"

"Animal medical school. Hydrogen sulfide can build up in manure pits or other areas where animal waste accumulates, so they taught us about it on my farm rotation. It can be deadly—"

Josephine poked another finger toward Laurie. "A ha!"

"—but it's far more likely to be some teenage pranksters setting off a foul-smelling stink bomb they whipped up. Nothing sinister."

"Stink bomb, my patootie!" Carl shouted. "This wasn't some juvenile prank. That there was the godawful stench of death!"

A few customers glanced over curiously.

I gave them an apologetic smile.

Carl came over to our table to continue his tirade. "Mark my words, someone's letting loose deadly fumes in this town. Wouldn't surprise me one bit if that's what did poor Luna in." He shook his head. "But do the police care? Nope. They'll just sit on their doughnut-filled behinds until we've all been gassed to death in our sleep."

"Well, that took a dramatic turn," Josephine muttered.

"Now, Carl, let's not go making wild accusations," I said. "I know things seem strange, but we should avoid leaping to conclusions without all the facts."

"I smelled the facts," Carl grumbled into his coffee. "My eyes watered at the facts. Smelled like the back end of a—"

"Carl," I hissed.

Landon turned to Laurie, his expression thoughtful. "Laurie, you were the one doing CPR on Luna right after she collapsed. Did you notice anything peculiar in the air?"

Laurie paused, brows knitting together as she cast her mind back to that distressing scene. "You know, now that I think about it, there was a faint but very unpleasant scent sort of hanging around her." She closed her eyes, revisiting the sensory details. "I assumed it was just some spilled food or drink from the festival attracting flies nearby. But... yeah, there was an almost sulfuric tinge to that odor." Laurie opened her eyes. "It was faint, though. Very faint."

"I think I might have, too," I added. "I remember people saying something about it, but I just figured someone ate something that disagreed with them and didn't want to admit they'd... well, you know." I turned toward Laurie. "Is this rotten egg gas fatal?"

"It can be, yes." The vet looked troubled.

Josephine smacked a hand down on the table. "Bad gas. I keep telling you."

"Now, hold on," Landon said. "Let's not get ahead of ourselves here. We don't have any solid evidence yet that this gas is anything related to her death."

"We have our noses!" Carl bellowed, his face turning a shade of crimson. "Clear as day, that whole dang street reeked to high heaven! Smelled like something mighty foul had sauntered through, leaving a wretched stink in its wake. Like the devil's butt expelled a mighty roar!"

He pounded a fist on the table, rattling the coffee mugs.

A mother seated nearby with her young son looked over, dismayed. She covered the boy's ears with her hands and shot Carl a stern, admonishing look that would curdle milk. "Carl Prince, do you mind? There are children here."

"What, Dora? Did I say anything with the wrong four letters? Last I checked, 'butt' ain't a dirty word! Is it? If so, I didn't get the memo! I coulda said the devil farted, but I didn't!"

The mother pursed her lips and turned away.

"Why don't we move this conversation somewhere more private?" I suggested, herding our gossiping group toward a back corner booth like a mother hen gathering wayward chicks.

Old Carl followed.

That old gossip hound couldn't resist a salacious

conversation any more than a dog could ignore the siren call of a juicy bone.

Once we were settled again, Josie leaned forward. "So let's think this through. If Luna was exposed to some sort of... rotten egg smelling gaseous emission..." she said, "could that really have caused her death?"

"I ain't no scientist," Carl said. "But I know what my nose told me. That rotten stench was enough to knock a horse flat on its backside."

"Like I said—if it was hydrogen sulfide, and if it was a high enough concentration, and if she was in an enclosed space, then yes. It's possible it caused her death. But"—Laurie looked skeptical—"she was outside when she collapsed. How could she have inhaled a toxic level of any gas while sitting in the open air?"

I leaned forward. "Could she have been exposed while inside that trailer? Then made her way outside before the effects set in?"

"You mean like a delayed reaction?" Josephine asked.

"Not even a delayed reaction. She could have inhaled something in that trailer that affected her. Maybe she left the trailer to go sit down because she was dizzy or coughing, and then when she did, the full effects hit her system and killed her. This whole thing could have been an accident."

Old Carl said, "We need to get in that trailer."

I realized Carl meant well, in his own cantankerous

way—and that even if it was expressed through long-winded harangues, he wasn't wrong.

"You're right," I said. "We should find out everything we can about that trailer, who ordered it, who had access to it, and what's inside it." I looked around. "Back to the festival?"

Carl looked taken aback that someone agreed with his tirade for once, rather than placating him with soothing rebuttals about patience and due process. I hid an amused smile at the sight of him momentarily struck speechless.

"Ellie?"

"Yes, Carl?"

"Can I get a ride?"

Chapter Sixteen

THE EARLY MORNING AIR STILL HELD A TOUCH OF nighttime coolness as our group made our way back to Estella's corner store near the town square.

The dawn light washed the dingy gray trailer parked at the curb in a muted glow, casting soft shadows that did little to diminish its worn, weathered appearance. Though the streets were still mostly deserted this early on a Sunday, I heard the distant toll of church bells beckoning the faithful with melodious chimes.

"I can't believe how quiet it is," I said.

Josie glanced around the street. "Better for us."

We gathered around the trailer, peering closely for any telling details we may have overlooked before, but in the bright morning light, nothing seemed amiss or suspicious about the metal box on wheels. The trailer sat there innocuously, giving no hints about whatever noxious cargo had been stored inside that was now being concealed.

Old Carl tapped his foot and crossed his arms. "Well, are you just going to admire that trailer all day like it's a diamond ring in a jewelry store window? Or are we going to take some action and see what secrets this metal box is hiding?"

"I don't think—"

"Well, that's no surprise." He cast a sidelong glance my way, one bushy eyebrow arched. "That trailer's as tight-lipped as a steel trap, but with the right persuasion, we might get it to squeal. Think that's going to start with breaking into it, though."

The front door of Garcia's Corner Store opened and Estella shuffled out carrying her broom, gray hair escaping her bun in wispy tendrils. She spotted our motley crew congregating by the trailer like conspiratorial delinquent teens.

"Oh, good morning!" Estella started sweeping as she addressed us. "Is everything all right over there?"

"Morning, Estella." Stepping closer, I asked, "Do you know who rented this trailer for the festival?"

Estella paused, her sweeping, leaning on the broom handle. She squinted at the trailer, lips pursed. After a moment, she shook her head. "That's one of the rentals that nice young man brought over for Luna's booth." She squinted, thinking. "Now let me recall... I believe his name was Miko? No, wait—Marco."

"Marco Jimenez?" Landon asked.

"I think that was it. He arrived a few days before the festival hauling this trailer and another big truck full of things Luna had rented."

That matched what Mario told us about the trailer being registered to Marco's Austin-based party rental business.

"Do you know what Mr. Jimenez provided for Luna's booth?"

Estella turned toward me and pursed her lips. "Well now, let's see... there were those big coolers to keep the margaritas chilled, some stainless steel buckets for ice, a couple patio heaters, festive string lights she hung up, propane tanks, helium tanks for balloons, those plastic cups, blenders..."

As she rattled off the exhaustive list of party supplies and decor Marco had delivered, I tried to imagine how such innocuous items could be connected to Luna's suspicious demise. On the surface, it seemed unlikely such standard rental equipment could be involved in any nefarious plot.

Yet my intuition prickled.

As I racked my brain trying to settle on a question that would extract pertinent details, Old Carl sauntered closer to Estella with all the grace of a three-legged crab. He leaned against her storefront in what I presumed he thought was a debonair pose, but to me resembled a top-heavy bowling pin about to topple over.

"Say there, Miss Estella," he began, "I've been meaning to tell you, you run a mighty fine establishment here." He gestured toward the shop. "Cleanest aisles I ever did see!"

That old goat was about as subtle as a wrecking ball.

Estella gave him a polite smile. "Well, I do try my best, Carl."

"I bet with a gracious lady like you at the helm, every aisle sparkles—especially when you're in it!" Carl punctuated his excessive flattery with an exaggerated wink.

Estella responded with the gentle tolerance of someone indulging a precocious child. "You're too kind," she murmured, resuming her focus on sweeping the sidewalk.

Carl, oblivious as ever, pressed on. "Tell you what— I'd be happy to stop by sometime and help stock those tidy shelves of yours." He leaned in closer, lowering his voice in what I assumed he thought was an alluring rumble. "And afterward, maybe I could take you out for a nice dinner..."

I had to turn away to hide my amused smile as Carl laid it on thick, throwing out his infrequent charm to impress the unimpressed Estella—who responded with a noncommittal hum, her expression steely as she focused on her sweeping.

Carl seemed to get the hint, muttering "Fiddlesticks" under his breath as he stepped back from Estella's space.

"What happened to all the equipment and rentals after Luna passed away?" I asked, steering the conversation back on track.

"It's all still here, far as I know," Estella replied,

dumping a dustpan of sidewalk debris into the trash can. "After what happened, Rosa Vargas wanted to use Luna's booth stand and everything since it was just sitting here empty, but I wouldn't allow that. It didn't seem right." Her lips pressed into a firm line. "She didn't seem to care that Luna died and considering they weren't friends, I can't see any reason she should profit off Luna's misfortune. Luna paid good money out of her own pocket to rent all that."

Laurie nodded. "I can understand that."

"It just didn't sit well with me to let her contest competitor swoop in like a vulture, you know?"

"Do you know if the police have shown any interest in the trailer or equipment?" Landon rubbed his chin. "Did they search it or look through it in connection to Luna's death?"

Estella shook her head. "Last night I looked out the window, and they were sniffing around it, but as far as I know, its all been sitting here untouched since... well, you know." Her expression grew somber. "Such an awful shame what happened to that girl."

A heavy silence descended as we all stared at the trailer.

Luna's musical laughter from our last conversation still echoed in my mind, haunting me, and I could picture her dancing to the Latin music at the festival last year, her skirt twirling around her.

After a moment, Josephine broke the somber atmosphere. "Well, thank you for satisfying our curiosity,

Estella," she said. "We appreciate you taking the time to explain."

"Of course." Estella glanced at her watch. "Well, I better get back to my chores now. You folks let me know if you need anything else."

As she disappeared inside, Carl turned to us. "Am I the only one who finds it mighty peculiar the police hadn't bothered much with that trailer?" he asked, hands on his hips. "Could be clues to Luna's death inside, for all we know!"

I didn't disagree with the crotchety man. "You're right, Carl. It is frustrating that they didn't investigate it, especially after the concerning smell Landon reported last night. But you have to remember they don't think Luna's death was anything but natural. They don't have a reason to go in there."

Landon nodded. "It does seem like an obvious thing to check out."

"This trailer is someone's private property, their own personal metal fortress, sealed up tight behind that rusty padlock," Josephine said. "The police can't just go rummaging through another person's belongings on a whim. There are these pesky things called laws. Of course, it's ironic the one time we want Tablerock's Barney Fife police force to disregard proper protocols and shake this trailer down like an olive tree, they're sticklers for due process."

Carl harrumphed, displeased with Josie's law-abiding take. "Bah! The so-called proper authorities don't know their elbow from a hot rock." He gestured at the trailer. "We ought to take a peek ourselves, I say."

Landon chimed in, eyes glinting with a mix of mischief and resolve. "I have bolt cutters in the truck."

"Now Carl, let's not get ahead of ourselves. Josie makes a good point—we shouldn't overstep legal bounds." I raised a hand. "Maybe we could call Chief Rollins and tell him what we suspect, suggest he send someone to do another canvass of the trailer, just to be thorough."

Carl crossed his arms, scowling, but Josephine stepped in before he could begin one of his fiery tirades. "It's pointless. They still won't be able to unlock it."

I peered again at the dirt-streaked metal box. Despite its innocuous appearance in the quiet morning light, I couldn't shake the ominous prickling that Carl was right—somehow that trailer held answers about Luna's demise.

I looked at Landon. "Get the bolt cutters."

Landon hurried off to retrieve the bolt cutters while Josephine stood there with her arms crossed, tapping her foot.

"What is it?"

"Ellie Rockwell, I sure hope you aren't suggesting we should break into that trailer. Being bound to the ethical standards of the legal profession, I cannot and will not be an accessory to any shenanigans that would make my sainted mother rise from her grave and whack me with Black's Law Dictionary. My law degree did not come with instructions for abetting and aiding felony burglary." She paused, narrowing her eyes at us. "Well, it sort of did, but we're not supposed to use it for that."

"If you don't want to know the answer to a question, Josie, don't ask the question." I smiled, not wanting to admit to my legally questionable plans, even if I felt morally justified.

"You know what? Y'all just keep me in the dark like a mushroom. If any sort of unlawful trailer trespassing takes place, my ears don't need to hear a peep about it," Josie announced. "That way, I can keep my blissful ignorance and plausible deniability as an officer of the court. For now, I'll just mosey along and make myself scarce, conveniently oblivious to any potential shenanigans."

Laurie chuckled. "You do that."

Josie squinted at her bare wrist as though peering at an invisible timepiece. "Oh, would you look at the time?" Her brows pinched together in exaggerated concentration before she nodded, dropping her arm. "Seems I'm suddenly remembering a very important early morning meeting I need to get to. Somewhere else. And not here."

With that, she hurried off just as Landon returned with the bolt cutters.

Carl cupped his hands around his mouth and called after her, "Don't you worry none, Miss Josie! If any unlawful mischief takes place, you'll hear nary a peep from these lips!" He mimed zipping his lips, then made an exaggerated show of tossing away the invisible key over his shoulder. "You have your deniability!"

Laurie tipped her sunglasses, peering over them. "I don't think people in Austin heard you, Carl. Speak up next time."

"Oh, I think they might have heard me."

"Did I miss something?" Landon asked.

"She's pretending she has no idea we're about to break into that trailer." Laurie glanced toward Josie's retreat with a smirk. "Not very well, mind you. But she did try."

"Gotcha. All right, let's see about getting this trailer open, shall we?"

The bold cutters crunched through the lock with ease, the metal giving way like a stale cookie. I yanked it free and pulled open the latch; the hinges squealing in protest as I eased the door open.

Peering inside the trailer's gloomy interior, I saw a jungle of rental equipment crammed elbow to elbow. Bulky coolers hunkered in the shadows, propane tanks stood at attention in rows, and an army of metal cylinders were stacked along the walls at precarious angles, leaving a narrow pathway in the center to maneuver.

"Well, would you look at that," Old Carl muttered.

"What?"

"Um. I don't know. Just that. None of it looks dangerous," he told me.

Stepping between the helium tanks, I let my fingers trail over their cool metal surfaces. My nails caught on the edges of the block letter labels and I glanced at the canister.

CAS No. 7440-59-7
WARNING: COMPRESSED GAS
HELIUM (He)
Non-Flammable Gas

"Ellie," Landon said, his voice taut with worry.

"I don't smell anything at all. Do you?"

Landon stood motionless as a statue and sniffed the air, head cocked. "No," he said. "But if that changes I'll yank you out quick as a jackrabbit."

"Fair enough." I nodded, peering closer at the tanks. The air maintained its stale but inoffensive odor. If danger lurked in here, it wasn't apparent to my nose yet. I pressed on, shifting cans aside, hyper-alert for any change carrying a warning on the stale, stuffy air.

"If one of these helium canisters leaked, it could have caused Luna's issue," Laurie pointed out from the trailer's entrance. "But that would just be an accident, or maybe negligence, not murder. But we can't discount it —if the concentration of helium in the air becomes high enough, it can lead to asphyxiation because there is insufficient oxygen to breathe."

"Someone would have to shut her in here, though,

wouldn't they?" I asked. "Could this really kill her if the back doors of the trailer were open?"

"I don't know," Landon said, scratching his head. "But what I do know is helium doesn't smell like rotten eggs."

I was about to suggest we re-lock the trailer and slip away before someone spotted us nosing around, when I noticed something peculiar. Four of the helium tanks had identical CAS numbers printed on their labels, but the fifth tank's number was different.

That seemed odd.

Wouldn't all the helium tanks share the same number? I would think, anyway—though I didn't know what a CAS number was.

"Landon, do you know what this number means?" I asked.

"CAS stands for Chemical Abstracts Service Registry Number," he explained. "It's an identifying number assigned to chemical substances."

"So helium would only have one CAS number?"

Landon nodded, scratching his chin. "Yep, why?"

I pointed. "That canister's number is different."

"Huh. There should only be one CAS number on all these tanks if they contain the same thing."

"That's what I thought," I murmured.

I stepped closer to the tanks, examining the labels once more.

Sure enough, I confirmed that four of the cylinders

had "7440-59-7" printed in neat block letters—the CAS number for helium. But the fifth tank—marked as helium—had a different number: "7783-06-4."

I traced my fingers over the numbers. "Then what's in this tank? The number's different, so it can't be helium. Right?" I carefully detached one of the tanks from its bungee cord restraints and turned it around. As I shifted the metal cylinder, the large identifying sticker pulled away slightly at the corner. I tugged it a bit more.

Then I froze.

"Landon," I said slowly. "This says 'hydrogen sulfide' on it. Someone just slapped a helium sticker over it so no one would know."

His head jerked up, eyes widening. "You sure?"

I nodded, my throat tightening.

He moved beside me, eyebrows furrowing as he inspected the label. His fingers fished out his phone and tapped the number in. Landon's eyes widened.

"This here's the CAS number for hydrogen sulfide, too," he said. "That rotten stench we got a whiff of would match up with that."

"So now we know. Is it more dangerous than helium?"

"By a lot. This says it can be lethal at concentrations of just a few hundred parts per million. That doesn't sound like much to me." He met my gaze, the color draining from his face. "We need to get out of this trailer. Now. Carefully, but now."

As I placed the tank down with trembling hands, I heard a soft hissing sound. My heart stuttered in my chest.

Oh no.

Was the hydrogen sulfide tank leaking?

"Go, now! Now, all of you! Get out!" Landon ordered.

My heart thundered against my ribs as a surge of adrenaline propelled me forward. Landon's urgent grip on my arm half-flung, half-guided me toward the open doors where Old Carl was staggering out as fast as his rickety legs allowed. Fear and panic screamed through every nerve, narrowing my dizzy focus to one thought—escape. Get out, get out, get out pounded with each frantic beat of my pulse.

Carl wheezed but pushed on, feet shuffling, and finally, blessedly, we burst out into sunlight and fresh air just as a wave of that horrendous rotten egg odor slammed into my nostrils. I doubled over, gagging. Beside me, Carl wheezed and coughed.

"Back up from the trailer. Give yourselves some space!" Landon called out.

After a few moments of gulping fresh air, the nausea and dizziness subsided. But a chill slithered down my spine as I imagined what could have happened if we'd lingered any longer in that metal tomb leaking deadly fumes.

Luna must have been trapped in there with concentrated exposure.

As the pieces clicked together, sorrow and outrage battled within me.

Luna's death had been no accident.

Chapter Seventeen

THE INITIAL RUSH OF FEAR AND PANIC WAS FADING, but my hands still trembled no matter how much I tried to steady them. Beside me, Landon stroked my back as I gulped down deep breaths, trying to calm my racing heart.

"You okay?" he asked, his own voice shaky.

My mind was a jumble of panicked thoughts—the top being that we had barely escaped from that death-trap. Instead of giving voice to it, I just nodded, not yet trusting my voice not to shake. The fresh morning air had never tasted so sweet.

Old Carl leaned against the corner store's brick wall, wheezing like a three-pack-a-day smoking asthmatic who'd just finished running a marathon. His face had taken on a sallow, greenish cast that lent him a certain swamp creature chic quality—though I shouldn't poke fun given that I likely looked equally attractive. "Good...

goodness gracious," he sputtered between wheezes. "We're lucky... to be alive."

"No kidding," Laurie rasped. "Let's back up a bit more, just to be safe."

We shuffled farther down the sidewalk, putting more distance between us and the trailer with the swift steps of a bomb squad technician performing a very urgent evacuation. My pulse still hammered, echoing in my ears, but as the adrenaline ebbed, my hands stilled and my breathing normalized.

Luna must have been trapped in there, I realized with dawning horror. Or she just didn't run fast enough once her eyes stung. Either way, she must have been exposed to concentrated fumes in that enclosed space.

Deliberately.

Someone deliberately changed the canister.

Which meant her death had been no accident.

The front door to Garcia's Corner Store opened and Estella hurried out, wisps of gray hair fluttering loose from her bun like errant feathers escaping a bird's nest. Sadie trailed behind her, face creased with concern. "What's going on out here?" Estella asked. "We heard shouting and then saw you all staggering around. Is everything all right? You all look terrible."

Inhaling a deep, fortifying breath, I stepped forward to explain the dire situation we had uncovered, and details spilled out about the swapped tanks, the hidden deadly fumes, and our chilling close call with the leaking gas.

Estella pressed a weathered hand to her heart. "Dios mío! That's the gas that killed poor Luna?"

"We think so. Someone switched the tanks and left that one in the trailer. I barely jostled it and it started leaking. That must have been loosened on purpose."

Sadie exchanged an uneasy glance with Estella, and then said, "I hear what you're saying, Ellie, but if someone wanted to hurt the poor girl, wouldn't there be simpler ways than swapping gas tanks and hoping she'd climb inside that trailer and then jostle a loose top?"

"Sure, but—"

"And not realize what was happening?"

"Sure, but—"

"And then not get out fast enough?"

Well...

When she put it like that, it does sound complicated.

Estella nodded. "It does seem a very complicated way to create an accident."

Carl, having recovered his wind, shuffled over to join the conversation. "No accident! We're talking cold-blooded murder here! Mark my words."

"Regardless of intent," Laurie said, "we now know this was no natural death. That hydrogen sulfide likely caused Luna's demise based on what I know of its toxicity. At the very least, it's criminal negligence that those hazardous tanks were mixed up if it was some strange accident—it nearly gassed us just now."

Landon nodded. "You're right. Intentional or not,

something fishy led to that deadly gas canister being in that trailer."

"Should we go talk to the rental guy? Miko? Marco?"

"At this point, I think we need to call Mario, get him to send a team back here to investigate properly this time. Who knows what else they missed if they didn't notice this?"

Landon was right, as much as I hated to admit it.

Wild speculation and interviewing potential murderers might not get us the answers we needed right now—no matter how tempting it was to point fingers at Rosa's ambition or Diego's evasiveness or Blanca's jealousy, any of which could be a motive for murder.

We needed to contact the authorities and lay out only the confirmed facts—the switched tanks, the deadly gas, and the implications for Luna's demise.

And we needed to hope for fingerprints.

"That poor child," Sadie murmured, shaking her head. "To think she died in such an awful way, it's just heartbreaking."

Estella squeezed her hand. "We'll make sure whoever is responsible is held accountable. Justice will be done for Luna and her family. We're Tablerock, Texas. We may stumble and bumble through, but usually land our butts in the right mud puddle."

I looked at Sadie, swallowed my sarcastic impulses, and stepped away to phone Mario, quickly explaining finding the swapped tanks and our near miss with the leaking fumes.

"What were you doing in the trailer? Wasn't it locked?"

"Sorry, what? I can't hear you."

"Hydrogen sulfide?" Mario repeated, his voice louder. "Are you certain, Ellie?"

"Positive. Landon confirmed the CS number on the tank matches hydrogen sulfide."

"The CAS number?" Mario let out a low whistle. "Okay, I'll be right over with a team to take control of that trailer as a crime scene. Don't let anyone else near it." He paused. "You all okay?"

I exhaled a quavering breath that might have been an anxious giggle. "We're still catching our breath, but we're all right. Just..." I trailed off, emotion clogging my throat.

"I know," Mario said. "Stay put—I'll be there shortly."

Two patrol cars came screeching around the corner, sirens blaring, followed closely by the white crime scene van. Mario leaped out of the lead car, his usual easygoing demeanor replaced by crisp, attentive efficiency.

"Cordon off this area," he directed the officers accompanying him. "I want a twenty-foot perimeter and when hazmat gets here, they can make it smaller if needed. Tape it off."

I let out a small sigh of relief at seeing him jump into

action and take control of the scene. The full weight of what we'd discovered still pressed on my shoulders, but now at least we had the professionals here to investigate Luna's suspicious demise without bungling or half-measures.

Mario held up a hand like a crossing guard halting traffic as he faced the trailer. "No one goes in that trailer until we process it," he ordered, his voice sharp and authoritative. He stared down one of the uniformed officers who had drifted closer to the entrance, and the man took a hasty step back under Mario's flinty gaze.

Satisfied the scene was secured, he turned to us, his expression softening as he pulled out a notepad and pen. "I know you all have been through a lot this morning already, but I need to get official statements on the record about finding that tank and your exposure to the gas." He focused those alert dark eyes on me and clicked his pen, ready to capture every detail.

I recounted the terrifying ordeal again—the hissed warning, the dizzying stench, those desperate moments of scrambling panic before we burst back out into blessed fresh air and sunlight.

He nodded, face grim.

"You're awful lucky you all got out in time," he said. "I called hazmat on the way here to see if I need to shut down the whole square, and while I didn't, that gas is still toxic." He shook his head. "I should have insisted on processing that trailer right off, not just a quick sniff test. We dropped the ball."

He was right.

At least he admitted it.

"You didn't have any reason to think foul play was involved," Landon pointed out.

"Doesn't matter. Procedure is procedure. We took our eye off the ball." Mario's jaw tightened. "We should have ruled out any risks associated with that trailer and its contents during the initial canvassing of the scene."

"Maybe," Landon told his friend. "The important thing is we know now. Let's focus on making sure whoever did this doesn't get away with it."

Mario's expression softened. "You're right. No sense brooding over what's past. We'll handle things from here." He glanced over at the trailer. "Our crime scene techs will process every inch of that thing. We'll get it right this time."

One of the officers approached Mario. "Perimeter is taped off, sir."

"Excellent. Let's get some photos, then go over this thing inch by inch."

We stood back as the police began photographing and documenting the trailer, their gloved hands dusting for prints, searching for fibers, and cataloging every minute detail. I watched with a profound sense of relief as they treated the scene with the rigorous care and attention it deserved.

Finally, the authorities were giving Luna's suspicious death the serious investigation it warranted from the start.

"We'll need statements from everyone here," Mario said. "For the official report. But that can wait until the scene is processed."

One of the techs poked his head out of the trailer. "Sir, you need to see this."

Inside the trailer, the tech stood motionless as a statue, one gloved finger pointing to the sinister green tank of hydrogen sulfide nestled against the wall. My gaze traveled to where he indicated.

"What is it?" I asked.

No one answered, but with the bright lights inside the trailer, I could see what I couldn't see before.

The regulator valve and attached gauge on the deadly tank looked different from the others. While it matched the basic shape and connections of the helium tanks, the fittings appeared loose rather than securely fastened, with smears of sticky residue around the edges, as if someone had swapped out pieces.

The duct tape wrapped around the tank valve struck my eye next. It looked hastily done, uneven and wrinkled in places, not smooth and purposeful like the professional setups on the other canisters. Unease prickled down my spine as I studied the sloppy, irregular assembly.

"That's why it vented when you jostled it." Mario's expression darkened. "Whoever tried to make this one look like all the others didn't set up the regulator properly," Mario declared through gritted teeth. "This was no accident."

The morning sun warmed the stands, which were set up and waiting, rather than lively with music, mouthwatering scents, and chatter. They appeared to hold their breath in anticipation of the crowds (post-church and post-hangover) that would soon arrive on the festival's last day.

I recalled learning in school years ago that Cinco de Mayo commemorated Mexico's victory over French forces at the Battle of Puebla in 1862. Beyond that history lesson, I'll admit my knowledge was fuzzy.

In my mind, Cinco de Mayo meant people from all walks of life coming together, differences set aside as we swayed and spun to traditional mariachi music under the twinkling lights. It meant the air heavy with enticing aromas, my friends' smiling faces around me and a lightness in my heart. The rich heritage and history behind the holiday were important, but the connections and delight it inspired right here in our little corner of the world each year made it special.

Could someone really do this?

I thought of Mario's words—that Luna's death was no accident...

It seemed like we kept saying that, over and over, but it was looking like all our instincts—and Josie's Ouija board—had been right.

Luna's death?

It really was no accident.

I spotted the tall peaks of the Ferris wheel soaring above the square, backdropped by pastel morning skies. The metal spokes reminded me of curled fingers stretching toward the heavens.

It stood quiet, waiting.

"You know, I don't much care for those newfangled contraptions," Carl groused, following my gaze. "Ferris Wheels, Tilt-a-Whirls, Scramblers, Zippers—seems nowadays they'll strap near about anybody to anything and fling 'em every which way for kicks." He shuddered. "Give me solid ground under my feet any day. None of that hoisting in the air and twirling about."

"The Ferris Wheel was invented in the late 1800s, you know. Back when medical advice involved bloodletting and cocaine toothache drops," Laurie informed him. "It's not newfangled."

Carl narrowed his eyes at her. "What are you implying?"

"I'm not implying anything. I'm saying Queen Victoria was on the throne and germ theory was still a radical notion. It's not new."

"I've been around the block enough times to spot shoddy workmanship and questionable materials." The old man eyed the looming Ferris wheel dubiously. "Mark my words, one stiff breeze and that whole rickety structure will collapse faster than a house of cards in a fart storm."

"Oh, I don't think so," Laurie replied. "Where's your sense of adventure?"

"I get plenty of thrills from bingo night at the community center, thank you very much. A good bingo gives me an excellent shot of adrenaline right where it counts. By the way, where are we going?"

"Around," Landon told him. "To look for anything out of place."

Laurie and Carl's friendly bickering continued as we made our way past the rows of booths, the chatter fading to background noise as I scanned each stand we passed. Vendors eyed us curiously as they set out their wares to prepare for closing day, no doubt surprised to see folks meandering about before the official start time.

We offered friendly, distracted waves and rote "good mornings" to those beginning their setup rituals, but my focus stayed locked straight ahead, alert for any sign of the missing tank.

"Morning!" called a cheerful voice.

We turned to see Rosa Vargas arranging colorful bottles of premixed margaritas and cocktails on ice at her booth.

"Well, good morning, Rosa!" Laurie greeted her. "Your booth is looking wonderful—so colorful!"

Rosa smiled at Laurie's compliment, though it seemed guarded, not quite reaching her eyes. "Thank you. I want everything looking perfect this year so there can be no question I deserved that trophy." She fussed with a tray of fruit, adjusting each slice just so. "The Austin newspapers are coming in today, too, so I need to impress." Her dark eyes darted over our group with veiled curiosity as she took in our early morning presence. "You're all out and about early."

"We are. I wanted to ask you—"

Landon's fingers encircled my wrist in a gentle but firm grip. I glanced up, startled, to see him giving an almost imperceptible shake of his head, eyes warning me not to reveal too much.

I paused, mouth still partially open, confusion furrowing my brow, and I grappled for a harmless question to cover my stumble. "If you, uh, have a bottle of water?" I finished somewhat lamely. "Thirsty."

Rosa nodded and pulled a bottle from a cooler beneath the counter. "Here you go." She handed it over with a polite smile before returning her attention to the fruit trays, dismissing us.

As we walked away, I leaned in and whispered, "Why did you stop me?"

Landon's warm breath tickled my ear. "She doesn't need to know we're looking into this. Not yet. Keep things close for now, especially since the police just ratcheted everything up."

Carl grumbled under his breath, "She don't seem too tore up about Luna passing. More concerned with her margaritas than Luna, if you ask me."

We pressed onward through the maze of booths and tents, scanning each one. Most vendors were too distracted with last minute setup tasks to do more than nod or wave absently as my eyes combed over the displays, hungry for any glimpse of the vanished tank.

Booth after booth revealed tables overflowing with wares—vivid woven blankets, handmade pottery, rows of scented candles, displays of leather goods and jewelry.

An eye-catching treasure trove, to be sure... but not the treasure I sought.

After we circled around a section of food stands pumping out savory scents, I spotted the familiar banner for the art center up ahead and as we approached, the tables out front remained empty. A few framed paintings leaned against the side of the building, but the booth lacked any of the finishing touches I would expect.

"Doesn't seem very set up," Landon commented. "And no one's around."

"The doors are open. Maybe Diego is running behind schedule," Laurie suggested.

"Right. Maybe he's just inside," I said.

Landon raised an eyebrow. "And maybe he's on a train out of town after hearing about the trailer. The gossip tree must have reached half the town by now."

"What train? The only train that comes through here is that tourist steam train from Cedar Park." Carl cupped his hands around his mouth. "Ahoy there! Anybody home?"

No response.

"Should we take a quick peek inside?" I asked Landon.

He considered it, then nodded. "A little look-see couldn't hurt."

We walked up the steps and through the open doors.

Inside, the musty, earthy scent of potting soil filled the air. My eyes adjusted to the shadows, and I realized why—the space was dominated by elaborate plant installations.

"Wow," I breathed. "This wasn't here two days ago."

"This here's what they consider art nowadays?" Carl grumbled behind me, narrowly avoiding plowing straight through a delicate hanging garden suspended from the ceiling. "Looks like my backyard after a week-long bender with a truckload of Miracle-Gro."

I shot him a look over my shoulder. "Don't start, Carl."

"What I'm just asking is, does tossing some weeds in a wheelbarrow make it a masterpiece? Are you trying to tell me that's talent?" Carl prodded a nearby sculpture that resembled a giant Venus flytrap molded from metal and moss. It wobbled precariously. "You could hide Jimmy Hoffa in this foliage and no one would ever find him."

"Oh, I think some of it is lovely." I admired a nearby installation resembling a tree crafted from twisted driftwood and living plants. It was quite exquisite. Diego had certainly taken the art center in an unconventional direction this year.

My gaze traveled over the bohemian scene. Tucked away in a shadowy corner, half-hidden behind fronds, I spotted a metal cylinder.

A helium tank.

Chapter Eighteen

My eyes fixed on the metal cylinder tucked away in the corner, half-concealed by the lush fronds. In the morning light filtering through the art center's windows, I could make out the block letter label reading "HELIUM" across the tank.

This was the missing tank that was exchanged for the deadly hydrogen sulfide canister from the trailer. It had to be. What was it doing here, hidden among Diego's plant art installations?

I hesitated, fingers twitching with the urge to reach out and examine the suspicious cylinder, to confirm if this was the same tank that matched the others in the trailer, but an anxious inner voice warned me not to disturb the scene and risk contaminating potential evidence.

But then my frustrated inner voice scolded my anxious inner voice, chiding her for being a skittish guard dog who started howling five minutes after we'd just stomped through the literal crime scene—in other words, she was a little late to the party as usual.

They continued bickering like squabbling sisters as I edged closer, reaching out a tentative hand to examine it.

"Don't touch anything!" a voice barked out.

I jumped, my heart lurching into my throat. Whirling around, I found Diego standing in the doorway clutching a potted ficus, his expression shifting from surprise to suspicion quicker than a chameleon changes colors.

"What are you all doing in here?" Diego demanded.

"We, uh...we were just on a walk and when we peeked in, we were stunned at how incredible the art center looked!" I stammered, forcing a smile that felt more like a grimace. "The doors were open, but no one was around, so we thought we'd poke our heads in. Did you need any help setting up?"

I cringed at how unconvincing the excuse sounded tumbling from my lips. Subterfuge had never been my forte—my father once told me I had a glass face that broadcast every fleeting thought.

Now that I think about it, it's something I probably should have considered before I became an amateur small town busy body that randomly poked into criminal conspiracies thanks to cat gossip.

Diego's eyes darted between us. "The art center isn't open to the public yet."

"Right, no, we can see that, but the doors were open

and, um—" I faltered, grasping for something else to say that wouldn't arouse more suspicion.

Laurie jumped in. "Like Ellie said, we noticed your doors were open while we were walking by, saw the plants, and popped in out of curiosity." She smiled. "We love what you've created in here, Diego. It's wonderful."

Diego's tense posture relaxed by small increments at Laurie's artful compliment, his defenses softening under her strategic flattery like butter melting in a pan. I should have remembered that even the most guarded soul couldn't help but preen under positive feedback.

"Well, I do appreciate you taking an interest in my work," he said slowly. Diego's expression lost some of its confrontational edge as he basked in Laurie's praise, though wariness still lurked in his eyes. "But I still have much to finish before the festival opens, so I'm afraid I must ask you all to—"

Just then, the side door flew open with a resounding bang that echoed through the art center like a gunshot, making us all flinch. Before my nerves could settle, the door ricocheted off the wall with a teeth-rattling crack that almost rivaled the initial concussive blast.

Blanca strode in, the beads and bangles clattering with each furious stomp. Her dark eyes blazed with wrath and her full lips were pulled into a taut, angry line. She jabbed one finger toward Diego like a prosecuting attorney zeroing in on a hostile witness.

"There you are, you snake!" Blanca strode through the entrance, eyes flashing with fury. She jabbed an accusing finger at Diego. "And I catch you in the act with these people! I know what you're trying to do, calling the geriatric gang of small town P.I. wannabes to search my shop!"

"Geriatric?" Carl looked insulted.

"How old are you, again?" Laurie asked, one eyebrow arched as she eyed him with veiled amusement.

"Back off, why don't ya, before you find yourself on the pointy end of my walking stick," he added with a harrumph, brandishing his gnarled cane like a saber. "I'll show you geriatric right across your backside."

Diego's eyes bounced between Blanca and Old Carl like a spectator at a heated tennis match. "What are you talking about, Blanca?" he asked. "I didn't call anyone!" He shook his head, his shaggy dyed blond hair whipping around his face like an agitated mop.

"Don't play dumb with me," Blanca spat. "I know you've been trying to pin this whole thing on me from the start. Why? I have no idea. But now you called in these Amateur Sleuths R Us wannabes to, what, search my shop? Question my customers?" Her voice rose in both volume and hysteria. "Interrogate me? Because I have no answers about Luna! None." She took a menacing step toward him, red painted nails curling into claws. "I've had it with your mixed signals!"

Whoa, boy. This escalated quickly.

Diego backed away, nearly tripping over his own feet in his haste to evade Blanca's impending fury. "I haven't accused you of anything or sent anyone to investigate you. And I didn't invite these people here. They showed up unannounced." He gestured to where we stood watching the confrontation unfold.

"It's true," Landon said.

"We did just walk in here," Laurie added.

I offered an awkward half-wave under her piercing stare.

"I don't know these people," Carl said like a toddler denying they ate the missing cookies (while their face was still smeared with chocolate).

Blanca's scowl only deepened.

She stood with fists planted on her curvy hips, tilting her chin up. "I'm supposed to believe that? Believe any of you? All of you here meeting before the center opens up right after the police swarmed the area around Estella's store?" Her narrowed gaze slid from Diego to scrutinize Landon, Laurie, Carl, and me in turn. "I think it's you who needs to be investigated. I think you're using these people to take the suspicion off you."

"You're out of your mind, woman," Diego sputtered, throwing his hands up in exasperation. "I called nobody. You're conjuring up wild accusations from the thin air."

"You're so desperate to divert suspicion that you'd throw me under the bus." Blanca stepped closer, eyes blazing. "But your little plan failed. I won't let you smear my name and accuse me of hurting Luna when you know full well I cared about her. She was my customer for years, and my friend."

"Cared about her?" Diego let out a brittle laugh. "Is

that what you call it? Sneaking around, trying to break us up while we were together? That's care?"

Blanca's cheeks flushed. "I told you, that was a mistake, a foolish lapse in judgment. It meant nothing."

"Didn't look like nothing to Luna when she caught you all over me outside the Cinco de Mayo planning meeting," Diego shot back.

Blanca crossed her arms. "You're not still hung up on that, are you? I apologized afterward. It was just... physical attraction. I was lonely—and I thought you liked me. You flirted with me enough!"

"I flirt with everyone!" Diego dragged a hand over his face. "Do you know how much it hurt to have her think I betrayed her like that?" His voice shook with emotion. "You have no idea what it did to me, how it broke my heart."

"You went out with other women when you and Luna were having problems," Blanca said, her tone softening. "That had nothing to do with me. That was your choice. I just happened to be the person you used to try to make her jealous. But all of this? This is pointless. Dredging up the past won't bring Luna back." She hesitated, biting her lip. "We all made mistakes when it came to her and when it came to us. Let this go and move forward. Unless you killed her—and if you did, I hope you rot, Diego."

Diego sagged against the wall. "You're right," he admitted. "As much as I want someone to blame, it won't change anything. And much of it rests on me." He looked up at Blanca. "Did you kill her, Blanca? Just tell me. I can handle it."

"You are impossible!" Blanca shouted, anger flaring anew. "Kill Luna? Are you insane? Did you not hear a word I said? Are your ears packed with cotton?"

Diego raked both hands through his hair in exasperation. "Look, I know you, Blanca, and I know Luna was furious at you—"

"Aye, I can't believe I ever liked you." Blanca's lip quivered almost imperceptibly as she spat the words at Diego. She blinked, her dark lashes fluttering like the wings of a distressed butterfly. Breaking eye contact, she turned her face away, staring at the floor as she wrestled to compose herself.

I watched Blanca, noticing her rigid posture soften by degrees as the tense silence stretched on. Her clenched fists relaxed, her breath steadied. When she turned back around, the fiery wrath had drained from her eyes, replaced by a profound sadness that reminded me of a child who had just realized fairy tales weren't real.

"I care about you, but for you to think I would kill someone over some man?" After a weighty pause, she continued, her voice barely above a whisper. "I can't stop thinking that if I had done something differently, she might still be here." A single tear slipped down her cheek. "Maybe she'd still be with us now if I'd just left you alone, ignored your flirtations. She tried to talk to me woman to woman, and I denied you and I were still talking even though we were. I will regret lying to her for the rest of my life."

The room fell silent except for Blanca's muted sniffles.

Despite her combative entrance, seeing the flash of anguish in her eyes made my heart squeeze with pity. Losing a loved one always invited regret and questions— an endless reel of what-ifs replaying on loop.

Diego stepped toward Blanca, reaching to rest a comforting hand on her shoulder. She stiffened, but didn't pull away.

"Look, if you didn't kill her, this wasn't your fault," Diego whispered. "However things went between you two at the end, Luna cared for you. I know she wouldn't want you torturing yourself over what you could have done differently. How could any of us have known this would happen? I always thought there would be time to fix it."

Fresh tears spilled down Blanca's cheeks. She swiped at them with the back of her hand as Diego reached out and pulled Blanca into a comforting embrace. She collapsed against him, face buried in his shoulder, her body shaking with grief. Diego held her, patting her back.

"It's okay. We keep assuming someone hurt her, but who would want to hurt her?" he murmured. "It was probably like the police said, a terrible accident. A horrible tragedy."

The rest of us exchanged uneasy glances, but it was Carl who spoke up.

"Now don't you go burying your heads in the sand pretending this was just some freak mishap," Carl scolded, wagging his finger so it resembled a metronome on overdrive. "The facts here are plainer than grits without butter or salt—blander than oatmeal, too, and just as lumpy once you chew 'em over a spell. That poor girl didn't just up and die by happenstance. No, sir. She was gassed, I tell ya, and quicker than a June bug trapped in a Mason jar on a hot summer's day."

Diego's brow furrowed in confusion. "Gassed? What on earth are you talking about?"

Landon stepped forward, expression grave. "I'm afraid Carl's right. This morning we discovered evidence that Luna's death was no accident. The police are over by her area now—"

Carl rapped his walking stick on the floor for emphasis. "Because she was gassed! Intentionally, mind you. Maliciously, even. By someone with villainous intent that would curdle the cream in your coffee. Mark my words, there's a killer on the loose in Tablerock, and they ain't gonna rest until we've all been picked off! one by one!" He gave them a meaningful look over his spectacles, his bushy white eyebrows knitting together. "Is it one of you?"

"Carl!" Laurie hissed.

"While Carl's being dramatic, he's not entirely wrong about everything." Landon explained how we found the swapped canister in the trailer, the hydrogen sulfide fumes leaking, and how it likely caused Luna's demise either intentionally or through negligent mishandling of hazardous materials. "Whether it's a tragic accident or deliberate murder, we can't say—but someone put that tank in that trailer, and someone disguised it so no one would think it was harmful."

Diego paled, shaking his head in disbelief. "No, that can't be true." He stepped back until he bumped against the wall. "Who would do such an awful thing?"

Blanca pressed a hand over her heart. "That's terrible."

Diego and Blanca seemed surprised, but I couldn't help but remind myself the canister was just a few feet from where we all stood. I didn't know how to bring it to Landon and Laurie's attention without alerting Diego and Blanca, and I wasn't sure those two were innocent.

Their shocked expressions seemed genuine, but I couldn't ignore the skeptical voice in my head (that sat alongside the frustrated and anxious voices up there) reminding me that the mysterious canister sat right there, half-concealed amid the artful foliage. Its presence here raised questions, and I floundered for a way to alert Landon and Laurie without also tipping off Diego and Blanca.

If they were faking, though, they deserved Oscars for their performances.

I swallowed a frustrated sigh, cursing the canister for being so near, yet out of reach. As vexing as it was, it occurred to me Blanca's earlier comment provided a thread I could tug on. She had rushed in, accusing us of searching her shop.

But we didn't.

"Earlier, you mentioned thinking we'd searched your shop," I said, keeping my tone light. "What made you think that?"

Blanca sniffled, dabbing at her eyes with a handkerchief produced from her embroidered skirt pocket. "When I opened my shop this morning, I could tell someone had gone through the back room and rummaged around my desk area. Things were all in disarray."

"You thought it was us?" I asked.

"Well, yes." Blanca tilted her head, studying me. "My neighbor told me Estella's grandson was poking around my back entrance earlier this morning. Him and your daughter."

I frowned, a crease forming between my brows.

Evie had mentioned nothing about her and Matt investigating anything this morning. As far as I knew, they were just having breakfast together. A twinge of parental concern needled me. I picked up my phone and typed out a text to Evie: "Hey. Where are you and Matt? Thought you were just getting breakfast?"

"I also found something unfamiliar tucked in my desk drawer—some sort of machine part," Blanca continued. "It looked like it belonged to one of those gas cylinders. I started wondering if someone was trying to frame me for Luna's accident."

I stared at the unanswered text, feeling a swell of apprehension.

Where had they gone? What were they looking into?

I drew in a measured breath, trying to temper the protectiveness flaring inside me.

Evie was an adult, I reminded myself. I couldn't expect her to share every detail of her morning, even if my instincts screamed that something felt off.

Still, a follow up text couldn't hurt.

"Everything okay?" I added. "Just want to make sure you're safe."

I hit send and waited, watching the little text bubble that showed my message was delivered. The bubble stayed solitary, without Evie's usual rapid response.

Unease trickled down my spine.

"Evie's not answering back at the moment, but as far as I know, she hasn't searched your shop or placed anything there. The two of them wouldn't break in."

"But you walked in here," Diego pointed out.

"This is a public place," Landon responded. "Your door was open."

I stared at my phone, willing it to ping with an incoming text from Evie, but the screen remained dark and silent, almost mocking in its lack of response. I knew her generation was glued to their phones—for Evie not to text back right away was odd and out of character.

I tapped out a message to Matt, hitting send with a decisive jab of my thumb.

The delivered notification popped up instantly.

But again, no quick reply appeared.

I bit my lip, my pulse kicking up another fretful notch. The continued lack of response from both Evie and Matt honed my parental concern into a sharper, more visceral sense of alarm.

Something didn't feel right.

I turned my attention back to the conversation unfolding around me, hoping for information. "About the neighbor who claimed to see Matt and Evie snooping around your shop, Blanca—who said that?" I asked.

Blanca shrugged, looking uneasy. "Well, it wasn't the neighbor herself, but her boyfriend. Marco Jimenez. He said he saw them skulking around the back door of my shop while he was loading up his work truck."

Landon, Laurie and I exchanged a startled glance as this news landed with an almost audible thud.

Marco Jimenez—the mysterious man who owned the trailer that delivered the deadly canister.

Chapter Nineteen

I COULD ALMOST FEEL THE MENTAL PIECES FITTING together as we made our way to the spot where Marco had parked his truck.

Marco's rental trailer had delivered the deadly gas canister that killed Luna. Blanca said Marco claimed to see Evie and Matt snooping around her shop that morning—but Evie and Matt hadn't mentioned anything to me about investigating shops or back alleys. The suspiciously convenient parking spot for Marco's van snugged right up by Rosa's front door.

My thoughts flickered to the helium canister we'd found tucked away amid the plants at the art center. Diego had seemed shocked to learn of the deadly gas tank, but that cylinder in his art center raised questions. How did it get there?

Blanca mentioned about finding a strange object in

her desk drawer that morning. Was someone trying to frame her by planting evidence?

Like the canister...

They were both planted.

To cover for—

"What's on your mind?" Landon glanced over, noticing my pensive expression. "You look like you just solved a Rubik's cube in your head."

Before I could respond, Marco emerged from behind his truck.

His eyes widened and his mouth fell open as he noticed our group, his body tensing as if he'd stumbled upon a snake in the grass. He blinked, his hand tightening on the rolled-up papers he carried, the knuckles turning white.

Landon raised a hand. "Morning!"

Marco stood frozen, his gaze darting between us like a cornered animal seeking an escape route. Then, just as quickly, he seemed to collect himself. His taut shoulders loosened, though the smile he forced looked like a mask, disconnected from his evasive gaze. He took a step forward, the papers crinkling in his grip as he raised his free hand in a halfhearted wave.

"Good morning," Marco said, recovering his composure. "Can I help you folks with something?"

Old Carl leaned forward, his weathered face set in a scowl. "Oh, I'll tell you how you can help, Marco." He tapped his temple with a gnarled finger. "You can start by spilling the beans, confessing your sins, and letting the cat out of the bag."

"Subtle," Laurie told him.

Carl mimed raising a glass in a mock toast.

"We just had a question for you, Mr. Jimenez," Landon replied.

"Call me Marco."

"Okay, Marco—Blanca Cruz said you told her you saw my friend Ellie's daughter Evie and her boyfriend Matt snooping around Blanca's shop early this morning. Is that right?"

Marco shifted his weight from foot to foot, glancing around. "Oh, uh, yeah, I did see those two kids kinda hanging around the alley beside Blanca's place when I was loading up supplies. Must have been around seven thirty or so."

As Marco spoke, his words seemed to tangle together, his gaze skittering away from mine like a startled rabbit. His hand crept up, fingers kneading the back of his neck as if trying to work out a persistent knot. The corners of his mouth twitched, a fleeting grimace that vanished as quickly as it appeared, replaced by a forced smile that didn't quite reach his eyes.

I let my gaze wander, my attention drawn to his work van once more.

The truck's location, Marco's shifty demeanor, the way his words seemed to dance around the truth—it all pointed to something lurking beneath the surface, a secret waiting to be uncovered. My gut churned, a mixture of anticipation and unease.

"Excuse me," I asked, keeping my voice casual despite the dread curdling in my gut. "You wouldn't happen to know Rosa Vargas, would you?"

Marco's eyes darted away as he shifted his weight. "Uh, yeah. We're kinda dating, actually." He let out an awkward chuckle. "Why do you ask?"

And that was it. The puzzle assembled itself in my mind.

It was Rosa who killed Luna.

She was the one who swapped the gas canisters with Marco's help. He had means and access through his rental business. They made sure there would be other suspects by stashing the helium tank at Diego's art center. And they tried implicating Blanca by planting something in her shop.

Marco must have lied about seeing Evie and Matt to throw suspicion off himself and onto them, too. He wanted the police chasing phantoms while Rosa and Marco finalized covering their tracks.

And that could mean Evie and Matt were in danger.

"Where are Evie and Matt?" I demanded. "What have you done with them?"

Landon shot me a puzzled look. "Ellie, what are you talking about?"

I kept my focus locked on Marco. "It was Rosa, wasn't it? She killed Luna, and you helped her do it."

Marco's already pale face blanched whiter than sun-bleached bones. "W-what? No, I don't know what you mean." He took a step back. "Why would you say something like that?"

"Because it all adds up," I said, advancing toward him. Out of the corner of my eye, I saw Laurie and Carl exchange confused glances. "Rosa wanted that trophy, so she got rid of her biggest competition. You provided the means with your rental trailer and access to the gas. You stashed the helium tank at Diego's to throw suspicion on him, you stashed something at Blanca's to throw suspicion on her, and now you're trying to throw suspicion on Evie and Matt by claiming you saw them snooping around when I know they didn't."

I jabbed an accusing finger toward him. "So I'll ask you again—where are Evie and Matt? If you've hurt them..." My voice trailed off into a threatening growl.

"Whoa, let's slow down a minute." Landon grasped my shoulders. "Ellie, what's gotten into you? Where is this coming from?"

I shrugged out of Landon's grip and whirled around to face them. "Can't you see it? His truck parked right beside Rosa's house? The swapped gas canisters?"

"What gas canister?"

"I saw one at Diego's, behind the plants. Marco telling Blanca he saw Evie and Matt poking around even though they never told us they were going to and now they're not responding?"

"Now hold your horses," Carl admonished. "Don't go leapin' to conclusions quicker than a springbok crossed with a jackrabbit." He twirled a finger beside his temple. "Use your noggin, woman. Take a step back before you go clear off the deep end."

"Carl?"

"What?" the old man asked Laurie.

"You're not helping." She looked at me. "It does seem suspicious, but we can't just start hurling accusations without proof in the middle of the street." Laurie turned to Marco. "Though everything she said does stack up to a pretty good circumstantial case, Mr. Jimenez. So, tell me—what do you have to say about what Ellie said?"

Before he could respond, the front door of the house flew open and Rosa Vargas stormed out, her expression clouding over when she spotted us crowded around Marco's truck.

"What in blazes is going on here?" Rosa's voice lashed out like a whip, her hands planted on her hips. Her accusing glare raked over our faces before zeroing in on Marco with laser-like intensity. "Well? Were you supposed to be bringing more supplies over or standing around here?"

Marco cowered under her imperious stare, shriveling like a wool sweater in the dryer. "Y-yeah, I was just, uh, loading up the last of the stuff for you, honey. Honest!" He gestured at the van.

I watched him, noting how the supposed "last of the stuff" still sat untouched at his feet while the van doors remained closed.

Rosa's eyes narrowed to slits. "Then why are you just standing around jawing with these people?" Her lip curled in distaste as she looked over our group. "What do you want? We have things to do here—move along."

Rosa was really taking that Margarita Queen title seriously.

I stepped forward, shoulders squared, meeting Rosa's challenging stare with a defiant tilt of my chin. "Maybe because Marco here was just about to tell us where Evie and Matt are. Weren't you, Marco?"

Rosa's laughter rang out sharp and brittle as glass. "What kind of nonsense accusation is that?" She arched one groomed eyebrow. "Marco knows nothing about those kids of yours." With a dismissive sniff, she examined her ruby-red nails. "We're too busy getting ready for the festival's big day to care about your drama."

Marco's gaze darted around like a trapped rat seeking an escape. "I do, though," he mumbled. "I know about them poking around Blanca's this morning, remember?"

Rosa's head whipped around.

Marco shrank under her scowl.

After a tense moment, Rosa gave an exaggerated eye roll. Shaking her head, sunlight glinted off her large gold hoop earrings. "Now, if you're quite finished harassing my boyfriend, we need to finish setting up." She flapped a hand at us. "Get lost."

"This here's a public street!" Carl's voice boomed out, echoing off the nearby buildings. He shook his cane at Rosa like an angry schoolmaster. "We don't have to get lost or scram or vamoose or any other dadgum thing! We can plant our rears right here on this curb and watch you do whatever it is you're gonna do!"

He leaned forward, bushy white eyebrows drawing together. "Now you listen here, little missy. I've tangled with bigger fish than you, so don't go getting high and mighty." Carl's wrinkled face reddened with mounting outrage. "You're a very rude young lady, you know that? Why, in my day, a child didn't dare step a toe out of line, or they'd get a swift paddling!"

Rosa—in her early thirties, I'd guess—opened her mouth, but Carl barreled on, wagging a gnarled finger in her face. "Your elders deserve respect! But you— prancing around, barking orders like the Queen of Sheba —you're about as pleasant as a porcupine in my britch- es." He thumped his cane. "I've got underwear older than you, so you watch your tone, young lady!"

The three of us—Laurie, Landon, and me—stared at Carl, jaws dropped.

I couldn't believe the tirade that had just poured from Carl's mouth. My shock gave way to a swell of admiration for the cantankerous old man. He didn't mince words—that was for sure.

And it seemed like Rosa's imperious facade cracked

just a bit under Carl's verbal onslaught. She pressed her lips together, nostrils flaring. "I didn't mean to tell you to leave so rudely," she said, visibly struggling to inject some politeness into her clipped tone. "We're swamped with last minute tasks before the festival's big day."

Carl harrumphed, thumping his cane. "Busy hiding something more like it."

Laurie and I exchanged a glance.

"The contempt in your voice when you shooed us away like bothersome flies was unmistakable. You wanted us gone." I nodded, folding my arms across my chest. "Why?"

A loud thump echoed from the back of Marco's work van.

Rosa and Marco wore matching expressions of shock, eyes widening.

"What was that?" Landon asked.

"Hey now, let's all just remain calm," Marco pleaded, holding his arms out in front of him. "We can talk this all out. It ain't what you think."

"What do we think?" Carl glanced at me, wild eyebrows drawing together in confusion. "What do you think we're thinking?"

Another thump sounded from the truck, followed by a muffled yell.

"Who's in there?" Landon darted left, then right, trying to get around him, but Marco moved with my boyfriend, blocking him at every turn. "Who do you have in your van?"

"No one!"

Another thump and yell sounded from the truck.

"Get out of his way!" I shouted.

Two more thumps and a muffled, "Mom!"

That was Evie's voice!

Anxious terror surged within me.

My daughter was in that van.

Estella came barreling around the corner, with Mario and Josie close behind. Estella had her cellphone pressed to her ear, and was shouting into it, "What do you mean they're right here? We should be on top of them? But I don't see them!"

Mario skidded to a halt next to me, his handsome face creased in confusion. "What's going on?" He asked, his dark eyes darting around. "Matt's supposed to be here, and he's in trouble—have you all seen him?"

Landon looked at the van. "I think he's in there—we heard thumping. Why do you think he's here?"

Estella's cell glinted in the sun as she thrust it upward, her eyes wide. "Javier says Matt hit his panic button and that he must be right here!" She gestured at the van, confusion and fear mingling on her face. "You said you think he's in the van? Has anyone checked?"

Marco shifted his weight, avoiding her gaze.

"Open the van," Landon told him.

Marco did not open the van. He scrubbed a hand

across the back of his neck. "What, uh... what is a panic button?" he asked, his nonchalant tone betrayed by the nervous bob of his Adam's apple.

"Matt's a private investigator," Mario explained, his words clipped and terse. "He's got a panic button that alerts his boss if there's trouble. A GPS distress signal."

"You fool!" Rosa spat. "How could you miss something so obvious?"

Marco's shoulders hunched. "Hey, I didn't think to search for stuff like that. How would I know?"

"They know we can hear them, right?" Carl asked Landon.

Mario's piercing gaze snapped to the van. "That your vehicle?"

"Uh, yeah," Marco mumbled, unable to meet Mario's intense stare.

"Open it. Now."

"Huh?"

"I said open it." Mario bit out each word like a command, his tone brooking no argument.

Rosa leaped in front of the van's rear doors, feet planted wide, arms splayed outward. Her eyes blazed with defiance as she barred access. "You got a warrant to be poking around in here?" she challenged, her voice ringing out sharp as a gunshot.

Two more resounding thuds reverberated from within the van's confines. Muffled cries of "Help!" and "Get us out!" seeped through the walls.

Mario's eyes narrowed. "Exigent circumstances. Now move."

"I don't know what that means," Rosa fired back.

"I do," Josie said, "and he's fine."

Mario's piercing gaze bored into Rosa. "It means we've got cause to think folks are in trouble inside. So I can tear those doors right off with my bare hands if I have to." His arm sliced the air as he signaled the other officers over with a sharp jerk of his chin. They flanked Marco and Rosa, cutting off any escape. "Make sure they don't wander off anywhere," Mario bit out, his eyes on Rosa's defiant face. Turning to Marco, he said, "Now open the doors—unless you want us to rip them open ourselves."

Rosa protested, but it died in her throat as an officer took hold of her arm in an unbreakable grip. She fell silent, eyes smoldering as her boyfriend wavered, glancing between the doors and Mario's outstretched hand. Finally, he slunk aside, shoulders hunched in defeat, turned, and opened the doors.

"It's not what it looks like."

What it looked like was a kidnapping. Evie and Matt lay bound hand and foot, silver duct tape plastered across their mouths. Their wrists strained against the coarse rope biting into tender skin. Eyes blinked in the sudden sunlight, conveying wordless relief.

"Oh my heavens, Evie!" I cried, rushing forward. Mario helped me untie my daughter and peel the tape from her face while Landon freed Matt.

"Mom!" Evie threw her arms around me as soon as she could, hugging me tight.

Matt swayed as he stood, shaking his head to clear it. "Thank goodness you found us," he rasped, relief heavy in his voice. His gaze hardened to flint as it fixed on Marco and Rosa. "These two snatched us after catching them red-handed coming out of Blanca's place."

"That's a lie!" Marco protested, but it rang hollow and unconvincing. "You broke into my vehicle, not the other way around."

Matt arched an eyebrow. "Oh yeah? So I tied myself up for kicks?"

"Hey, man, I don't judge what you and your girl are into." His joking tone couldn't disguise the nervous tremors in his voice. "Takes all kinds."

Mario's expression darkened as he glared at Rosa and Marco. "You two are under arrest for kidnapping and suspected murder. You have the right to remain silent—"

"We didn't hurt anyone, I swear!" Rosa insisted, her voice rising in desperation. "We only wanted to talk to them, and we didn't kill anyone!"

Did she expect us to believe that?

"We just wanted to sabotage Luna's booth a little, that's all!" Marco burst out, the words spilling from his lips. "I figured that gas would just make her area reek something awful so the judges wouldn't give her first place. How was I supposed to know it could kill somebody?"

Rosa whirled on him. "You idiot, shut your mouth right now!"

"What?" He threw his hands up in a gesture of innocence, but his eyes held a frantic, cornered look. "They oughta put big warning labels on that stuff if inhaling it is deadly. I never would've messed with it if I knew!"

Mario's stony expression showed he wasn't buying it, either. "You can spin your excuses for the judge," he said. He lifted his chin at the officers flanking Rosa and Marco, issuing an unspoken command. They grabbed hold of the two suspects. "Get them out of my sight."

The officers hauled a protesting Rosa and sniveling Marco away to the waiting squad cars like parents dragging tantrum-throwing toddlers from a toy store.

Chapter Twenty

I PULLED EVIE CLOSE, MY HANDS SKIMMING OVER her as I checked for injuries. My protective parental instincts, which never go away no matter how old my child gets, roared to life after the scare we'd just endured. What if we hadn't found her in time? What if she'd been hurt by those criminals? My mind spun through terrifying what-ifs that made my stomach churn.

Focus, I told myself, shaking off the dark thoughts.

"Are you sure you're okay, sweetie?" I asked, unable to keep the shrill note of concern from my voice as I examined the raw marks left on her wrists. "We should get you checked out by a medic, just in case. Maybe even take you to the hospital just to be sure. What do you think? Did anyone hit you in the area around your pace-maker? Should I call Dr.—"

"Mom! In the name of all that's holy, just take a chill

pill." Evie gave me a brave smile, though she winced as she rubbed at the tender skin. "I'm fine, really. More shook up than anything. Don't fuss, okay?"

Don't fuss, she says.

My shoulders slumped as I exhaled a shaky breath, trying to loosen the anxious knot in my chest from its viselike grip around my own heart.

Evie was safe.

I repeated that fact to myself like a mantra until my galloping pulse steadied.

"I'm sorry, you're right." I hugged her tight, as if I could shield her from all harm through my embrace alone. My little girl was safe. That's all that mattered. "I just want to be sure you're okay."

"I'm fine."

"Can you tell us what happened?" Landon asked, glancing between Evie and Matt. "How'd you end up in the back of that creep's van?"

Matt shook his head, still looking dazed from the ordeal. "We were just grabbing a coffee en route to the festival when we noticed Marco and Rosa huddled together, acting all suspicious."

"We didn't even know they knew each other," Evie added.

"When they took off down the alley by Blanca's shop, we got curious and followed them."

"You followed them?" I interrupted, my voice rising in disbelief. I swirled in the parental maelstrom of consternation and grudging awe that resulted whenever my spitfire daughter's impulsiveness plunged her into impetuous waters way over her head. Honestly, where does the girl get it from? Certainly not her stick-in-the-mud, play-it-safe, crazy cat lady mother. "Why on earth would you do that instead of calling someone?"

Evie gave me a classic youthful eye roll. "Mom, we're not helpless kids. And we figured we could get evidence if something fishy was going on." She squared her shoulders. "Obviously, it turns out we were right to be suspicious."

Carl shook his head, clucking his tongue in disapproval. "Now that's just dumb as a sack of hammers. You were investigating a murder, but you decided to just follow two suspicious suspects to see what they were up to?" He rapped his cane against the sidewalk. "You kids oughta use your heads for more than hat racks."

"We did use our heads," Matt protested. "We caught the bad guys. It worked out."

"We nabbed the culprits," Laurie said, giving Matt an affectionate but pointed look. "While you were hanging out and catching up on your beauty rest in the back of a van and experiencing your kidnapping ordeal to the fullest, the rest of us geriatrics were out here saving the day, thank you very much."

Matt flushed under her veiled, good-natured scolding.

"What matters is you're both safe now," Landon said. "Though if you find yourself in a situation like that in the future, calling Mario as backup would be the wiser course of action."

Carl grumbled under his breath about "dang fool kids" and their lack of sense.

"We didn't want them to spot us, and besides, Matt had the panic button Uncle Javier gave him when he started working at Lodestar. He just had to roll over and smash his hip into it if we did get kidnapped—which is what he did," Evie explained. "Anyway, we crept up real quiet-like, and that's when we saw them coming out of the back room of Blanca's shop carrying stuff."

Matt nodded. "Looked to me like they were planting evidence—they went in with a bag, and came out with nothing. But before we could do anything, Marco spotted us." His jaw tightened, reliving the memory. "We hid behind the van, not realizing it was his. I guess he hustled Rosa into it and they threw open the back doors..." He trailed off with a rueful shrug.

"And that's how we ended up bound and gagged inside," Evie finished, a visible shudder coursing through her slender frame at the memory. She bit her lip, hazel eyes growing over-bright and distant, and I could see the vivid recollection of those terrifying moments playing out across her delicate features. When she spoke again, her voice hitched. "I'll admit I was more than a little nervous that he was going to drive off and..."

Wordlessly, I wrapped her in a fierce, protective embrace, cradling the back of her head as I pressed a fierce kiss to her hair. For a moment, she relaxed into me, drawing comfort from my touch.

But then the headstrong independence that defined my daughter reared up, and she gently but firmly extracted herself, shooting me a self-conscious glance as she smoothed her disheveled locks, a hint of color rising in her cheeks.

"Mom, I'm fine," Evie insisted.

Mario shook his head. "I can't believe we didn't see the danger. And you guys figured it out." He sighed. "Some detective I am."

"Aw, don't beat yourself up, son." Carl thumped him on the back. "Your heart was in the right place. Not every day we get cutthroat criminals in this sleepy town plotting murders over homemade margaritas."

"Feels a little like it's at least quarterly, though," Matt said.

Laurie shook her head. Her warm brown eyes held a pensive, almost sorrowful look. "It's hard to fathom how things spiraled so horribly out of control over something as innocuous as a margarita competition."

"It just goes to show you never know what someone is capable of when the right motive arises." Josie shrugged, letting her arms fall back to her sides. "Not even in a sleepy small town like ours."

"Not so sleepy anymore," I pointed out.

Landon nodded. "Not so small, either, if those developers have anything to say."

"Still, we should have taken it more seriously from

the start." Mario's dark eyes clouded with regret. His gaze traveled over the colorful booths and rides dotting the square, the festival coming back to life for its final celebratory day. Laughter and music filled the air. "Luna deserved better."

"Luna would be happy to see everyone having fun," I said.

Evie nodded, leaning into Matt's comforting embrace. "She brought out the best in Tablerock. We won't forget that."

Jessa Winthrop's raspy laugh cut through Evie's sentiments as she sauntered toward us, flanked on either side by the smirking faces of Town Prosperity Investments's developers.

Her bleach-blond hair was teased and curled into an elaborate updo that looked one stiff breeze away from toppling over. Garish jewel-toned eyeshadow complemented her bright fuchsia lipstick, giving her the appearance of an aging beauty queen clinging to faded glamour.

My heart sank. It seemed the trouble wasn't over yet after all.

"Well, well, if it isn't Tablerock's very own Scooby Gang!" Jessa trilled, her crimson talons flashing as she gave a little finger wave. "We just had to come to thank you all for your detective work catching that dreadful pair of killers."

The men on either side of her chuckled, exchanging knowing glances.

"Yes, you've done the whole town a great service," piped up Daniel Patrick.

"We appreciate you helping take a dangerous criminal off the streets," added lanky William Woodfield. The predatory gleam in his gaze reminded me of a hawk spotting prey. "Truly admirable work."

Jessa tittered, slapping William on the arm. "Our little band of heroes! Why, you should have your own detective agency."

"I work for Lodestar Investigations, and my uncle works with all of us here when needed," Matt said, gesturing between himself and Evie.

"Well, aren't you just the cutest little Nancy Drew and Hardy Boy!" Jessa trilled, her voice dripping with so much exaggerated sweetness it could cause a toothache. She eyed Evie and Matt with a patronizing smile that didn't reach her heavily lined eyes.

"What can we help you with, Jessa?" Evie asked, eyes narrowed.

Jessa's smile never wavered, but a master jeweler couldn't have cut a finer edge. "How precious," she purred. "Learning attitude from her momma already."

I crossed my arms, fixing Jessa with a pointed look that could blunt knives.

"Oh, we were just on our way to the station to have a little chat with that dreadful Rosa creature about her property." She examined her nails. "With her facing criminal charges now, she'll have to unload that café posthaste. A quick sale for whatever pittance she can get will be her only hope of affording a lawyer, I would think."

"One woman's tragedy is another's opportunity, as I always say," Robert added with a sly smile.

"We're swooping in to take that sad little plot off her hands before it crumbles into ruin from neglect," William explained. "And we intend to offer a generous price—well, relatively speaking. Considering the circumstances. We're doing that neighborhood a favor by replacing an eyesore with something beautiful and productive."

Carl thumped his cane. "The only eyesores here are you newcomers with your fancy suits and fat wallets looking to gobble up our town like a Christmas goose!"

"Change is inevitable, Carl. Progress marches on." Jessa pivoted, her shadowed eyes locking onto me with the unerring focus of a marksman taking aim. "Why, just imagine the economic boon luxury condos and upscale shops will bring. You'll be thanking us soon enough."

"What happens to all of Rosa's employees?" I asked. "Driving out hardworking residents and pricing out families struggling to get by doesn't sound much like progress to me."

Josie nodded. "We don't need or want you displacing

our community and erasing the culture that makes this place special."

Her smile remained steady, but her eyes glittered with impatience. "Now, I admire your quaint little notions. I do. But the numbers don't lie. What we offer will improve home values and attract high-income residents."

"At the cost of what makes this place home," Landon argued.

"You can't put a price tag on community," Laurie added.

"Community fades," Jessa told us, "but cold hard cash doesn't. Why on earth are you people clinging to the past when we're offering you a glittering future?"

"Because a place isn't just buildings, it's people," I told her. "What good is neighborhood revitalization if it drives out the very neighbors that give it heart and character?"

"Here, here!" Carl bellowed.

Jessa's eyes narrowed to slits as she appraised me with the keen scrutiny of a scientist examining a new species of insect."When did you move here from Austin, Ms. Rockwell?"

I fumed.

"Well, now, we're trying to have a reasonable discussion, but I can see emotions are running high." Robert held up his hands in a calming gesture. "How about we all cool down and revisit this another time with level heads?"

"That's a good idea, Robert. We said what we came here to say." William's calculating gaze traveled over our group. "Let's go do what we need to do. You all have a good rest of your day."

They turned and departed without another word, their expensive shoes clipping against the pavement.

I watched them go, chest tightening. No matter how firmly we resisted, these corporate vultures kept circling closer, waiting for the right moment to swoop in and pick Tablerock's bones clean. We had won today's battle against Rosa and Marco's scheming, but it seemed there was a war for the spirit that animates our small corner of the world looming.

I faced my friends, a swell of warmth and appreciation blooming in my chest as I looked upon their courageous, compassionate faces. Here stood people willing to fight for what was right, no matter the cost or risk to themselves. In this group, I saw the center and foundation of our community—the connections that bound us together and gave meaning to this place we called home.

"Screw them," I said, the words slipping out before I'd realized what I was saying.

Laurie and Josie's jaws dropped in perfect synchronicity, their startled eyes swinging my way in disbelief. I couldn't blame them—such casual almost-profanity was uncharacteristic coming from mild-mannered me. I avoided curse words like most people avoided dentist visits.

Josie fanned herself theatrically. "My word, I do believe I need a fainting couch. However will my delicate sensibilities recover?"

"Sorry," I mumbled. "Not sure what came over me."

"Don't you apologize! You keep right on speaking your mind, honey. Polite society can clutch their pearls if they want."

"You're darn tootin' screw them," Carl growled. "We'll give those buzzards the what-for if they try any funny business." He shook his cane.

Mario nodded. "Tablerock looks after its own. We won't hand our town over."

"We'll save the heart and soul of this place, even if we have to chain ourselves to the park gazebo to stop the bulldozers," Evie said, just as laughter drew my attention to the festival.

The rides whirled and music played as residents celebrated with carefree joy, the pall of sadness morphed into true celebration now that Luna's killers were caught. Kids chased each other, clutching prizes won at carnival games, while adults clinked margarita glasses, toasting one more Cinco de Mayo festival's drama concluded.

Maybe there was still trouble brewing on the horizon with TPI and Jessa Winthrop, but today, at least, our community could come together and remember what mattered.

"C'mon, let's go join the fun," Josie said. "We've earned a break."

I slipped my hand into Landon's, giving it a grateful squeeze. No matter what challenges loomed ahead, as long as we stuck together, I knew we would find a way through. Just like we solved Luna's murder, we'd protect the soul of our town.

Because we weren't just fighting for buildings or businesses. We were fighting for community—the sense of belonging that couldn't be bought or sold.

"You ready for some rides and fried food?" Landon asked me.

"Absolutely." I smiled up at him.

His laughter mingled with the music and chatter enfolding us as we lost ourselves in the celebratory atmosphere of the festival's last day—a welcome chance to leave heavier burdens aside for a few precious hours.

"Step right up, win a prize for your sweetheart!" a voice bellowed. I turned to see a carny gesturing at a shooting gallery booth, his smile flashing gold under the morning sun. "Test your skills and claim a treasure!"

Landon's eyes glinted with playful competitiveness. "What do you say I win you something, Ellie?" He gave my hand an affectionate squeeze. "Any requests?"

I grinned up at him. "Surprise me."

Minutes later, we walked away from the booth with Landon victoriously toting an oversized cat, its fluffy bulk dwarfing me. I laughed as I peeked around it.

My cheeks hurt from smiling. After the stresses and

scares of the last few days, it felt good to laugh together again, basking in a lighthearted moment.

I stood on tiptoe to plant a kiss on Landon's scruffy cheek. "My hero."

He leaned down to steal a quick kiss. "All in a day's work."

Laurie and Josie waved us over. "We're about to ride this thing," Josie called. "You in?"

I eyed the looming metal frame. The Ferris wheel towered over the town, its apex seeming to graze the clear blue sky. The peaked center rose as the outer rim turned with musical creaks and groans.

"I don't know..."

Evie appeared at my elbow. "Come on, Mom! It'll be fun."

My feet felt cemented to the ground and my stomach flip-flopped nervously.

Sensing my unease, Landon smiled. "I'll hold your hand the whole time."

Heartened by his support, I mustered my courage. "Okay, let's do it."

We crammed into the compartment, metal pinching flesh as the worker secured us inside.

With a lurch, the ride jolted into motion. I sucked in a sharp breath, gripping Landon's arm as our compartment ascended into the night sky. We rose steadily, the people below shrinking to miniature size.

"Breathe, El," Landon soothed, palm smoothing over my white knuckles. "Just keep your eyes on me."

I focused on Landon's handsome, bearded face as we climbed higher, leaving my unease far below. His steady presence calmed my fluttering nerves.

Our compartment slowed to a stop at the wheel's pinnacle, the compartment swaying gently. For a moment, we hovered, the world spread out below us. Festive colors glimmered around the square, faint music drifting up along with the happy murmur of the crowd.

"It's beautiful up here," I whispered. "So peaceful."

Landon's arms encircled me. "It is. But you're far more beautiful."

He leaned in, lips capturing mine in a tender kiss as we lingered high above it all, a rare moment of stillness amid the ceaseless turns of life's Ferris wheel.

All too soon, the Ferris wheel jolted back into motion, our blissful moment of stillness at its pinnacle coming to an abrupt end as our compartment began its descent back to earth—but as we plunged downward, the fluttery nervousness that had gripped me on the way up didn't return. Enveloped in Landon's muscular arms, any lingering unease evaporated.

"Ready for whatever comes next?" he asked.

I squeezed his hand, my own small smile dawning. "With you? Absolutely."

Thank you for reading! I hope you enjoyed the sixth book in the Silver Circle Cat Rescue Mysteries!

As the last page turns, things continue to unravel in the seventh installment, "Fluffy, Flip Flops, and Foul Play."

Follow the trail of sandy paw prints into a case where every clue could be as mismatched as a lone flip-flop. Join Ellie and Evie as they get sucked in to this cozy mystery that's more twisted than a beach towel after a windy day!

KEEP UP WITH LEANNE LEEDS

Thanks so much for reading! I hope you liked it! Want to keep up with me?

Visit leanneleeds.com to:

Find all my books...

Sign up for my newsletter...

Like me on Facebook...

Follow me on Twitter...

Follow me on Instagram...

Thanks again for reading!

Leanne Leeds

Find a typo? Let us know!

Typos happen. It's sad, but true.

Though we go over the manuscript multiple times, have editors, have beta readers, and advance readers it's inevitable that determined typos and mistakes sometimes find their way into a published book.

Did you find one? If you did, think about reporting it on leanneleeds.com so we can get it corrected.

Artificial Intelligence Statement

Portions of this book were created with the assistance of AI tools used for editing, proofreading, and refining the text. However, the ideas, storyline, characters, and overall creative vision remain my own original work.

While some aspects of the cover image were generated using AI tools, it was done so under my creative direction and curation.

I want to acknowledge the use of these technologies as part of my creative process, while affirming that the essence of this work comes from my own imagination and effort.

Leanne Leeds